14TH

DEADLY SIN

JAMES PATTERSON is one of the best-known and biggest-selling writers of all time. Since winning the Edgar™ Award for Best First Novel with *The Thomas Berryman Number*, his books have sold in excess of 300 million copies worldwide and he has been the most borrowed author in UK libraries for the past eight years in a row. He is the author of some of the most popular series of the past two decades – the Alex Cross, Women's Murder Club, Detective Michael Bennett and Private novels – and he has written many other number one bestsellers including romance novels and stand-alone thrillers. He lives in Florida with his wife and son.

James is passionate about encouraging children to read. Inspired by his own son who was a reluctant reader, he also writes a range of books specifically for young readers. James is a founding partner of Booktrust's Children's Reading Fund in the UK.

Why everyone loves James Patterson and the Women's Murder Club

'It's no mystery why James Patterson is the world's most popular thriller writer. Simply put: **nobody does it better**.'
Jeffery Deaver

'**Boxer steals the show** as the tough cop with a good heart.'
Mirror

'No one gets this big without **amazing natural storytelling** talent – which is what Jim has, in spades.'
Lee Child

'James Patterson is the **gold standard** by which all others are judged.'
Steve Berry

'A compelling read with great set pieces and, most of all, that **charismatic cast of characters**.'
Sun

'Patterson boils a scene down to the single, telling detail, the element that **defines a character** or moves a plot along. It's what fires off the movie projector in the reader's mind.'
Michael Connelly

'James Patterson is **The Boss**. End of.'
Ian Rankin

Have You Read Them All?

1ST TO DIE

Four friends come together to form the Women's Murder Club. Their job? To find a killer who is brutally slaughtering newly-wed couples on their wedding night.

2ND CHANCE
(with Andrew Gross)

The Women's Murder Club tracks a mystifying serial killer, but things get dangerous when he turns his pursuers into prey.

3RD DEGREE
(with Andrew Gross)

A wave of violence sweeps the city, and whoever is behind it is intent on killing someone every three days. Now he has targeted one of the Women's Murder Club . . .

4TH OF JULY
(with Maxine Paetro)

In a deadly shoot-out, Detective Lindsay Boxer makes a split-second decision that threatens everything she's ever worked for.

THE 5TH HORSEMAN
(with Maxine Paetro)

Recovering patients are dying inexplicably in hospital. Nobody is claiming responsibility. Could these deaths be tragic coincidences, or something more sinister?

THE 6TH TARGET
(with Maxine Paetro)

Children from rich families are being abducted off the streets – but the kidnappers aren't demanding a ransom. Can Lindsay Boxer find the children before it's too late?

7TH HEAVEN
(with Maxine Paetro)

The hunt for a deranged murderer with a taste for fire and the disappearance of the governor's son have pushed Lindsay to the limit. The trails have gone cold. But a raging fire is getting ever closer, and somebody will get burned.

8TH CONFESSION
(with Maxine Paetro)

Four celebrities are found killed and there are no clues: the perfect crime. Few people are as interested when a lowly preacher is murdered. But could he have been hiding a dark secret?

9TH JUDGEMENT
(with Maxine Paetro)

A psychopathic killer targets San Francisco's most innocent and vulnerable, while a burglary gone horribly wrong leads to a high-profile murder.

10TH ANNIVERSARY
(with Maxine Paetro)

A badly injured teenage girl is left for dead,
and her newborn baby is nowhere to be found.
But is the victim keeping secrets?

11TH HOUR
(with Maxine Paetro)

Is one of Detective Lindsay Boxer's colleagues
a vicious killer? She won't know until the
11th hour.

12TH OF NEVER
(with Maxine Paetro)

A convicted serial killer wakes from a two-year
coma. He says he's ready to tell where the
bodies are buried, but what does he
want in return?

UNLUCKY 13
(with Maxine Paetro)

Someone returns to San Francisco to pay a visit to
some old friends. But a cheerful reunion is
not on the cards.

A list of more titles by James Patterson is printed at
the back of this book

14TH

DEADLY SIN

JAMES PATTERSON

AND MAXINE PAETRO

arrow books

3 5 7 9 10 8 6 4 2

Arrow Books
20 Vauxhall Bridge Road
London SW1V 2SA

Arrow Books is part of the Penguin Random House group of companies
whose addresses can be found at global.penguinrandomhouse.com.

Penguin
Random House
UK

First published by Century in 2015
First published in paperback by Arrow Books in 2015

www.randomhouse.co.uk

A CIP catalogue record for this book is
available from the British Library.

ISBN 9780099594567
ISBN 9780099594574 (export edition)

Typeset in Berkeley Oldstyle (11.5/16pt) by SX Composing DTP, Rayleigh, Essex
Printed and bound by CPI Group (UK) Ltd, Croydon, CR0 4YY

For Suzie and John, Brendan, Alex, and Jack

PART ONE

Chapter 1

IT WAS A blindingly sunny morning in May, and Joe Molinari was out for a walk in the park with Martha, his smart and funny dog, and Julie, his adorable nine-month-old baby girl.

Julie was in a sling, her belly against her great big daddy's chest, looking over his shoulder and waving her fingers toward the lake with every confidence that she was making real words and that her dad would be happy to take direction.

"Do you have a license to point those things?" Joe said to the child.

"Damn right," Joe replied in his best imitation of how Julie would speak if she could. "We all know who's in charge here, Daddy. I only need to point and babble. Heh-heh. Race you to the bench. By the ducks."

Joe ruffled Julie's hair and got a better grip on Martha's leash as he took in the scene again. He ran his eyes across the path to the bench, checking out the people with dogs and strollers, the shadows between the trees, and the traffic beyond the glare of the water; then he paused to double-check a middle-aged guy smoking a cigarette, staring deep into his phone.

These were the habits of a former federal agent and until recently the deputy director of Homeland Security. He was now a consultant specializing in risk management assessment for big corporations, government agencies, and other authorities.

Currently, Joe was six months into a job he'd been working eighteen hours a day, mainly from his office in the spare bedroom. It was a complex project, an obstacle course of practical and political complications. He felt fine about how it was coming along. And he also felt good about the lay of the land as he settled onto an empty bench with a fine ducky view of the lake.

Julie laughed and beat the air with her hands as he unstrapped her from the sling and sat her on his lap. Martha came over and tried to wash Julie's face before Joe interceded and pulled the border collie to his side. Julie loved Martha and giggled a long peal of baby talk just as Joe's cell phone rang.

It wasn't Lindsay's ring. Pawing his shirt pocket, he saw that the caller was Brooks Findlay, the exec who'd commissioned his assignment with the Port of Los Angeles. Joe pictured the man: a former college football player, fit, thinning blond hair, dimples.

It was odd to get a call from Findlay first thing in the morning, but Joe answered the phone.

Findlay said, "Joe. It's Brooks Findlay. Is this a good time to talk?"

Findlay's voice was shaded by a dull metallic tone that put Joe on alert.

What the hell is wrong with Findlay?

Chapter 2

"I'M FREE TO talk," Joe said to Findlay. "But I'm not at my computer."

"Not a problem," said Findlay. "Look, Joe. I've got to terminate our arrangement. It's just not working out. You know how it is."

"Actually, I don't know," Joe said. "What's the problem? I don't understand."

A crowd of young boys entered Joe's field of vision, shouting to one another, kicking a soccer ball along the asphalt path. At the same time, the baby was giving Joe a new set of directions. He kept his hand on her tummy and hoped she didn't start screaming. Julie could *scream*.

"Brooks, can you hear me OK? I've put a lot of

time into this project. I deserve an explanation and a chance to correct—"

"Thanks, Joe, but it's outta my hands. We'll take it from here, OK? Your confidentiality contract is in effect, of course, and, uh, your check's in the mail. Listen, I've got incoming. Gotta sign off. Take care."

The line went dead.

Joe held the phone for a few long moments before he returned it to his pocket. *Wow.* No apologies. Not even a face-saving explanation. Just a needlessly brutal chop.

Joe reviewed his last conversations with Findlay, looking for clues to something he might have missed, some hint of a complaint—but nothing lit up the board. Actually, Findlay had seemed happy with his work. And Joe was sure his preliminary analysis of the container security protocols at the Port of Los Angeles was solid.

He really hadn't seen this coming.

After pushing through the initial shock and confusion, Joe glimpsed his new reality. First there would be the loss of income, then the humiliation of having to explain this sinkhole to the next guy interviewing him for a job.

That thought was just about intolerable.

He wanted to call Lindsay, but on the other hand, why ruin her day, too?

"Hey, Julie," Joe said to his now fussing daughter. "Can you believe it? Daddy got fired. Over the phone. *Bang.*"

Joe buckled the baby back into her sling, and she reached up and touched his cheek.

"I'm OK, Julie Anne. I'm thinking we should all go home now. I'm in the mood for a banana smoothie. Sound good to you?"

Julie looked like she was going to cry.

His little girl was mirroring his feelings.

Joe said, "OK, OK, sweetie. Don't cry. We can come back and see the ducks later. We can come back every day into the foreseeable future. I can put peaches in that smoothie, all right? You like peaches."

"I sure do, Daddy," Joe said in his baby voice. He swept his gaze around the park and then stood up with Julie.

"You ready, Martha? That's the girl."

She woofed and jumped, so he gave her the full length of her leash till they were leaving the park, then pulled the lead in for the couple of blocks toward home.

By then, Joe wasn't thinking of fruit and ice and yogurt. He was thinking of Findlay, pressing that gutless piece of crap through the blender.

Chapter 3

I WAS BEHIND my desk that morning as light streamed through the Bryant Street windows and slashed across the squad room's linoleum floor.

My partner, Inspector Rich Conklin, was standing behind me to my right, and Chief of Police Warren Jacobi loomed impatiently over my left shoulder.

Jacobi had caught a couple of bullets in his leg and hip a few years ago and the injuries had aged him. He was fifty pounds overweight, his joints crackled and popped when he walked, and the pain had drained the fun from his salty sense of humor.

He grumbled, "Wait till you see this," and handed me a disc; then he sighed loudly as we waited for my "lazy-ass computer" to boot up.

I slid the disc into the drawer. The drive whirred, and then a video, time-dated 3:06 this morning, appeared on my screen. The camera had been positioned under flickering streetlights in a nearly deserted block in the notoriously sketchy Tenderloin. The footage was grainy, shot with a cheap surveillance cam of the type used more as a prop than as a tool for actually identifying people.

"That's Ellis Street," said Jacobi. "And that's what I call crud," he added, stabbing a sausage-like finger at three figures entering the frame. The men wore black billed caps and navy-blue Windbreakers with white letters reading SFPD across the back. They also held automatic handguns as they headed smartly toward an all-night check-cashing store with a yellow sign above the window reading Payday Loans. Checks Cashed.

I straightened in my seat, then turned to shoot a look at Jacobi.

What the hell is this?

"Balls on these bastards," he said. "Boxer. It's hard to make out. Can't you focus that picture?"

"What you see is what you get," I said.

For long, gritty seconds, we watched the cops advance along the dark commercial street lined with low, blocky buildings. Then they converged on the lit-up storefront and went through the door in single file.

A moment later, the lights inside the store went out. The door burst open and one of the "cops" ran out with a satchel under one arm, followed by the other two men, who were carrying similar bags.

Now that they were heading toward the camera, I looked for facial features, something that could be run through facial-recognition software.

But *the faces were all the same.*

Then I got it. The bad guys were wearing latex masks that completely disguised their features. Seconds after leaving the store, the men in the SFPD Windbreakers had run out of camera range.

Jacobi said, "Christ. Someone please tell me that these men are anything but cops."

Chapter 4

I FELT SICKENED at what I had just seen on the footage. Like Jacobi, I hoped we were looking at holdup guys with a bad sense of humor, not actual police officers pulling off an armed robbery.

I asked Jacobi, "Were there any fatalities?"

"One," he said. "The owner wouldn't give up the combination to the safe until he was shot to pieces. He managed a few words with the EMTs before he bled out on the floor. He said cops did it. The kid who worked for him was interviewed on scene. He said there had been about sixty grand in the floor safe."

Conklin whistled.

Jacobi went on, "This is the second one like this. A few days ago, three men in SFPD caps and

Windbreakers robbed a Spanish market. A mercado. No one died, but it was another big score. It goes without saying, these guys have to be stopped or every man and woman in uniform is going to take shit for this whether we deserve it or not."

Conklin and I nodded, and Jacobi kept going.

"Robbery squad is already working the case, but I told Brady I want the two of you to work with them now that we've got a homicide.

"Boxer. You know Philip Pikelny, who heads up Robbery? Call him. You and Conklin work with his guys. This is the most important case in the house."

"We've got it, Chief."

Muttering to himself, Jacobi stumped out of the bullpen.

About now, Robbery would be canvassing Ellis Street and Forensics would be taking apart a check-cashing shop called Payday Loans. Checks Cashed. All we could hope for was a snitch or that this professional crew had left evidence behind.

I called Phil Pikelny and repeated Jacobi's instructions. The sergeant told me what he knew about the case so far.

"The scene is still off-limits," Phil said. "CSU

has barred the doors until they're done, which could be later today."

Phil told me he would get us the footage of the first "Windbreaker heist," the armed robbery of a mercado.

"It's with the DA's Office, but I'll put in a request to get a copy to you ASAP."

I called Administration and asked for time sheets for every cop at every rank in the Southern Station, thinking maybe we could at least make a list of cops who were off duty when those heists went down.

And for me, question number one was: Were these robbers really cops? Or just crooks in cops' clothing? Either way, wearing police Windbreakers probably gave the robbers a few seconds' grace before the victims knew they were being hit.

My good-doin' partner made a breakfast burrito run and I put up a fresh pot of coffee in the break room. Then we settled into our facing desks, ready for a roll-up-your-sleeves desktop investigation.

Chapter 5

HOURS AFTER TALKING with Phil Pikelny, Conklin and I were still waiting for the DA's Office to send over the video of the Windbreaker cops' first known heist. I checked my watch. I could still make it. I told my partner I'd be back in a couple of hours.

"I have a date and I can't be late."

Richie opened his desk drawer, pulled out a slim, brightly wrapped package with a bow and a gift card, and handed it to me.

"This is for Claire. Try to bring me back some cake." He grinned winningly. He's a handsome guy who has somehow avoided becoming vain.

I took the gift, as well as the one I'd stashed inside my top drawer, then got my car out of the lot across the street. Two twisted streets and ten minutes later, I parked my ancient Explorer at the curb in front of the Bay Club. I put my ID on the dash. Then I walked around the corner to Marlowe, a fabulous eatery housed in a brick building with wine and food quotes etched on the large-paned casement windows.

I peered through the glass and saw Yuki and Claire in the back at a table for four. They seemed intensely involved in conversation, and from the looks on their faces, they were taking opposite sides. I came through the door into the bright, industrial-style interior, and Yuki spotted me right away. It almost looked like she was hoping for rescue.

She called out over the loud conversation that was bouncing off the tile and steel surfaces: "Lindsay, over here."

I headed toward my pals, and Claire stood up for my hug. She looked gorgeous, wearing black pants, a V-neck sweater, and a diamond pendant shaped like a butterfly around her neck. Claire is usually trying to lose a few pounds, but she always looks perfect to me.

I said, "Love you, Butterfly. Happy birthday, girlfriend."

She laughed. "Love you, too, Linds."

She hugged me back, and I swung into a chair across from her and next to Yuki. Small-boned Yuki was impeccably dressed in a blue suit, her sleek hair falling to her creamy silk collar. A string of pale angel skin coral beads at her throat. When I'd last seen Yuki a week ago, she'd looked a little happier than she did now.

"You OK?" I asked.

"I'm good," she said.

We embraced, and I had just hung my jacket over the back of my chair when Cindy sailed up to the table, glowing like a rose at sunrise.

There was more hugging and kissing all around, Cindy adding a gift to the growing pile of sparkly paper and ribbons in the center of the table. We high-fived each other and I signaled to the waiter.

I was hungry for the specialty of the house: a hamburger made with Niman Ranch beef, topped with caramelized onions, bacon, cheese, and horse-radish aioli, nestled between halves of a hot, buttered bun. With fries. And even more than that upcoming delight, I was very glad to be with my best friends.

It was Cindy who had named our little group the Women's Murder Club. It was kind of a joke, and at the same time entirely for real, because the four of us certainly surrounded the subject of murder: me in Homicide; Claire, San Francisco's medical examiner; Yuki, a rising star in the DA's Office; and Cindy Thomas, a top-tier crime reporter at the *San Francisco Chronicle*.

Cindy was a new author, too. Her nonfiction book, *Fish's Girl: A True Story of Love and Serial Murder,* was grounded in a case Conklin and I had worked and two killers we had both known very well. Cindy had followed up the case and helped bring one of those killers down.

Her book was coming out at the end of the week. I was pretty sure that was why she was glowing.

After we'd ordered drinks, Claire piped up. "Yuki's quitting her job."

Cindy and I both said, "No way!" at the same time.

"I'm *thinking* about it," Yuki said, "just *thinking* about it. It's, like, an idea, you know? Geesh, you guys."

Cindy jumped in with what I was imagining.

"Oh. My. God. I know what's going on with you. You're *pregnant*."

Yuki was married to my boss, the tough but fair Lieutenant Jackson Brady—but they'd only been married for four *months*. I didn't have a chance to get my mind around the idea of Yuki and Brady having a child, because Yuki was answering Cindy in her typical rapid-fire style.

"No, no, *no*, I'm not pregnant, but if you don't mind, all of you, we have to order lunch *now*, because I absolutely have to be in a deposition in an hour."

And that was when my phone rang.

I looked at the caller ID while everyone stared bullets at me. We had one rule for our no-holds-barred get-togethers.

No phone calls.

"Sorry," I said. "I've got to take this."

And I did.

Chapter 6

I LEFT THE girls and found a niche where I could take the call in private.

"What's wrong?" I said to Lieutenant Brady.

"A dead body at Twenty-Fourth and Balmy Alley," he said. "I need you and Conklin to do a preliminary workup. Lock down the scene and sit tight until replacements arrive. Jacobi wants you and Conklin on the check-cashing heist, nothing else."

I rejoined my friends.

I said, "Sorry, guys. That was the boss. I've got to go."

Yuki tossed her napkin a few inches into the air in exasperation.

Cindy said, "What can you tell me?"

21

You can take the reporter out of the *Chronicle*, but you can't take the reporter out of Cindy.

"Nothing," I said. "I can't tell you even one little thing."

"How many times do I have to prove I'm trustworthy?" said Cindy. "Plus, you owe me."

Actually, Cindy was right. On both counts. I trusted her. And a few months ago, she'd saved my life.

"I still can't tell you anything. Not a word."

I grabbed for my jacket and had just about secured it when Claire said, "I cannot believe this is happening *again*."

The expression on her face stopped me. She was pissed. Highly.

"*What's* happening again?" I asked her.

"This is almost exactly what happened last year on my birthday," said Claire. "And the year before *that*."

"Are you sure?"

"I'm *damned* sure. Although as I recall, last year we actually ate most of our lunch before you bolted from the table. Check your memory, Lindsay. When was the last time you saw me blow out the candles?"

"I'm sorry. I can't get out of this. I'll make it up

to you, Claire. To everyone. Including myself. That's an iron-clad promise."

I apologized some more, blew kisses, and fled the restaurant. I called Rich Conklin from the street, and while I walked to my car, I said, "I'm ten minutes away."

"Same here."

The engine started right up. I peeled out and pointed the Explorer toward a busy intersection in the Mission.

Chapter 7

BALMY ALLEY AND Twenty-Fourth looked like a freeway pileup.

I counted three hastily parked cruisers, and another one was coming in behind me. Both streets were cordoned off, causing traffic to back up in the one open lane on Twenty-Fourth. Pedestrians had gathered three deep at the barrier tape with cell phones in hand, evidently having nothing better to do than gawp at a bleeding corpse in the crosswalk.

I parked on the sidewalk, got my point-and-shoot Nikon out of the console, and found Conklin, who was talking to a young cop. He introduced me to Officer Martin Einhorn, a rookie who'd been writing up a parking ticket when the incident occurred.

Einhorn's black eyes flashed back and forth between Conklin and me as he walked us through the scene. He was sweating through his uniform and his speech was high-pitched and staccato. Very likely he'd never seen a body before, and now he'd been this close to an actual murder as it happened.

He said, "I was putting a ticket on that red Mazda over there. The victim was crossing the street. There were a lot of people crossing at the same time, both ways. Tourists mostly," he said, pointing his chin in the general direction of the sightseer magnet: vividly colored murals protesting human rights abuses over the last fifty years.

"I didn't see the attack," said the rookie. "I heard the screaming, and when everyone scattered, I saw . . . her." He took a moment to get himself together before continuing.

"I called it in and the EMTs got here like a minute later. They said the victim was dead and I told them to leave her body in place. That this is a crime scene."

"Exactly right," I said.

Einhorn nodded, then said a squad car had arrived after a few minutes and the officers had strung tape. "We got as many names as we could, but people were trying to get out of here and we didn't have enough manpower to detain them. Those two witnesses hung in. Mr. and Mrs. Nathan Gosselin, right over there. Mrs. Gosselin saw the attack."

While Conklin approached the couple standing outside a smoke shop, I took a wide-angle view of the crime scene and got a fix on where the victim lay in relation to cars, buildings, and people. Then I ducked under the tape and identified myself to the officers who were protecting the body and the scene.

One of the cops said, "Right this way, Sergeant. Mind the blood."

"Got it," I said.

I gloved up, then moved closer so that I could get a good look at the victim.

Chapter 8

IT WAS A terrible sight.

The dead woman was lying on her side. She was white, had shoulder-length brown hair, and looked to be in her late forties or early fifties.

She had cared about her appearance, and wore expensive clothing: an unbuttoned tan raincoat over blood-soaked beige knit separates. The source of the blood looked to be a long slice through her clothes from her lower abdomen up to her rib cage that had likely required strength, determination, and a long, sharp blade.

The victim had bled out fast. She might never have known what had happened to her.

I trained my camera on the conspicuous wound. Then I shot close-ups of the victim's hands—no wedding band—and of her face, and of her stockinged feet, which lay like beached fish where she'd fallen out of her shoes.

An authentic and pricey large Louis Vuitton handbag lay beside her. I opened the bag and photographed the contents: a pair of good running shoes, a makeup kit, a Jimmy Choo sunglass case, a paperback novel, and a brown leather wallet, new and of good quality.

When I opened her wallet, I learned that the victim's name was Tina Strichler. Her driver's license listed her age as fifty-two, and her home address was about six blocks from the scene of her death. Strichler had a full deck of credit cards, and business cards identifying her as a psychiatrist. She also had receipts for recent purchases and two hundred twenty-two dollars in cash.

I typed Strichler's name into my phone, using an app that linked up to SFPD databases—and got nothing back. Which didn't surprise me. So far, I had nothing to explain why this woman of means had not been robbed. She'd been gutted in broad daylight on a busy street where cell phone cameras were pointing in every direction.

I circled the body and took photos of the crowd

on the sidewalks on the chance that whoever had killed this woman was watching the activity at the crime scene.

Conklin came toward me and summarized the witness statements, using his hands to point out the direction the victim had been coming from.

"The Gosselins were crossing Balmy Alley toward the victim," he said. "Mrs. Gosselin didn't notice the killer until he struck or punched out at the victim's midsection. All she saw was a medium-size white guy in a black jacket or coat or shirt with the tails out. She *thinks* he had brown hair."

Conklin looked exasperated, and I felt the same way. So many pairs of eyes, and one of the only two witnesses had seen practically nothing.

My partner went on.

"After the attack, the doer kept going and disappeared into the crowd. Mr. Gosselin saw none of this. He went to his wife when she started screaming. The rest was chaos. A stampede."

An unmarked car pulled up and two guys from our squad got out: Fred Michaels and Alex Wang, both new hires by Brady.

Conklin and I greeted them and brought them up to date on the details of the crime as we knew it. I told them I'd send them a typed version of my notes and the photos as soon as I got back to the Hall. And then, as sorry as I was to do it, I turned the case over to the new guys.

Conklin and I had our own horrible murder waiting for us at our desks. We got back into our separate cars and were headed back to the Hall when, as I turned onto Bryant Street, something came to me. It was a realization that just about reached out and hit me like a slap across the face.

Claire had been *right*.

There *had* been murders on each of her birthdays for the previous two years. And I was almost positive that those cases hadn't been solved.

Chapter 9

WHEN THE WRETCHED day finally ended and I came through the front door of our apartment, Martha wiggled her butt, barked, and sang me an excited welcome-home song. I hugged her, held her front paws, and danced a few steps with her. Then I called out to Joe.

He called back.

"I'm giving Julie a bath."

OK, then.

I hung up my jacket, kicked off my shoes, and put my gun in the cabinet, locking it up. I walked with Martha to the open kitchen of our airy apartment on Lake Street, where I'd come to live with Joe as his bride. A year later, this was where I gave birth to Julie during a

31

blacked-out and very stormy night while Joe was out of town.

That was at the top of the list of the most memorable nights of my life.

I topped up Martha's dinner bowl and poured two chilled glasses of Chardonnay. With Martha trailing behind me, I went to the master bathroom.

I knocked, opened the door, and saw the two people I love the most. My smile stretched out to my ears.

"Awwww," I cooed. "Look how cute and clean she is."

I leaned down and kissed Joe, who was kneeling beside the tub. Julie grinned her adorable face half off, lifted her arms, and squealed. I put the wine-glasses on the vanity. Then I kissed Julie's hand, making funny noises in her palm. I handed Joe the pink towel that was appliquéd with OUR BABY GIRL.

I understand that first-time parents are a little goofy, but this towel had been a *gift*.

"I need a bath myself," I said as Joe lifted the damp baby into his arms.

"You go ahead," said my handsome and most wonderful husband. "You OK with Pizza Pronto? I'll call in an order."

"Brilliant," I said. "Sausage, mushrooms, onions, OK?"

"You forgot the jalapeños."

"Those, too."

The pizza arrived, pronto.

Over our down-and-dirty dinner, I told Joe about the Windbreaker cops. When the pizza box was in the trash, the baby was asleep, and Joe was working in his home office, a.k.a. the spare bedroom, I brought my laptop to the living room and took over the big leather sofa.

I'd worked the Windbreaker cops case at both ends of my day, but I found I couldn't stop thinking about Tina Strichler, the shrink who'd been gutted in the street.

Now that I had a full belly and some free time, I felt compelled to check out the homicides that had happened on Claire's birthday the two previous years.

I was almost positive that these cases had somehow slipped through the cracks.

Chapter 10

MY HUSBAND STOOD behind me, his hands working on the clenched muscles in my neck.

"Oooh, I think I like working at home," I said.

"Yes, well, I'm the legendary man with the slow hands."

I laughed. "Yes, you are."

"More wine?"

"No, thanks. I'm good."

"OK, then," he said, giving my shoulders a squeeze. "Martha and I are going for a run."

"I'll wait up."

As soon as Joe and Martha had left the apartment, I checked on our sleeping little one, and then I went back to work.

I typed in my password and opened the SFPD

case log to kick off my search. The index to the files was little more than a list of the victims; each case was dated and marked either active, closed, or pending. The name of the lead inspector on each case was listed under the victim's name.

Since I was searching for murders on specific dates, it didn't take long to find the two women who'd been killed on Claire's birthday. I stared at the names, and I remembered the occasions.

Just the way it had happened today, I'd been called from the table to go to the crime scene because I was a ranking officer, on duty, and near the location when the body had been discovered.

I clicked open the older of the two unsolved cases.

Two years ago a woman named Catherine Hayes had been killed outside her father's coffee shop on Nob Hill. Hayes, who worked for her father during the day, went to night school for accounting and finance. On that twelfth day of May, she'd been having a smoke outside while talking to a friend on the phone when she'd been stabbed in the back. Then her throat had been slit.

There were no witnesses, and the friend who had been on the phone with Hayes had heard only the victim's screams. Hayes hadn't been robbed. The killer took his knife and left nothing behind; no note, no DNA, no skin cells under the victim's nails. The leads were thin to nonexistent, and nothing panned out. Catherine Hayes left devastated friends and family, and her open file was still chilling.

So was the file of Yolanda Pirro, a poet who'd been seen competing in last year's 12k Bay to Breakers Race, a huge attraction that had been run annually for over a hundred years. Many of the runners wore costumes; some even ran nude, or dressed like fish and ran backward, as if they were swimming upstream. Go figure.

Pirro's body was found the day after the race in a thicket of shrubs at the end of the course. She'd been wearing runners' gear, nothing that would make her stand out.

Pirro had multiple stab wounds, any one of which could have been fatal. Her devastated husband and close circle of friends said she had no enemies. She was a poet who worked as a volunteer at a community garden and liked to run.

She hadn't known Catherine Hayes, and the two women had no common friends, family, or acquaintances. The Northern District had caught the case and had *no* suspects and no witnesses—and at the same time, tens of thousands of suspects who'd participated in the race or watched from the sidelines. And so, without a clue, Yolanda Pirro's case went cold.

The Pirro case reminded me a lot of Strichler.

Lots of people in a crowd, but no witnesses.

Including Tina Strichler, all three victims who were killed on Claire's birthday were attractive white females between the ages of thirty-four and fifty-two, living within three densely populated miles of one another.

Did anything connect them?

Well, yes. *They'd all been knifed.*

I was staring over my laptop, searching my mind for anything else that would link these three women's deaths, when someone kissed my temple.

I put my arms up the way Julie does, and Joe gave me a big crinkly smile and another kiss. He came around the sofa and sat down next to me.

"What are you doing?" he asked.

"Prowling around in some old case files."

"Oh, yeah? Why?"

I told him all about it.

Chapter 11

MY EYES OPENED at 3:15 a.m. Maybe the spicy pizza had given me a bad dream. Or maybe I just sensed that Joe was lying beside me with his eyes open.

Either way, I knew something was *wrong*.

I rolled over to face my husband and put my hand on his pajama sleeve.

"Joe? Are you OK?"

He heaved a sigh that almost stirred the curtains across the room. Something was keeping him awake, but what? I quickly reviewed our evening at home, and apart from my asking him "How was your day?" to which he'd answered, "Pretty good," our conversations had been all about *my* cases and *me*.

That made me feel terrible.

I shook his arm a little bit.

"Joe? What's going on?"

He said, "I didn't mean to wake you."

"You didn't. What's wrong?"

Joe sighed again, then plumped the pillows, rearranged the duvet, and drank some water.

Then he said, "Brooks Findlay, that little shit. He fired me. Man, I was not expecting *that*."

"*What?* But *why?* "

"He gave no real explanation. Just change of direction, blah-blah. Which was a lie. 'You're out. Your check's in the mail.'"

I was shocked by the news and equally blown away by how coldly Findlay had axed my husband, and not just because what hurts Joe hurts me. I say this because Joe was deputy Homeland Security director. He is supremely knowledgeable, has a good bedside manner, and has top credentials from DC to the moon. Port authorities are his specialty.

Brooks Findlay, on the other hand, had gone from business school to an office job in LA. If you ask me, hiring Joe might have been the highlight of Findlay's career. Maybe he didn't like standing in Joe's shadow.

"I can't *believe* this, Joe. You were completely blind-sided?"

"I had not a clue. If I'd screwed up, Findlay would have been happy to tell me what, when, and how. So it's gotta be that Findlay doesn't like me. Or someone above Findlay doesn't like me. It stinks. But it doesn't really matter."

"Why's that?" I asked.

"Because I'm not ready to retire. I'll get something better, but I have to close the door properly before the next door opens."

Joe grabbed his phone and tapped some keys.

Geez. It was still only 3:30 a.m. I heard a cracked voice at the end of the phone. My husband said, "Brooks, it's Joe Molinari. Listen, you cut me off this morning, so I didn't get a chance to tell you. I had a breakthrough on the project. Yeah. Big one. Key to the whole damned puzzle.

"But you reminded me that we have a confidentiality agreement, so I deleted the work. Don't worry. I scrubbed the disc. The info is unrecoverable. No one will ever see it."

I could hear a squeaky protest coming over the phone, but I couldn't make out the words.

"No, no. That's all. I wanted to tell you that you

didn't have to worry. It's like it never even existed. Sleep tight."

Joe clicked off the phone and said, "You little prick."

He had a devilish Cheshire Cat grin on his face as he said to me, "Now, *that* was priceless." Joe started to laugh and I did, too. Then he turned off the phone ringer and lay back down beside me.

I pictured Findlay cursing, trying to call back, getting the voice mail, getting nowhere.

I fell asleep in my husband's arms and when I woke up, Joe was in the kitchen with Julie and Martha, and he was making apple pancakes.

It was a yummy start to what would turn out to be a very bumpy day.

Chapter 12

YUKI WAS WRESTLING with a bear of a conflict as she parked her car in the wide-open parking lot at Fort Mason Center. She had a job interview with the Defense League at ten, and although they'd called *her*, she'd been borderline nauseated since she'd agreed to talk with them.

The main reason for her queasiness was that she liked her job and she liked her boss, Leonard "Red Dog" Parisi, who had been her biggest booster. She hadn't told him or anyone else at the office that she was thinking of making a switch. So going on a job interview made her feel sneaky.

Just as important, she also hadn't told Brady about the interview. Her husband was decisive and opinionated, and she wanted to make up her own mind before Brady had his say. And she was pretty sure he would tell her, "Do *not* take that job."

Yuki stared out at the always astonishing panoramic view of the bridge stretching across the glistening bay. Then she locked up her car and crossed the lot to a sidewalk running alongside one of the former fort's barracks. She passed several identical rusty brown doors before she saw the one marked THE DEFENSE LEAGUE.

Entering the office, Yuki gave her name to the young woman behind the plain wooden desk, took a wrapped peppermint from the dish, and sat down on one of six identical wooden chairs. Apart from the receptionist, Yuki was the only person in the small, unadorned, pretty-close-to-shabby room.

She couldn't help comparing this out-of-the-way place with the district attorney's office in the Hall of Justice. There, she was one of hundreds of legal professionals and cops working both sides of criminal cases all day, and most nights and weekends, too. The DA's office energized her, tested her, and plugged her into the heart of the San Francisco justice system, where she was finally beginning to distinguish herself.

And thinking about all that made her wonder

once again what in God's name she was doing *here*. But she knew.

The one thing that nagged at her conscience was her growing awareness that people with money got far better representation in court than those without. Light-years better. Nearly every day, some poor guy who'd been represented by an overworked and overwhelmed postgraduate public defender got out of jail after twenty long years because the DNA evidence came back saying he wasn't guilty.

Yuki couldn't ignore her feeling that two-tiered justice wasn't really *just*.

She'd been thinking quite often, really, that perhaps she should be *doing* something about this inequity—and then she'd gotten a call last week from Zac Jordan at the Defense League.

Jordan had said, "I've heard what a fighter you are, Ms. Castellano. I think we should talk."

It was ten to ten, so Yuki used the few minutes of utter silence to review what she knew about this not-for-profit foundation sponsored by a secret-Santa megabucks philanthropist. And she remembered a scrap of headhunter wisdom she'd relied on when she was looking for her first job.

Get the job offer. Then you can always turn it down.

A phone buzzed on the receptionist's desk.

The young woman answered the call, then said, "Ms. Castellano? I can take you back to see Mr. Jordan now."

It was showtime.

Chapter 13

YUKI GATHERED HER impressions of the long-haired Mr. Jordan as he rose from his desk chair to greet her. He was in his late twenties, casually dressed in a nubby beige cotton pullover and jeans. He wore a wedding band and had a firm handshake, and his diploma from Harvard Law was inconspicuously placed on the wall, almost hidden by the hat rack.

He definitely looked the part of a liberal-leaning do-gooder. In fact, Yuki liked him immediately.

The two exchanged "nice to meet yous," and Mr. Jordan said, "Please. Call me Zac. Thanks for coming in. Have a seat."

"I haven't taken an interview in a long time, Zac. But I am aware of the Defense League and what you do here. I have to say I'm intrigued."

"Intrigued by the opportunity to work long hours for low pay in a grubby office? Because I always find that to be a good recruiting tool."

Yuki laughed. "Actually, my current job provides some of the same benefits."

Jordan smiled, then said, "We've got a few perks I'll tell you about some other time, but first, let's talk about you. I've read your résumé, and I have a few questions."

"OK, shoot," Yuki said.

And then the laughs were over and the *real* interview began. Zac Jordan asked about her first job in corporate law and her reasons for going to the DA's Office, and then he started drilling down on the cases she'd worked from the beginning of her time with the DA.

Yuki had lost nearly all the cases she'd prosecuted in her first three years, and Zac Jordan seemed to know each case as well as if he'd been sitting in the courtroom. He questioned her on every soft opening statement, every missed opportunity, every time opposing counsel had trampled her with superior litigation experience.

Well, yeah, she'd been outgunned in several

cases, but there were usually contributing factors: faulty police work, a witness who changed her testimony, a defendant who committed suicide before Yuki made her closing argument. Depressing, deflating "not guilty" verdicts had made her even more determined to sharpen her game. Which she had done.

Meanwhile, here she sat, having to defend her fairly pathetic win/loss ratio to a man she didn't know, who might or might not offer her a job she didn't necessarily want.

When Zac Jordan dug into the infamous *Del Norte* ferry shooter's trial, in which the defendant had killed four people and had been found legally insane, Yuki really had had enough.

By definition, the shooter *was* crazy.

But she *had* to try him for multiple homicides. That was her job.

So she forced a smile and said to the hotshot across the desk from her, "Well, gee, Zac. I have always done my best, and I've been promoted several times. I really don't understand why you asked to see me. Did you just bring me in so you could stick it to me?"

"Not at all. I needed to hear your side of these

cases because we're *always* the underdogs. How would you feel about defending the poor, the hapless, and the hopeless?"

"I don't know," Yuki said, abandoning her plan to get the job offer knowing that if she didn't want it, she could turn it down.

"See if this is of interest to you, Yuki," Zac said, handing her a file. "I have a case that desperately needs to be tried. The victim was arrested outside a crack house where some dope slingers had been shot. He was running. He had a gun. The cops had probable cause to arrest him, but this kid was fifteen and had a low IQ and for some damned reason, his parents weren't there. Although he maintained that he only found the gun, that it wasn't his, the cops muscled him into waiving his rights, and then he was squeezed until he gave a confession.

"While this poor schnook was awaiting trial, maybe a week after his arrest, he was murdered in jail. If he'd had a trial, he might have proven his innocence, and I do believe he was innocent. I believe he was victimized by the cops who interrogated him and that he should never have gone to jail at all.

"I'm going to have to ask something of you, Yuki. Think about this overnight and see how you feel tomorrow morning. You're my first choice for this job, but I'm talking to someone else, too, and I have to make a hire right away.

"Give me a call either way, OK?"

Chapter 14

YUKI HAD BEEN lying awake in bed since Brady got up at four and started bumping into things as he tried to dress in the dark.

"You can turn on the light," she said.

"I'm good. My socks. I can't tell if they're blue or black even when the light is on."

He came to the side of the bed, sat on the edge of it, and kissed his wife.

"Why are you up?" she asked him.

"A drug lab was shot to shit. Go back to sleep. I'll call you later."

Yuki thought, *Later might be too late.* He was checking his gun, strapping on his shoulder holster.

"Brady?"

"Hmm?"

"C'mere a sec."

He came back to the bed and stood above her in the dark, zipping up his Windbreaker.

"I have to tell you something big," she said. "I'm going to leave the DA's Office."

"What? Yuki, what are you talking about?"

"I have a job offer with a not-for-profit. The Defense League. Impeccable credentials. I'll get the same salary, don't worry. But I'll be defending people with inadequate representation. They already have a case for me."

"Can we talk about this later?" Brady said. He unhooked his phone from its charger and put it in his pocket.

"Sure. We can talk about it," she said. "But I've got to give the Defense League an answer."

"Today?"

"Yes. And I've got to tell Parisi before I accept, and he's on his way out of town at the end of the day."

Brady took his wallet off the dresser and put it in his back pocket. He was moving in a pretty herky-jerky fashion. Yuki read his body language. He was processing something he really didn't like. She knew her timing sucked.

"Sounds like you've made up your mind."

"It was sudden. I just met with the director yesterday, and I wanted to think about the offer overnight."

"Thanks for your faith in me."

Yuki trusted Brady with her life. This wasn't about faith in Brady.

"OK," he said after five or six silent seconds had elapsed. "I guess you should do what you want. I hope it works out for you."

"Brady? Please don't be like this."

"People are waiting for me, hon. I'll see you later."

She listened to him leave the apartment, closing the door hard; she heard the door lock. And she heard her dead mother's voice inside her head.

You hurt your husband's pride, Yuki-eh. Why didn't you ask him if he approved of this move?

She didn't have to answer her mother. She felt defiant, knowing that truly, Brady would have pressured her out of the job. And he would have had valid reasons. He would have said it was good for her to work in the Hall, to be near him.

As a lifetime cop, he would have told her patiently that it was good for her to be part of the city government, where her job was secure, where she was moving up, making a reputation, and locking in a pension plan. He would have said that her hours might be long, but they were predictable. And he would have said that he wouldn't be able to stop worrying if she was working in bad neighborhoods.

And he would have been right on all those points.

But he would also have been wrong.

Safe was good. But she had another idea about what she should be doing with her life and her abilities. She wanted to do work that would make her feel good about herself.

Yuki looked at the clock, then slipped a sleep mask over her eyes.

She tried to fall back to sleep, but there was no way.

As bad as it was fighting with her husband, she couldn't stand thinking about what Red Dog was going to say to her. It wasn't going to be good.

But she had to get it over with.

Chapter 15

YUKI SAW THAT Leonard Parisi's office door was open and that he was at his desk, with its wide, uninspiring view of traffic and the handful of gritty low-rent businesses on Bryant Street.

Parisi's assistant was away from her post, so Yuki rapped on her boss's door frame. He smiled at her and waved her in, pointing to the phone at his ear.

She came inside and closed his door behind her. Then she took the chair across from him at his leather-topped desk and stared past his shoulder to the wall hanging behind him that showed the caricature of a big red dog gripping a bone in its teeth.

Yuki had thought about what she was going to

say to Len; she knew that in some ways, it was as critical as an opening statement to a jury. Len was that important a person in her life. But she knew that once she'd made her speech, the meeting could go very wrong, depending on what Len said to *her*.

Parisi was talking to a witness for an upcoming trial. The man had just had an emergency quintuple bypass. Yuki let her mind float until Parisi hung up the phone.

"Sorry, Yuki. That was Josh Reynolds. He's not feeling too well."

Parisi himself had had a massive heart attack a few years ago. Yuki had been with him when it happened and had gotten medical assistance for him, PDQ. Later, he'd said she'd saved his life. It wasn't true, but she knew he felt that way.

He certainly regarded her as a close friend. Which was why having to tell him she was quitting was going to royally suck.

"So what's on your mind?" he asked her. "Something wrong, Yuki?"

Yuki gripped the edge of his desk and said, "Len, I got a job opportunity that I want to take."

There was dense, soundproof silence. Yuki could hear her words echoing in her head. She'd been honest, respectful, and direct. What was Len going to do now?

Would he hug her? Or tell her to go fuck herself?

He rocked back in his chair, then leaned forward, put his forearms on the desktop, and clasped his hands, looking directly into her eyes. He said, "Oh, man, what terrible timing. You know I'm going away tonight for a week. There's just not enough time for me to get you a counteroffer today, but I will put it in motion. Give me some ammo. What kind of job? How much are they offering?"

"That's so nice of you, Len, but I don't want a counteroffer. I don't want to leave, either."

"Well, don't. Problem solved."

She smiled. "But I need to do it. It's the Defense League, and there's an urgent case that I feel drawn to. I think I'll regret it if I turn this opportunity down."

"The Defense League. Really? You'd rather go into a nonprofit than stay here? I thought we had the same goals for this office. You've been working the best cases. I mean, not just Brinkley, I gave you Herman, too. I had to fight off piranhas to do that. Every ADA in the office wanted a piece of that guy."

"I know. I know, Len, and I don't want you to think I'm not grateful."

"Yuki, speaking from personal experience, let me just say that a near-death event changes a person. I know that's what happened to you. You're still processing that you could have died, and for someone your age, that's heavy. You will feel differently in six months, I promise. Turn down the offer. Let me work on making this a dream job—"

"Len, I got hooked by a dead teenager," Yuki said. "He was wrongly arrested and killed while awaiting trial. His family is devastated, rightfully so. The Defense League—"

Parisi already knew where she was going with this. She felt thunderheads gathering.

"You're going to sue the City? The SFPD? You're coming after *us*?"

"It's the right thing to do."

"I *hear* you," Parisi said, "but I don't understand you." There was a look of outrage on her friend's face that Yuki had seen before, just not directed at her.

Parisi's chair spun noisily as he got out of it. He crossed the room and opened his door wide.

He said to her, "Human Resources will bring

you some empty boxes and walk you out. You'll surrender your card, your laptop, and your keys, immediately. I'll have Payroll cut your check. "

"Len, I'm indebted to you. I know how much—"

"Save it," he said. "I'll see you in court. And I do mean *me*. Personally."

He returned to his desk chair and picked up the phone. He punched in some numbers, then swiveled around so that his back was to her. He said, "Michelle, it's Parisi."

Michelle Forrest was head of Human Resources. Yuki left Len's office and, dazed, walked to her own.

She hadn't intended to tear up her life. She wanted a different job. And now her husband was pissed at her. Len was threatening to destroy her in court. And she hadn't even told Zac Jordan that she was accepting the position.

Well, she *was* taking the job, and she was going to win compensation for the Kordell family for the wrongful death of Aaron-Rey.

There was no turning back now.

Chapter 16

I WAS OBSESSING about Tina Strichler as I drove to work that morning. Yesterday, Strichler had been ripped up her midsection with a long, sharp blade, a vicious murder that felt personal. I couldn't shake the feeling that there was a connection between her and the other women who had each been killed with knives on May twelfth, now three years in a row.

Brady has a keen investigative mind, and I really wanted his thoughts on this.

I walked through the gate to the squad room and saw that Brady was in his small, glass-walled cubicle at the back of the bullpen. He was behind his desk, his blue shirt stretched across his chest and his bulging biceps. His white-blond hair was pulled back into a short pony, revealing where a part of his left ear had been shot off during a fierce gunfight in which he had acted heroically and saved a lot of lives.

Right now, however, he was fixated on his laptop.

I said "Hey" to Brenda, waved at a few of the day-shift guys who looked up as I strode past, then rapped my knuckles on Brady's door. He waved me in and I took a seat across from him.

I said, "About that homicide yesterday on Balmy Alley—"

"Yep. Michaels and Wang are working it."

"I know. What I'm thinking is that there's something familiar about this killing—"

"Tell Michaels. Jacobi's calling me three times a day about the Windbreaker cop robberies. I'm worried about Jacobi. I know he doesn't want to retire with the stink of these douche bags all over him. Or all over *us*. And now the press has sniffed it out. I've got questions from I don't know how many papers and TV reporters, and, of course, a ton of e-mail from the concerned citizens."

He waved his hand at the laptop.

"I understand, Lieutenant," I said. "We're on it."

"OK," he said, fixing his ice-blue eyes on me. "Bring me up to date."

I summarized the footage of the first Windbreaker cop holdup in the mercado, saying that the quality was worse than the footage of the one at the check-cashing store. But still, we were able to see three men in SFPD jackets, carrying guns.

"The job took about five minutes from A to Z," I said. "They scored about twenty grand. Sergeant Pikelny interviewed the store owner, who said the men in the SFPD Windbreakers locked them in the back room and then shot up the cash drawer. Hardly any words were spoken. No one was hurt."

"Did they leave any evidence?"

"Nothing. They picked up the shell casings. They wore gloves. Conklin and I are going to look at the scene of last night's check-cashing robbery, where the owner was killed. And we're doing a follow-up interview with the survivor."

"OK. Come back with *something,* will you?"

Brady was done. I left him hunched over his

computer and met Conklin in the all-day parking lot on Bryant.

We were both impatient to interview Ben Viera, the young man who'd been working at the check-cashing store when his boss had been shot to death.

Luckily, the kid had lived to talk about it.

Chapter 17

BEN VIERA, THE surviving witness to the robbery-homicide at the check-cashing store, cracked open his door about four inches, which was the length of the chain lock. He demanded to see our badges, and we held them up. He asked our names, and after we told him, he closed the door in our faces.

I heard his voice on the telephone; he spoke and listened for a couple of minutes.

The door opened again, this time wide enough to let us in. Viera was of medium height and build, wearing green-striped boxers and a Giants T-shirt. He was saying, "I called the police station. To make sure you are who you say you are."

"OK. I get that," Conklin said.

The one-room apartment on Poplar Street was dark, and messy with pizza boxes and soda cans, dishes in the sink, and laundry on the floor. Viera folded his futon bed into a sofalike object, offered us seats, then got into a reclining chair and leaned back.

"I'm on Xanax. Prescribed for me. Just so you know."

"OK," said Conklin.

"I already talked to the police the night of the . . . thing," Viera said to the ceiling.

"I know this is hard, Ben," said Conklin. "You've told the story, and now we want you to do it again. Some new thought could jump into your mind. Right now we don't have a clue who those guys were. They're *killers*. You saw them, and we have to catch them."

Viera sighed deeply before describing the holdup and the shooting, which had clearly traumatized him.

"Like I said, there were three of them. They were wearing police jackets and, like, latex masks. They came through the door fast. One aimed at us through the Plexiglas teller window, and another one kicked open the security door. Then one of them told Mr. Díaz, 'Give us the money and no one will get hurt.'"

The young man went on to say that his boss had a gun but never got off a shot. One of the masked robbers shot Díaz in the right arm. Another of them got Viera in a chokehold, put a gun to his head, and demanded that he open the safe. Viera told them the safe was in the floor and that he didn't know the combination, "I swear on my mother."

Throughout the telling of this story, Viera's flat affect hadn't changed. But there was a tremor in his voice, and I could feel the terror bubbling up just below the tranquilizer.

He said, "Mr. Díaz was rolling on the floor screaming, but he wouldn't give up the combination. So then they shot him in the knee. Oh, God, it was—bad. And then Mr. Díaz screamed out the combination.

"I opened the safe and they took the money and left. I thought maybe Mr. Díaz was going to make it. He was always good to me. I don't even know why I'm alive."

Conklin and I took turns asking questions: *Did you notice anything unusual about any of the men? Did you recognize anyone's voice? Did any of the men seem familiar? Like they'd been in the store before? Did any of them take off his gloves or mask? Did any of the men call anyone by name?*

"Maybe one of the guys called another of them Juan."

It wasn't much, but we'd take it.

I gave Viera my card and told him to call me day or night if he remembered anything else.

He said, "I guess. God knows I can't sleep and I can't forget."

He walked us to the door, and as soon as it was closed behind us, I heard the lock and the chain.

Our next stop was the check-cashing store with the sign over the window: PAYDAY LOANS. CHECKS CASHED.

CSU was wrapping up, and CSI Jennifer Neuenhoff walked us through. She showed us where the robbers had kicked in the door between the public space and the back of the store. She showed us the massive bloodstain where Mr. José Díaz had bled out. We looked into the open safe in the floor. It was like looking into a grave.

Neuenhoff said, "Not more than thirty million prints in here. They shouldn't take more than three lifetimes to process."

Conklin said, "Save yourself some time, Neuenhoff. The witness said the shooters wore gloves."

When we were back in the car, I called Brady and told him everything we had, which was pretty much a textbook case of how to stick up a store and make a clean getaway. I said we'd be back in the house in a couple of hours.

"We've got a stop to make first, Lieutenant. Personal matter."

After I hung up with Brady, I pulled the rubber band out of my hair, shook out my pony, and tried to shake off my sour mood at the same time. I pulled down the visor and slicked on some lip gloss, and even gave my eyelashes a thin coat of mascara.

When my face was presentable, I said to my partner, "OK. Now you can step on it, Inspector."

"You want sirens, Sergeant?"

"Whatever you have to do."

He snapped off a salute, which made me laugh, and not long after that, we parked outside the Ferry Building.

Chapter 18

THE SAN FRANCISCO Ferry Building is not only the dock for ferries going to and from Alameda and Oakland, it's a spectacular marketplace. The Great Nave is more than six hundred feet of arched arcade, with a clock tower, and the entire building is a lively hub of restaurants, shops, offices, and a vibrant farmers' market.

Conklin and I entered the building from the thirty-foot-wide bayside wharf, skirted the tables of people grabbing quick lunches, and entered Book Passage, an expansive bookstore with floor-to-ceiling windows facing the San Francisco Bay.

My partner and I made our way between the displays of new fiction and the long shelves of other books and reached the back corner of the store, where nine or ten people had taken seats facing a speaker at a lectern.

The speaker was our own girl reporter, Cindy Thomas.

She looked adorable, as always, wearing a soft blue cashmere sweater dress and rhinestone combs in her curly blond hair. She was talking about her hot new book and skipped a beat when she saw us. Then she grinned and neatly recovered as we took seats.

She said, "*Fish's Girl* is the true story of two killers who were bound together by love and serial murder. If that makes you think of Bonnie and Clyde, this pair was nothing like them, but just as crazy. *Crazier*, actually. And *deadlier*.

"Randy Fish and MacKenzie Morales killed separately, almost as if they were inside each other's minds."

Cindy held up the book so her audience could see the grainy cover photo of her subjects walking hand in hand, the only known picture of Fish and Morales together. And then she told her small audience that as a crime reporter for the *Chronicle*, she had begun covering Randy Fish after he'd been convicted of killing five women in and around San Francisco.

"Fish had a preferred victim type," Cindy said. "His victims were slim, dark-haired college girls, and MacKenzie Morales was exactly the kind of woman Fish liked to torture and kill.

"But for some reason, Fish didn't kill Morales.

"In fact, he loved her and spoke her name with his last breath. And she loved him, too."

Cindy went on to say that after Fish's death, she began to investigate MacKenzie Morales, who was the prime suspect in three murders, but that she had escaped police custody. While on the run, Morales was suspected in the murders of several women of the type Randy Fish had once targeted for torture and death.

Cindy said, "I had met Morales once, and I had inside information as to her possible whereabouts. I thought if I could create a safe place for her to talk, I could appeal to her ego. I hoped she would tell me why Randy Fish had become her mentor, her lover, and the father of her son.

"Sounds risky, right? Or maybe it sounds totally *nuts* for a reporter to chase a psychopathic killer in order to write a newspaper story.

"But I was hooked, and I thought the Fish-Morales story could be the crime saga of a lifetime. While researching the book, I came to understand that you don't always get the answers you're looking for. But the answers you get often tell it all.

"The whole story is in this book."

She'd done it—whipped up her audience, who clapped enthusiastically, asked questions, and then lined up at the table so Cindy could sign their books.

I couldn't stop beaming. I was so damned proud of her.

I stood off to the side of the table, but I heard Conklin saying to Cindy, "Sign this one to me. Don't spare the *Xs* and *Os*. And sign this one to my mom."

Cindy laughed and said, "You betcha. Whatever you like, handsome."

Cindy and Conklin had been having a hot off-and-on relationship for years, and right now, they were *on*. I hoped that this time they were on for good. Cindy signed books for her man and maybe her future mother-in-law. When Conklin stepped aside, I asked the lady in line behind him if she could do a favor and take a photo.

"You bet," she said.

I handed her my phone and grabbed my partner and my good friend. We put Cindy in the middle, linked arms around her, and said "Cheese," and then we said it again.

Cindy said, "Let me see." We all gathered around that little piece of tech that had caught all three of us, looking good—how often does that happen? A banner had been strung behind the podium. It was centered right over our heads: AUTHOR CINDY THOMAS, TODAY.

"Wow, this is totally great," Cindy said, doing a little dance in place. "A perfect photo of a perfect day."

Chapter 19

THE MAN WHO called himself One was in the back-seat of the four-door sedan, directly behind the driver. The two other guys in his crew were numbered Two and Three to prevent the accidental blurting out of an actual name.

One knew that human stupidity was the only thing that could screw up this job. Everything else was easy. There were no security guards. No camera. There was plenty of cash in the drawer and there was only one person in the store.

Unlike bank jobs, where security was tight and the average take was about four Gs, check-cashing stores ordinarily had fifty to a hundred thousand in the drawer. And while mercados had less, this one had an impressive stash on the premises from its Western Union franchise.

One and his crew were quiet as they watched the light foot and car traffic on this commercial block of South Van Ness Avenue. When he was ready, One used a burner phone to call the cops.

He said urgently, "Nine-one-one? The liquor store at Sixteenth and Julian Avenue is being *robbed*. I just heard *shots*. Lots of them. Send the cops. Right away."

He clicked off as the operator asked his name, but he knew she would put out the radio call. This diversion would draw any random cruisers patrolling the neighborhood and send them to a location a half mile away.

Across the street, the girl in the brightly lit Spanish market was behind the counter, taking cash from a customer, an old man. One thought the girl looked to be in her midtwenties. She was wearing a long tan cardigan over a shapeless brown dress. When she'd put the groceries into the customer's striped fabric bag, she came from behind the counter and walked him to the front door, saying a few words to him in Spanish as they stood on the sidewalk.

Then she went back inside the shop, closed the

glass door, and flipped the sign inside the door to CLOSED. One watched her walk to the back of the long, narrow store.

When she was out of sight, Two said, "She's alone, One. Did you want me to stay in the car? Save some time?"

One heard sirens now, the cruisers and unmarkeds heading over toward Sixteenth. It was time to go.

"Yeah. Good idea. That'll work."

One and Three got out of the car with their SFPD Windbreakers zipped up, masks in their pockets, and guns tucked down in their belts. It took only seconds to cross the street. When they stood in the deeply shadowed doorway of the little grocery store, they pulled on their masks.

One adjusted the bill of his cap and knocked on the door, looking down so that the girl would see the SFPD on his Windbreaker but not his masked face.

Three stood with his back to the store and looked at his feet while he waited for the locks to open. The locks clattered and the bell above the door rang as the girl opened the door.

The two men rushed the doorway. The girl

screamed. One grabbed her arm and pushed her inside while showing her his gun. Three threw the locks and flipped the switches at the left of the doorway, dousing the lights in the entrance and front section of the store.

The girl shouted, "Get out of here, get out!" She wrenched her arm free, spun around, and broke for the back door.

One shouted, "Stop or I'll shoot! I mean it!"

The girl stopped and cried out, "Don't hurt me! *Please!*"

One said to her, "No one wants to hurt you, miss. That's the truth. Now, hands up. Turn around. That's it. Now go to the cash drawer and open it. Do that and everything will be fine. Just do exactly what I say."

The girl put her hands in the air and said, "I'll give you the money, no problem." She walked to the counter, edged behind it, and faced the gunmen with her back to the wall of cigarettes and mouthwash and deodorant.

One spoke soothingly.

"That's good. Very smart. Now you can put your hands down and open the drawer. A minute from now we'll be out of your life forever."

The girl hit a couple of keys.

The cash register pinged and the drawer shot open.

"Way to go," said Three. He leaned over the counter and reached for the money in the drawer. He wasn't ready for the gun the girl pulled out of the pocket of her baggy brown dress.

Chapter 20

MAYA PEREZ HAD two babies. One was growing inside her body, fourteen weeks old now, and very precious to her. The other baby was this market. It had been her father's, and he had poured everything he owned and earned into keeping the shop open, to put food on their table and because he wanted her to have something of value when he died.

Then, a month ago, his cancer had killed him.

Ricardo Perez hadn't lived to see his grandchild, but he had felt the baby was a blessing and he had left Maya the deed to the store that had been named Mercado de Maya for her.

And she loved this place: every hand-lettered sign, the shelves her father and uncle had made from scrap lumber. She knew where every box, bottle, and tin belonged. Now that she was pregnant and on her own, the store meant survival.

She had moved upstairs to her father's flat and intended to run this place and bring up her baby right here.

There was no way she would let anyone steal from her. It was just not happening.

Besides, there was something else.

When the men in the police jackets came to the store, she thought they were looking for information on the check-cashing-store holdup on Tuesday a few blocks away. But when she saw the masks and the guns, she knew that as soon as they got the money, they would shoot her.

Like they had done to José Díaz.

Maya was having physical sensations she'd never had before. Tingling, light-headedness, her blood pounding almost audibly. She knew that this was her body reacting to the fear of imminent death. There was no way to run or to hide, but she was thinking clearly and she was determined. She thought, *No way they're killing my baby*.

She kept her father's little Colt in her pocket. And when the man reached over the counter to get his hands on her money, she saw her chance.

She had the gun pointing at his heart, her finger on the trigger, and she said very clearly and firmly, "Drop your gun."

Maya barely saw the second man move, he was so fast. His hand came down hard on her arm. She got off a shot, but even in that split second, she knew her shot had gone into the floor.

After that, the bullets punched into her and everything went black.

Chapter 21

IT WAS AFTER 8 p.m. when Conklin and I left the Hall, both of us wiped out and done for the day. My partner walked me to my car in the Harriet Street lot. We were making comfortable small talk about whose turn it was to bring breakfast to our desks in the morning. I told him I'd see him then.

I rolled up my window and had just fired up the engine when Brady called on my cell. I slapped my window, signaling to Richie to hang in.

Brady sounded edgy.

"Boxer, a tipster has reported multiple gunshots coming from a Mercado de Maya on South Van Ness Avenue. He saw cops exiting the store in a hurry. Sounds like a possible Windbreaker cop hit. Check it out."

He gave me an address and I said, "We're on the way."

Rich was still standing next to my car.

"On our way where?" he said.

I headed my car toward South Van Ness with sirens and lights full on, while Rich called Joe and Cindy to say we'd been detoured. Within five minutes, I pulled up to the sidewalk twenty yards down the street from a small market with a sign over the window reading MERCADO DE MAYA.

A cruiser pulled up behind us. I got out of my vehicle and asked the two uniformed officers to drive around to the rear of the shop. Then Conklin and I advanced on the front entrance to the little grocery store.

This is always the worst moment: when you don't know if the scene is still hot, if bullets are going to fly, if victims are being used as shields.

The front door of the market was wide open when my partner and I approached with guns drawn. The doorjamb was intact, lights out in the store. Smell of gunfire.

Hugging the doorway, I called out, "Police. No one move."

I heard a moan and then a woman's voice saying, "Over here."

We entered the store. Conklin found the lights and covered me while I followed the voice to the floor behind the counter only yards away.

I holstered my gun and knelt beside the victim. She was writhing in pain and bleeding from what looked to be several gunshot wounds.

"I've been shot," she told me. "He shot me."

The cash drawer was open. Bottles had fallen off the shelves. There had been a struggle.

I heard Conklin speaking to dispatch, and backup was coming through the back door. I said to the victim, "Hang on. Paramedics are on the way. What's your name?"

"Maya. Perez."

I said, "Maya, an ambulance will be here any minute. You're going to be OK. Do you know who shot you?"

"I'm pregnant," she said. "You have to save my baby."

"Don't worry. The baby will be fine."

I said it, but Maya Perez had lost a lot of blood. It was pooling on the floor, and she was still bleeding heavily from a gunshot wound to her thigh. I pulled my belt through the loops and cinched her thigh above the wound.

It really didn't help.

I asked her again, "Maya, do you know who did this to you?"

"A cop," she said. "Two of them."

She coughed blood, and tears streamed down her face. She groaned and cupped her stomach through the blood-soaked fabric of her dress. "Please. Don't let my baby die."

Chapter 22

I GRIPPED MAYA PEREZ'S hand and mumbled assurances I didn't quite believe.

Where were the EMTs? Where were they?

"This cop who shot you," I said. "Have you ever seen him before? Has he come into the store?"

She whipped her head from side to side. "They were wearing. Police. Jackets. Masks. Gloves. Latex."

"Is there someone I can call for you? Maya? Do you want me to call a friend, a relative?"

Colored lights flashed through the front window as the ambulance parked on the sidewalk outside the market.

Conklin shouted, "She's over here!"

I stood up to give the paramedics some room.

"Her name is Maya Perez. She's pregnant," I said.

The EMTs spoke to one another and to their patient, lifting her onto the stretcher and wheeling her out the door. I followed them.

My heart was aching for Maya, imagining her fear for her unborn child. I stood for a moment and watched the receding taillights as the van took her toward Metropolitan Hospital.

Then I called Brady.

He asked, "So, this was another cop heist?"

"'Fraid so," I said. "Windbreakers. Masks. Gloves. She didn't know the shooter."

As I talked to Brady, I was looking at all the likely places for a security camera to be positioned inside the store. I was hoping for an eye on the front door or the cash register. I found nothing, so, still talking with Brady, I went outside and looked for cameras on other shops that might be angled so that they caught the front of the mercado.

I said, "Brady. I don't see a security camera. Anywhere."

He cursed and we had a few more exchanges until I couldn't hear him over the sirens coming toward us from all points. Conklin and I closed the shop door and were waiting for CSU when I got another call from Brady.

"Maya Perez didn't make it," he told me.

"Damn it!" I shouted. "Killed for the contents of her cash register. Does this make sense, Brady?"

"No. Come back to the house. I'll wait."

Chapter 23

IT WAS CLOSE to midnight when Conklin and I got back to the Hall. Brady was in his office, and although we'd been in constant contact for the last four hours, he wanted to talk to us.

The fluorescent bulbs overhead cast a cold light over the night shift behind their desks in the bullpen, making them look as bloodless as zombies. Brady, too, looked half dead, and I would say that my partner and I didn't look any better.

Conklin and I took the two chairs in Brady's cubicle. My partner tipped his chair back and put his shoes on the edge of the desk, which Brady hates, but this time, he let it go.

"The MO was the same as the last two times," Conklin said. "The shooters left nothing behind except the rounds in Maya Perez's body. The ME is sending them to the lab."

"We have to turn over every stone," said Brady. "And the dirt under every stone."

I said, "Assuming these are the same Windbreaker shooters, they're slick, Brady."

I went on to say that in the morning we'd go through the cop records again and look for motive: cops who were ambitious but undistinguished, those who were disgruntled, or had been suspended, or had retired early. I said to Brady, "But even saying they're actually cops, they may not be from our station, or even our city."

Brady nodded.

Then he said, "I'm assigning additional people to this case."

I had been focusing on the work ahead, so Brady's comment totally snapped my head around.

I said, "Another team?"

"Inspectors Swanson and Vasquez are now on loan to me from Robbery, along with four guys who are working for them."

Ted Swanson and Oswaldo Vasquez were reputed to be great cops. But assigning them and their teams to this case, rather than other detectives from Homicide, only tangled the chain of command. I wasn't pleased. Brady read my expression.

He said, "Here's what we've got: three big-money heists, two DBs in six days, no evidence, media attention of the worst kind, and pressure from upstairs.

"So don't get territorial, Boxer. Swanson knows robbery homicide cold. Vasquez grew up on the streets. Whether the doers are cops or pretend cops, it doesn't matter. If we don't get those mopes into lockup, all of our jobs will be compromised. Understand?"

I admire Brady. Sometimes I even like him. But he was ticking me off. Swanson and Vasquez had nothing on Conklin and me.

"Get in touch with Swanson and Vasquez," he went on. "I want all of you canvassing around that shop until you get somewhere or someone. This spree has got to stop and I don't care who stops it."

"We're on it, boss," Conklin said.

"Read you loud and clear, Lieutenant," I said through clenched teeth. I felt a sleepless night coming on.

Chapter 24

THE SQUARE BRICK apartment house was at the dead end of a street lined with other plain three-story buildings on Taylor Street at Eddy: the worst part of the Tenderloin.

Yuki pushed in the outer door and pressed the intercom button marked KORDELL.

The buzzer blared and Yuki climbed three stinking flights of graffiti-tagged stairs and knocked on the door at the end of the hallway. A woman cracked the door open.

"I'm Yuki Castellano. Mr. Jordan from the Defense League sent me. Did you get a call?"

"Yes, yes, please come inside."

Mrs. Kordell was African-American, very thin, about forty; she wore a red bandana over her hair and had yellow rubber gloves peeking out of the pockets of her cargo pants.

Yuki walked behind her down a long, narrow hallway and entered a living room crowded with what looked to be generations of furniture. An elderly gentleman sat in a lounge chair, his hand on a carriage that he was rocking gently.

Mrs. Kordell introduced Aaron-Rey's grandfather as Neil Kordell and said her husband was at work.

"My husband is a total wreck," she said. "He doesn't sleep. He barely speaks. Aaron-Rey's death has destroyed him."

Yuki took a seat on a worn brown sofa, and Mrs. Kordell sat in a matching armchair. On the table between them were pictures of a smiling Aaron-Rey Kordell.

"Why don't you tell me about your son?" Yuki said.

The boy's mother picked up one of the photos and held it as she talked. "Aaron-Rey was fifteen. He was so big, he looked older than that—but he had the mind of a child."

Yuki nodded. Zac had told her that Aaron-Rey was mentally handicapped but had never been in any kind of trouble before his single, fatal incarceration.

"He went to school every day, or so we thought," said Aaron's mother. "I only found out later that he hung around bad places."

"After the shooting at the crack house," Yuki said.

Mrs. Kordell nodded, and then her father-in-law told the story.

"What happened is that Aaron-Rey saw that these three dealers got shot and he ran out onto the street. The cops came after him and arrested him for killing those men. It was a *joke*. Aaron-Rey had the mind of a five-year-old. He didn't even know *how* to shoot a gun."

Mr. Kordell seemed to realize that he was rocking the baby too hard, said into the carriage, "Sorry, sweetheart," and clasped his hands in his lap. He was agitated and clearly grieving for his grandson.

Yuki said to the elderly man, "As I understand it, the police found the gun on Aaron-Rey's person."

"Yes, that's true. He picked *up* the gun. He didn't think more than *Oooh. A gun*. And the police took him in and they questioned him for hours and didn't call *us*."

Mrs. Kordell picked up the story.

"If Aaron-Rey hadn't been wrongly arrested, if the police hadn't played him by saying how great he was for killing those drug dealers, my son wouldn't have waived his rights and he wouldn't have confessed. And he wouldn't have been killed in jail while waiting for *trial*. My son would still be alive."

Yuki felt the sharp pain of the people who had loved Aaron-Rey, and she could see that now that she was with the Defense League, terrible stories like this one would be her life.

Mrs. Kordell was saying, "The police should pay for what they did, right, Ms. Castellano? They should *pay* so that they don't do this to anyone else's child."

Yuki said, "I agree. We've already filed the case against the City and the SFPD. It's going to be difficult, Mrs. Kordell. The City is going to defend itself. You may have to testify. Tough questions are going to be asked, and the City's lawyers are going to put Aaron-Rey in a bad light, if they can."

"We're all in," said Mrs. Kordell.

"So are we," said Yuki.

Actually, joining the Defense League seemed

like a rash and very crazy idea. Was she even remotely cut out for this?

Yuki embraced the Kordells and said good-bye.

She hoped to hell she'd made the right decision.

Because when Parisi and his expensive law firm hired by the City were through chewing her up, she might never want to practice law again.

Chapter 25

AFTER LEAVING THE Kordells, Yuki drove four blocks and parked her car directly across the street from the crack house where three months before, Aaron-Rey's life had taken a very bad turn at Turk and Dodge Place. As Aaron-Rey's mother had said, the Tenderloin was a bad place to raise children. No kidding. It was the worst.

The impoverished district was an underworld of savagery, mayhem, and despair, populated with aggressive drunks and crackheads, runaways, derelicts, streetwalkers, and violent thieves. The best you could say of people who survived on these streets was that they were pitiable; most of them were doomed.

Yuki knew better than to get out of the car.

She was here to see the scene of Aaron-Rey's death, to get the picture in her mind so that she could make a moving and watertight narrative for a jury.

She stared ahead at the peeling, sagging wood-frame building with a Chinese restaurant on the ground floor. The abandoned second floor, according to Yuki's information, was a flophouse for junkies. The third floor was the trading floor, where wads of folding money and small packets of powder changed hands.

She saw the scarred metal door that opened from the interior of the house and emptied out to the street. It was clear from the numbers of men and boys who looked both ways before going through that door that the crack house was doing a brisk business.

Yuki imagined Aaron-Rey Kordell hanging out at this place because it was cool, then being shocked and confused when the shooting went down. She saw him picking up the gun—a shiny, valuable object—and running.

If this version of the story was true, and Zac Jordan believed it was, Aaron-Rey had suffered wrongful death and his family deserved justice that could only be delivered in the form of a multi-million-dollar settlement from the SFPD and the City.

Yuki was thinking about the work yet to do when there was a rap on the window. Startled, she turned to see a uniformed officer, making a circle with his index finger, indicating that she should roll down her window.

"Officer?"

"You having car trouble, miss?"

"No, not at all."

"You know it's not safe here, right? A woman got shot over on Hyde a couple of hours ago. Wait—"

The patrolman leaned down to get a better look at her face.

"Aren't you the lady who's married to Lieutenant Brady?"

"Yes. I'm Yuki Castellano."

"I'm Clark. John. That's *my* office," he said, hooking a thumb toward his cruiser, smiling at her. "You're working, Ms. Castellano? Because I gotta say, I wouldn't like my wife to be in a car by herself on this block."

"I'm OK, Officer. I'm looking into a multiple

homicide that took place a couple of months ago," she said, pointing to the crack house.

"Oh, right. Those drug dealers who were whacked over there. I arrested that poor mutt who did it."

"Aaron-Rey Kordell?"

Clark said, "That's him. He was a runner. Ran out for coffee, smokes, that kind of thing. I don't know why he shot those pushers. But he did the City a service."

"What did he say when you arrested him?" Yuki asked.

"Said he didn't do it," said Clark. "I asked what it was he didn't do and he said, 'I didn't shoot those guys upstairs.' So we went into the house and found the DBs."

Yuki thanked the officer, then pulled her car out into the congested three-lane street. This would be a twisted story to sell to a jury. And maybe an impossible case to win.

Chapter 26

BACK IN HER new office at the Defense League, Yuki slugged down half a bottle of water, kicked off her shoes, and locked her handbag in a desk drawer. She booted up her computer and pulled up the Aaron-Rey Kordell dossier Zac Jordan had compiled.

The cops who interrogated Aaron-Rey after his arrest were Inspectors Stan Whitney and William Brand in Narcotics/Vice Division, SFPD.

Yuki easily located the documents showing that Aaron-Rey had been booked and incarcerated upstairs on the sixth floor of the Hall, County Jail #3, pending trial. There was also a death certificate dated a day later showing the teen's cause of death as "sharp force trauma" to the liver, and a brief report from the correctional officer on duty that a fracas had broken out in the showers.

Eight suspects had been listed in the investigation of Aaron-Rey's death, but there had been no evidence, no proof, no confession—and no informant had come forward. Aaron-Rey's death had been subsequently written up as a killing by an undetermined individual and no further action had been taken.

The transcript of Whitney and Brand's interrogation of Aaron-Rey Kordell wasn't listed in the document file, but Zac Jordan had already obtained the video.

Yuki slipped discs into her computer. From the very beginning, the hairs on her arms stood up as she watched the masterful interrogation of a mentally challenged black kid by a team of experienced investigators.

She watched for about an hour. Then she called her new assistant, Gina, and told her that she needed to have a deposition notice served on SFPD inspectors Stan Whitney and William Brand.

Chapter 27

CONKLIN AND I had met up with Robbery Division's Edward "Ted" Swanson and Oswaldo Vasquez on the corner of Mission and Twenty-Third Street, down the block from the now shuttered Mercado de Maya.

Swanson and Vasquez got out of their unmarked Chevy and we all shook hands. Swanson was stocky, with a pleasant face, sandy hair, and light-gray eyes. He was exactly my height at five foot ten, probably my age, too.

Vasquez was muscular, shorter and younger than his partner, with an impressive grip. Looked like he'd once been a prizefighter.

The four of us, along with another team from Robbery, worked the streets adjacent to the mercado, canvassing dives and whorehouses and apartments in the area.

I personally went through Maya's apartment above the mercado, looking for anything that would indicate that her death was anything but a murder of convenience for the Windbreaker cops. I found nothing but a small, neat home and a tiny room Maya had prepared for her unborn child. This was as heartbreaking a vignette as you could possibly imagine.

The walls were a sunny yellow in a room that never got sunshine. The crib had been made by hand, as had the mobile of rainbows hanging over it. It was all too touching, too sweet—and if I never see a rainbow mobile again, it will be too soon.

I interviewed Perez's neighbors, who told me what a sweetheart Maya was, and a few of them cried. Feeling heartsick and angry, I rejoined the canvass, and between the eight of us, we came up with exactly no idea who had robbed the market and shot Maya Perez to death.

No one admitted to even seeing the robbery go down, and this time, there was no grainy surveillance footage.

When our shifts were over, the eight of us

refueled at a local diner and went back to canvassing both sides of the block again, catching up with people who had day jobs and had just returned home.

We still got nothing.

And then I got a call from Clapper, head of Forensics.

"We've run the slugs taken from Maya Perez."

"Good. What did you get?"

"Two thirty-eights. The gun that fired them isn't in the system. I wish I could give you something. A name. Another shooting. Something."

There are days when being a cop is challenging and worthwhile and days where the job is duller than watching a dripping faucet. Today was neither. A cold canvass in the Mission was stressful and dangerous, and it had been unproductive. A total bust.

Conklin and I went back to the Hall and briefed Jacobi and Brady on our great huge bag of nothing. That meeting took about five minutes, including the Q&A.

I walked with Richie out to the parking lot.

He tried to cheer me up, saying, "Someone is going to slip up. Bad guys almost always do."

I've said the same thing to Richie. Joe has said the same thing to me. It's the cops' version of "Everything is going to be OK."

Hah.

Whoever these Windbreaker bastards were, they were organized, they were disciplined, they had untraceable weapons, and their timetable was short. How long would it be before another low-tech, high-cash business was shot all to hell by men portraying themselves as San Francisco's finest?

My partner and I waved good-bye, got into our respective cars, and exited the lot.

As I made the turn up Bryant, I glanced up at the Hall and saw that Jacobi's office light was still on. I felt bad for him. The job was my former partner's entire life.

We had to get these shooters for a number of reasons, and one of them was surely that we had to do it for Jacobi, before he retired as chief of detectives.

Chapter 28

LIFE WAS GOOD chez Molinari. Martha, our loyal doggy, was asleep on the sofa next to my dear husband, and although he was on the phone, the wonderful aromas coming from the kitchen told me dinner was ready.

"Heyyyy, Blondie," said my husband, cupping the phone. I blew him a kiss and went to the baby's room.

Julie was sleeping on her back. She had kicked off her blanket, so I pulled it up to just under her arms. She waved a fist in her sleep and I kissed her sweet forehead. She pushed me away. I took this as a sign that my little girl was asserting her personality, even in her sleep. *Go, Julie.*

But seeing my beautiful child brought me

straight back to Maya Perez's apartment. I visualized the small, windowless room she had turned into a chick-yellow nest for her baby, who would never be.

I watched Julie breathing for more than a few minutes. Then I shucked my clothes and hit the rain box for fifteen delicious minutes. When I returned to the living room in my man-in-the-moon-patterned PJs, Joe was dishing up the chicken cacciatore.

I went over to him and got a big hug, a kiss, and a belated jumpety howdy-do from Martha.

I said, "Lucky, lucky me." And I meant it.

"Vino?" Joe asked me.

"You don't have to twist my arm," I said. "So what did the home team do today?"

"I've been doing a little work," he told me.

"Really?"

"Free work. I've been looking into the CBM case."

Joe seemed to be in a very perky mood. He pulled out a bar stool for me and another for himself and we sat down at the kitchen island to eat.

"What, I have to ask, is CBM?"

He poured out the glasses of wine and explained, "Claire's Birthday Murders."

"Really?" I said, repeating myself. "And you came up with something?"

"I think so," he said. "The start of something, anyway."

I liked what I was hearing, but at the same time, I felt a little bad. Here was this big-time law enforcement guy on the bench, now doing unpaid busy work—for me. But he wasn't complaining.

"Tell me about it," I said.

"I'm gonna do that. Eat your dinner before it gets cold."

I tucked in. Joe leaned closer and said, "I went back five years and found every crime that happened on the twelfth of May in San Francisco. A lot of shit happened, Linds."

"I'm guessing fifty-sixty murders a year," I said.

"Sixty-eight last year," he said.

We grinned at each other. I loved working with Joe. I was even a little envious that my husband had the time to focus on this case and work it from home.

"Although there was no shortage of violent crime, very little of it resembled the murder of your victim on Balmy Alley. Along with the three fatal stabbings from this year and the previous two, I found a stabbing fatality in each of the two previous years that met my narrowly defined parameters. And I didn't find any stabbing fatalities just like it on any other days or in the years preceding the one that happened five years back."

"Tell me about the stabbings in years one and two."

Joe grinned. "You don't have to beg."

He took our empty plates to the sink and brought two slices of pie to the island. It was apple pie, and he'd stopped to put ice cream on top. I looked up at him like, *Is this for real?*

"Nope. I didn't make the pie. But then, I was busy on a very twisted and highly interesting case."

I laughed at him, grabbed a plate, and stuck in a fork.

"Run it for me, will you?"

"Yes, I will, Sergeant," said Joe.

Chapter 29

"SO I DID a little time-traveling," Joe said. "The victim in year one of the five was an uptown lady, Ms. Alicia Thompson. She had been to Neiman's and she was on her way to her car."

"We know this how?" I asked.

"Shopping bags and keys in her hand. And she was killed a half block from Union Square Garage, where her car was parked."

"Did anyone see anything?"

"Nope, and Ms. Thompson got the full five-star investigation. Chi was the lead investigator."

"And how did the case play out?"

"Not only were there no witnesses, there were also no forensics, no footage, no nothing. Not even the knife. Make a note, Sergeant Blondie. Taking the knife is a common thread."

"Duly noted," I said.

"OK, next victim was very different than Ms. Thompson."

"Do tell," I said.

I took the empty dessert plates away and put them in the dishwasher while Martha and Joe headed to the living room. We all settled into the oversize leather sofa. Martha put her head on my lap, letting out a contented sigh.

"Victim number two, Krista Toomey, was homeless," Joe said. "Twenty-five years old, in bad shape even for a meth addict. She was sleeping in an alley in the Tenderloin. Olive Street. No witnesses, but plenty of people knew her."

"And were they able to contribute anything?"

"Nothing useful. I found the autopsy report. Like your victim who was stabbed in the back outside her father's diner, this girl was also stabbed from behind. The first or second blows were fatal, but the killer kept going. Stabbed her all over her back, arms, buttocks—thirty-five separate wounds.

"Based on the shape and depth of the wounds, the weapon was probably a paring knife, but it

wasn't found. Again, no witnesses, no evidence —
and because there were no leads, and no friends or
relatives stepping forward putting pressure on the
police, and there were a whole lot of open cases at
that time, this one went cold."

I understood. I might even have been aware
of this crime. All murder cases *should* be worked
and solved. But there's not enough manpower,
not enough time, and some cases just don't get
solved.

I said, "Whoever killed these women is smart,
aware of cameras and bystanders and what
constitutes forensic evidence. The victims were all
women, and it looks like the five you've identified
were all killed by a common type of knife that is
never left behind."

"Agreed, Linds. Add all that to the date they
were all killed, May twelfth. And that's why I
suspect one person killed the five of them."

"So you conclude what about the killer?"

"If my theory is right, this dude didn't know his
victims," said Joe. "He chose these women because
the circumstances were favorable to him. And
whatever his motive for murder, he was driven to
kill violently. This is a guess, but I'd say he was mad

as hell. He kills people he doesn't know in a ferocious *rage*."

"Yeah, I can see that. And since he kills in daylight, and no one sees him, he's got a cloak of invisibility."

"I decided to leave something for you to figure out."

"Awww. Thanks."

My husband patted my thigh. "I believe my work here is done. Let's go to bed."

Chapter 30

AT QUARTER TO eight the next morning, my partner and I met in the break room and made coffee. Conklin's face was lined from sleeping facedown, and I'm sure I looked like I'd gotten no sleep at all. Which was true.

When Julie wasn't calling for something, Martha was edging me off my side of the bed.

And then there were my vivid, disturbing dreams about Maya Perez, in which she begged me not to let her die. I knew enough pop-culture dream analysis to know that I was Maya in that dream and I didn't want to die or let anything hurt my baby.

Conklin and I sugared our coffees and went to our computers. I took A to M and he took N to Z as we started going through Human Resources files looking for "sore thumbs." That was what we were calling disgruntled cops who'd been demoted or dropped or had stalled in dead-end careers—the type of malcontent who might risk life in a federal pen without chance of parole in return for a quick payday.

We found plenty of sore thumbs, none of them named Juan, but every last one of them had guns and a navy-blue Windbreaker with white letters across the chest and back spelling out SFPD.

At eight thirty Brady called us into his office.

One look at him and I knew it was Groundhog Day. Just as he'd been every day this week, Brady was grouchy.

I almost said "What now?" but I kept my mouth shut.

Brady said, "I'm sorry I've been a pain in the ass."

What? Say that again?

"Jacobi thinks the whole station is going down the tubes This is between us three, OK?"

"OK," Conklin said. "What's happened?"

Brady said, "In the past year, a half dozen drug dealers have been shot in crack houses and stash pads all across the city. The cash and the drugs disappear, never to be seen again. Word on the street is that the robbers are cops."

No wonder Brady was pissed. There was a bad cop epidemic. And we were just about the last to know.

I said, "Are you thinking these cops who're ripping off drug dealers could be the same rogue cops we're looking at for the check-cashing stores?"

"Could be, or maybe not. We've got no surveillance of the shooters, of course, and no one's naming names. I'm just saying, keep this in mind."

When I got back to my desk, there was a note on my chair, handwritten on my own FROM THE DESK OF LINDSAY BOXER notepad.

The note was in block letters.

It read, WATCH YOUR BACK, BITCH. REMEMBER WHO YOUR FRIENDS ARE. THEY WEAR BLUE.

I looked around the squad room.

The night-shift guys were getting ready to check out while the day shift was just settling in. I saw about a dozen and a half cops I'd worked with for years. I loved some of them, liked many of them. But one of these guys was warning me not to cross the thin blue line.

Not even if catching bad cops meant catching murderers.

But then, blind loyalty was a bone-deep part of being a cop. I did wonder, though, if this note was from one of the Windbreaker cops. Could one or more of them work in this very squad? Or was the note from any one of the cops in this room who had simply seen the open investigation file I had left in plain sight on the computer?

I showed the note to Conklin, who gave me a questioning look. I shrugged and put the note in my handbag.

I would watch my back. But I was shaken. Next chance I got, I was going to have to report this to Brady.

Chapter 31

AT EIGHT THIRTY that morning Richard Blau had his keys in his hand and was about to open the folding metal gates in front of his check-cashing store on the corner of Market Street and Sixteenth. Blau was a careful man. He and Donna had successfully run their business for over thirty years and were closing in on retirement.

He had heard that a couple of stores like theirs had been robbed in the last week, making him glad he had an alarm tied into a central station and also had a shotgun behind the counter.

His wife had gone to park the car in the underground lot around the corner. Blau always opened the store. First he unlocked the padlock; he had started sliding the metal gates back from the plate glass window when he saw three men get out of a gray sedan two cars up from the entrance to the store.

The three men wore police Windbreakers and billed caps, which gave him pause, but then he caught a look at the identical latex masks they were all wearing.

They were latex pig masks. There was no unseeing that.

He had a panicky thought that if he could somehow get into the store and close the door behind him, this nightmare could be derailed. He could call the police—but he canceled the idea almost as soon as he had it. Last thing he wanted was for Donna to approach the store and get shot.

The men in the pig masks were coming toward him quickly. Their timing was good. There were no pedestrians, and the few drivers were focused on getting through the next traffic light. Blau saw that each of the men had a gun. He had to outthink them. He had to use his brain.

Blau raised his hands.

When the men were six or seven feet away, Blau said, "I'm not armed. I'll give you whatever you want. Just don't hurt me."

"OK, man. We don't want to hurt anyone," said one of the robbers. He seemed to be in charge. And he seemed to be a youngish man. His voice was young.

Blau tried to take in everything about him so he could give a good report of the robbery after it was over. He thought the guy who had talked to him was about five ten. And Blau saw from his hands that he was white. He couldn't describe the man's build because of the boxy shape of the Windbreaker, but he thought he might be able to recognize the guy's voice if he ever heard it again.

Blau said, "What do you want? My wallet is in my back pocket. Take it. I've got a few hundred in cash in there. And my watch is pretty new. Take that, too."

Blau was still holding the keys in his hand. There was nothing he could do about that.

A different one of the three men said, "Let's go into your store, OK, Mr. Blau?"

They *knew* him. They knew who he *was*. Blau felt faint. He'd never had a gun pointed at him before. He almost said, "Do I know you?" but shut the thought down.

If the guy thought Blau knew him . . . He

thought of Donna. He prayed she wouldn't show up now. She wouldn't be able to handle this.

Blau said, "OK. I'm going to open the door now, and let's do this fast before customers come in."

"Lead the way, Mr. Blau," said one of the masked men. "Let's go."

Chapter 32

BLAU FIDDLED WITH the gates and the keys and the double locks. His hands were shaking and he could smell his own sweat. He thought there was every chance he could be living his last minutes on this earth. He got the front door locks open, and then the door creaked and swung wide, and then he hit the lights so that when his wife showed up, she could see through the plate glass window. See that this was a holdup.

Please, Donna, don't come into the store.

One of the fucking armed robbers complained, "Hey. We don't need no steenking light, man."

"I have to see so I can open the *safe*," Blau said. "Believe me, I want you out fast. I'm happy to give

123

you the money, all right? Just trust me, OK? I'm working with you."

Blau didn't wait for a reply. He walked deliberately and quickly past the block of folding chairs, all the way to the back of the store where the lines were painted on the floor, delineating aisles leading to the teller windows. Next to the windows, on the far right side of the wall, was the security door that divided the store into the public space and the office area behind it.

The safe was in the office. Blau turned his back to the robbers to open the door, telling those shits, "After I give you the money, you can go out the back door. Be safer for you."

The men, maybe they were boys, the way they were all jumpy, were crowding into the office area with him. One of them, the smallest pig, was getting anxious, looking around, saying "Let's go let's go let's go."

Blau turned his eyes away from the credenza where he kept the shotgun and pointed out the wooden cabinet below the counter.

"The safe's in here," he said.

The one who had been saying "Let's go" was now saying "Come on come on come on."

Blau's hands were out of control. He could barely hold a key, and both the key and the cabinet lock were small. He poked at the lock until he finally got the key into it, turned it, and opened the lower cabinet where he kept the old cast-iron safe. Taking no chances, he angled his body so they could see the safe and said to one of the boys, "You're in my light."

He tried not to look at the kid, give him any sense whatsoever that he knew who he was, but his mind was running through the faces of all the kids, white, black, Latino, who came into this place to cash checks. His tellers talked to them. The transactions were brief. The only time he ever talked to a customer was when there was a problem.

"Step on it, Daddy," said a guy with a gun.

Blau said, "I *am* stepping on it."

He went for the safe with both hands, but at the last minute, he pressed the silent alarm, a button right under the lip of the cabinet. Then he turned the knurled knob of the safe. He knew the combination as well as he knew his own birthday, but he accidentally went past the second number and had to start over.

The kid standing closest to him put the muzzle

of his gun right next to Blau's temple and said, "You have till the count of three.

"One . . ."

That was when a lot of things happened at once.

The combination lock clicked into place and Blau swung the safe door open. The guys in the police Windbreakers focused on the envelopes of money inside the safe. And the front door of the shop was kicked open.

Cops swarmed in, yelling *"Everyone freeze! Hands in the air!"*

Blau crouched behind the counter and covered his head. He jerked with the sound of every cracking gunshot. And there were a lot of them.

"Please, God," he prayed, "make this all stop."

Chapter 33

BY THE TIME Conklin and I arrived at the Cash 'n' Go, Market Street looked like Red Hot Sales Day at a used-car lot. I counted a dozen cruisers with every grille and cherry light flashing, two ambulances parked down the block on Sixteenth, the ME's van pulling in, and the CSU mobile blocking the view of the store.

That must've been a disappointment to the many bystanders behind the barrier tape, crowding the sidewalks on both sides of the narrow street. But then a chopper appeared overhead, guaranteeing live pictures on Eyewitness News.

Windbreaker Cops Strike Again.

My partner and I left our car up on the curb between a Jilly's Gym and the Third Hand Rose

Consignment Shoppe and walked toward Swanson and Vasquez, our superstar Robbery squad partners also working this case.

They were standing outside the Cash 'n' Go. After a couple of days canvassing the area around Mercado de Maya with them, I'd found Swanson both efficient and kind. Vasquez was easygoing, and the pair of them were very professional.

I had to admit that Brady had made a good call putting them and their four men on the Windbreaker cop detail.

Vasquez smiled, relief written all over his face, saying, "I got my witnesses in the car. Taking the Blaus back to the house to take their statements. Then I'm gonna go out with my lady and celebrate."

After some fancy wheel work, Vasquez peeled off, and Swanson said to us, "Three John Does are down inside the store, all wearing Windbreakers, none of them breathing."

Conklin and I followed Swanson under the tape and through the door. The interior of the Cash 'n' Go was lined with pressed-wood paneling; counters ran at elbow height around two sides so people could sign their checks and fill out paperwork. There were a dozen metal folding chairs in the center of the store, all of which had been knocked out of line; white strips on the floor leading to three teller windows; and an open security door at the end of the room.

Two bodies lay sprawled on the floor between the chairs, blood pooling on the lino. I could see the body of a third where he had fallen across the threshold of the security door. Bullets had punched holes in the paneling, and shell casings were all over the floor.

Conklin said to Swanson, "Quite the shooting gallery. What happened exactly?"

Swanson called over one of the men on his team, Tommy Calhoun, a young guy, going bald at the back of his head, a cigarette smoker to judge by the nicotine stains on his fingers.

Calhoun gave us an animated summary of the Windbreaker cops' attack on the check-cashing store, including the owner tapping the silent alarm.

At about the same time Blau hit the alarm, his wife was seeing the robbery in progress through the plate glass. She called it in, then flagged down a cruiser for good measure.

"The uniforms came in," Calhoun told us

excitedly, making his hands into guns. He said, "Pow-ka-pow-pow-pow."

"I'm guessing the shooters had wallets on them," I said.

Swanson grinned. "Wouldn't that be nice? No wallets, but CSI just got started. We'll know who these guys are in an hour."

Was it over?

I was ready to exhale, I really was. I stepped around the blood and the CSIs taking pictures and stooped to get a look at one of the dead men.

He'd taken a couple of shots to the chest and one to his face through his mask—a pig mask. That was new. The Windbreaker cops on the video we'd seen were wearing plain face masks.

Then I noticed that the doer wasn't wearing gloves. I looked over at the second man, who'd taken out half a block of folding chairs when he was shot. Same kind of pig mask. And he wasn't wearing gloves, either.

Why had the slick gunmen we'd seen on surveillance footage changed their MO from nighttime robberies to morning, when there would be less money in the safe and more possibility that customers would enter the store?

Why had they gotten sloppy?

Swanson answered his phone, saying, "Yeah." And "Uh-huh."

"Amateur hour," Conklin said to me under his breath.

"Copy that," I said.

Swanson said into the phone, "Yeah, I think it's a done deal, Chief. When CSU finishes up, I think you can tell the press we got the bad guys."

I hadn't taken Swanson for an optimist, and while I hoped he was right, I knew he was wrong. The dead men on the floor of the Cash 'n' Go?

They were copycats.

I would bet my badge on it.

Chapter 34

YUKI ENTERED THE paneled and richly furnished conference room at Moorehouse and Rogers, Attorneys-at-Law.

Six of the firm's lawyers sat around the large mahogany table, and so did the first of the two narcotics cops she had come to depose.

Inspector William Brand was stout and muscular and had a two-day-old beard. She knew from watching him on video that he had the initials *WB* tattooed on the side of his neck, as if they'd been burned there with a branding iron.

He smiled at her when she came into the room. Like *What's up, honey?*

This was the problem with being small. And, OK, cute.

The pricey lawyers hired by the City of San Francisco introduced themselves, and hands were shaken all around. Someone offered her coffee while another pulled out a chair.

So far, all of this fit her expectations, right down to the oil paintings of the founding partners on the wall.

What she wasn't prepared for was the knock on the door, for one of the lawyers to open it, and for Len Parisi to walk in. The floor shook a little when he crossed it, and not just because he weighed almost three hundred pounds.

Len Parisi was like a force of nature.

She'd thought he would present himself in court at the most effective moment, but clearly, her case and his hinged entirely on Whitney and Brand's interrogation of Aaron-Rey Kordell.

She and Parisi exchanged the briefest of pleasantries, and when that was over, Yuki asked for the video to roll.

Then she said to Inspector Brand, "I've seen the footage of your interview of Aaron-Rey Kordell. I just need some background. What did you think his motive was to shoot those three crack dealers?"

"Motive?" said Brand. His eyebrows shot up and he pushed back a bit from the table. "It was a holdup. He wanted the money. Or the drugs. Or both."

"And what did he have on him when he was arrested?"

"The patrolmen who nabbed him just found the gun," said Whitney. "He either passed off the loot or it was taken offa him."

"Kordell confirmed that?" Yuki asked.

"He denied everything," Brand said. "And as the victims were dead, we didn't have anything else to go on."

"I see," said Yuki. "So when Aaron-Rey confessed, it was open and shut."

"We earned our pay," said Brand. "He denied everything until he couldn't deny it anymore. Then he spilled. Said he found the gun. He shot the dealers. He ran."

"And you believed him?" Yuki said. "He was fifteen. He had a below-normal IQ. He had no record."

"He said he was eighteen, and he was bright enough to put bullets into three scumbags," said Brand. "You have to commend him for that. Too bad the kid got killed. He did a public-service triple homicide."

"Were Mr. Kordell's hands and clothing tested for gunshot residue?"

"No. We had him in the box right after his arrest for carrying the weapon. We thought he would confess pronto. But it took longer and the gunshot residue just slipped our minds."

Yuki said, "But there's no doubt in your mind to this day that Aaron-Rey Kordell did those shootings?"

"None," said Brand. "I have not a doubt in the world."

Chapter 35

INSPECTOR STAN WHITNEY was more refined than his partner. He had fine features and a short beard; he was wearing wire-frame glasses and a blue denim shirt under his blue gabardine jacket.

Yuki asked Whitney the same questions she had asked Brand and got the same answers. Aaron-Rey Kordell had been arrested for carrying a gun that had recently been fired. He said he didn't shoot anyone, but his explanation of why he had the gun was weak and he was a prime suspect. And then he confessed to a triple homicide.

She asked Whitney why Aaron-Rey hadn't been represented by a lawyer, and the detective told her he had waived his right to an attorney. And because he had no record and had lied about his age, and didn't ask for his parents, his parents hadn't been present.

During the depositions, Parisi said nothing, asked nothing, just fixed Yuki with his brooding and steady glare. It was a look that was far from his customary benign countenance. And it was freaky. When Yuki finished deposing Stan Whitney, Parisi's co-counsel from Moorehouse and Rogers asked, "Anything else we can help you with, Ms. Castellano?"

"I'm good," Yuki said. "Thanks for your time."

She really couldn't get out of the conference room fast enough. Brand was an intimidating cop, and Whitney's straight-shooter manner could assure anyone of his good intentions—to their detriment. Having heard their testimony and seen clips from the videoed interrogation, a jury with an open mind would be moved and would see the cops' determined manipulation of a kid who had no resistance to them.

In the few minutes between leaving the law offices and reaching her car, doubt crept into Yuki's mind.

Parisi.

She would be going up against Parisi in front of

a judge and jury. Parisi had had fifteen years of litigation experience before he came to the DA eight years ago.

And he would do whatever he could do to build up Whitney and Brand and their lawful interrogation and subsequent arrest. That was the only thing he had to do. Show that the interrogation had lawfully produced Aaron-Rey's confession.

If he could convince the jury of that, the Kordells would lose their righteous lawsuit, and she would be humiliated. She just couldn't let any of that happen.

She could not.

Chapter 36

CINDY LEFT THE Chronicle Building and caught a cab the second she stuck out her hand—a lucky break at rush hour. She gave the driver the address of Quince, a terrific restaurant in the Jackson Square area. Then she sat back in the seat and thought about how mysterious Richie had seemed when he called and asked her to meet him for dinner. She hadn't been able to get anything out of him, but he was at a crime scene and unable to talk.

Still, she wondered what he *wasn't* saying.

She flashed back, as she always did, to their recent past: how they'd been wonderfully, fabulously engaged when their opposing issues had caught up to them and overwhelmed the magic of their living-together love affair.

They'd broken up, and bad times had followed for each of them in different ways. And then circumstances had thrown them back together and they'd connected on an even deeper level.

Now they were living together again, and Cindy was afraid.

Not by the closeness and the magic, but because she could see Rich loving her and them so much that he would want them to repledge their commitment and he would propose marriage again. Which, sadly, would bring them exactly back to their main point of conflict: Richie wanting kids. Which he wanted many of and soon. And Cindy figuring there was time for all that—later.

Take the last three weeks, for example.

She'd been working a hideous story about a man who'd killed his wife, mother-in-law, and two small sons. She had researched, written, and polished her five-thousand-word piece and had gotten it into Tyler's in-box three minutes before closing today. Tomorrow she was taking off for a ten-day book tour.

And her book was a tremendous source of pleasure. Not just that she'd been a big part of solving a terrible crime, but that she'd written a book-length work that had been published and was, if not exactly catching fire, performing well. Her editor had asked her to sketch out new book ideas for the publisher. Which was holy freakin' wow. A lot of great things were coming true, things she'd worked toward for years. Years!

But at the same time, she didn't want to lose Richie. She loved him so much, had missed him so much, loved coming home and getting into his lap and holding him while they breathed and hugged out the tension of the day.

Oh, please, Richie, please don't push this. Please don't try to close the deal.

"This where you wanted to go, miss?" the driver asked.

"Yes. Totally. Thank you."

Cindy paid the driver and went inside the restaurant. The maître d', a man named Arnold, took her to the more private back room, a very pleasant space with exposed-brick walls and Venetian glass chandeliers and aromas of wonderful house specialties floating on the air.

She took her seat, ordered a double Scotch, and had made progress with her stiff drink by the time Arnold brought Richie to their table. Her lover bent to kiss her and swung down into his chair, cool air from the street coming off him along with the smells of detergent and shampoo. He just looked great.

"Umm," he said, pointing to her glass of Scotch. "What's the occasion?"

She shrugged. "I was kind of in a mad lather all day. Got my pages in to Tyler on time. And now I'm thinking ahead to tomorrow . . ."

"I know. Almost two weeks away from home. That's why I wanted to have dinner at our favorite place. Have a little *us* time."

"Yeah?"

"Sure. Because, shit, Cindy. I miss you already."

Cindy pushed the glass away and took Richie's hands.

"You're the best guy I've ever known, ever. Ever."

He pulled her toward him and kissed her—with meaning.

"God, Richie," she said when the kiss ended. "I'm gonna miss you, too."

Chapter 37

I MET YUKI for lunch at Grouchy Lynn's in the Dogpatch neighborhood: a cute little greasy spoon with striped wallpaper and two-person booths and the best French fries east of the freeway. I ordered a club sandwich with everything and got my teeth into it while Yuki played with her salad.

Yuki has always been moody in the best possible way, meaning she can be sober and focused one minute, and in the next minute launch her contagious chortle, which could pull anyone's bad day out of the basement. But since her near-death experience during her honeymoon a few months ago, and it was really near death for hundreds of people, I've hardly heard her laugh at all.

And she wasn't laughing now when she told me she had taken a major fork in the road.

I pounded the ketchup bottle in the direction of my fries and said, "What fork?"

"I took the job," Yuki said.

She put down her utensils, abandoned her salad, and told me about a not-for-profit called the Defense League and that her client was *dead*.

"Who is this dead client and what are you supposed to do for him?" I asked.

"His name was Aaron-Rey Kordell, and he may have been coerced by the police into confessing to a triple homicide he didn't commit. Then, while awaiting trial in the men's jail, he was murdered in the showers by person or persons unknown."

I grunted. A big part of the job was to get confessions. Cops were allowed to lie, and it was conceivable that people got worked over or tricked and confessed to things they didn't do—but not often. Not that I knew about.

Yuki was saying, "Lindsay, if this story is in fact true, if Kordell was coerced into a confession and was then killed while awaiting trial, this is going to be a case against the city, the SFPD, and probably the cops who interrogated him, for I don't know how many millions."

I stopped eating.

A lawsuit against the police department would be a disaster for everyone in it, no doubt about it. A disaster. As Yuki's friend, I had to be a fair sounding board. But never mind me.

"Your husband is a lieutenant in the SFPD," I said.

"I know that, Linds."

"What does he say?"

"He's pissed off. We're barely speaking."

"Oh, man. You're pretty sure Kordell was innocent?"

"He was caught with the gun on him. He was fifteen. Low IQ. It would have been fairly easy to get him to confess. I've seen the video of the interrogation. The narcs lied their faces off, Linds. Like 'Tell us what you did and then you can go home.' Then they told him what he did—their version."

Yuki went on. "It might help me if I knew why Aaron-Rey was killed. Did he just piss someone off in jail? Or was he killed to avenge the deaths of those drug dealers? Because that would go to him being guilty."

"I hope I don't live to regret this, Yuki," I said, "but I'll see who was in lockup at the same time as Kordell. See what I can see. I don't promise anything."

"Just promise that whatever happens, we're still buds."

"*That* I can promise," I said.

Chapter 38

AT JUST BEFORE 5 p.m. that day, Yuki followed Officer Creed Mahoney through several steel doors and gates to the jail on the sixth floor of the Hall of Justice. From there she was escorted to one of the claustrophobic counsel rooms with high barred windows, reserved for meetings between prisoners and lawyers.

She'd been waiting for about ten minutes when the door opened and Li'l Tony Willis clumped into the room in chains from wrists to ankles, all five foot nothing of him, wearing an orange jumpsuit and two full sleeves of tattoos, twists in his hair and 'tude on his face.

"Who are you again?" Li'l Tony asked as

Mahoney threaded his chains through the hook in the table.

"Fifteen minutes, OK, Ms. Castellano?" said Mahoney. "I'll be back."

The door closed and locked.

Yuki said to the man-boy wife beater, drug dealer, and possible killer sitting across from her, "I'm an attorney. Yuki Castellano. I want to hear about Aaron-Rey Kordell getting killed. What happened?"

"Are you kidding me? You want to ask me did *I* kill him? Because no, I didn't. Got any cigarettes?"

"I hoped you might be able to tell me who might have killed Kordell, because that could be helpful."

"To who? I got nothing to tell you because I didn't do nothing to that retard. So if that's all, this is good-bye, Ms. Cassielandro."

"Here's what I know. You've given evidence against Jorge Sierra," she said, referring to a savage Southern California drug lord who was known as Kingfisher, a man whose whereabouts were unknown. Even his true identity was a mystery.

"You were one of his inner circle, weren't you, Tony? Don't bother to lie. I know a lot of cops and

I know you cooperated. If Sierra finds out, you're going to have a very short li'l life."

The kid looked scared for the first time. He shot his eyes around the small room, searching for a camera.

"Who said that?" he said. "Whoever said I ratted on the King is lying, lady. I'm no snitch."

Yuki said, pressing on, "Let me be very clear. I'm not looking to pin Kordell on you. I'm looking to find out why that kid was killed."

"Same thing," said Tony Willis. "OK, listen, it wasn't me. It mighta been a couple of guys in here working for the King that took him out. But tell you the truth, Kingfisher's name was in the air, but I don't think he had nothing to do with it.

"I'm spekalating, Ms. Cassielandro. I don't know shit about who killed A-Rey. That's all. And it's for free."

"I'll have cigarettes for you in the canteen."

"That's it?"

"Here's my card. You have any new thoughts about who killed A-Rey, get in touch. I'd consider that a big favor."

After Tony Willis was taken away, Yuki rode the elevator down to the street, went to the underground garage, and found her car. She drove to her office, her mind on what Li'l Tony had told her, which was nothing.

Shit. She thought of Aaron-Rey, that sweet look on his face in the picture in his mother's hands. She couldn't imagine that boy killing three drug dealers who'd befriended him.

No matter how many ways she looked at it, Aaron-Rey killing three drug dealers made no sense at all.

Chapter 39

WICKER HOUSE PURPORTED to be a wholesale showroom for imported wicker and rattan furniture. It was on the edge of Bernal Heights, on Cortland Avenue, a medium-rent light-industrial area that became more residential as the two-lane road ran uphill.

This particular building was in the middle of the block, blending in with the row of chunky, putty-colored or gray cinder-block two- and three-story buildings, some with wood siding under the eaves, several with fire escapes, none of them giving off a feeling of welcome.

The back of the shop opened onto a parking lot, which was accessed by a service road. The back door was made of reinforced steel and posted with signs reading TO THE TRADE ONLY and APPOINTMENT REQUIRED. The name of the shop wasn't posted, and neither was a phone number.

At just before three in the morning, there were seven cars in the parking area at Wicker House's back door. One was a Mercedes SL belonging to the proprietor of Wicker House, Nathan Royce. The other vehicles belonged to the staff.

Also parked in the lot, not far from Wicker House's back door but out of range of the surveillance camera, was an unmarked white Ford panel van. The man who went by the name of One was behind the wheel.

One had learned the Wicker House layout from an informant. The front part of the building's ground floor was a half-assed showroom. The back of the ground floor was a lab with rear-door access, convenient for moving chemicals and product quickly.

The lab techs made synthetic drugs: cathinones, known on the street as bath salts, and cannabinoids, synthetic marijuana. The second floor of Wicker House was a short-term warehouse for the product waiting to be shipped out. There was also quite a lot of heroin on that floor, and at certain times, a lot of cash was in transit through the premises.

One's informant had told him when shipments would move out of Wicker House to the hub of the larger enterprise, final destination unknown. Altogether, the payload was worth upward of five and a half million.

Men inside the building were armed and alert, which made this job riskier than taking out a couple of stoned junkies in a crack house.

One said to his crew of two men, "Ten minutes, OK? We waste men, not time."

There was tension inside the van as the three men put on Kevlar vests and their Windbreakers, gas masks, and SFPD caps. They screwed the suppressors onto their M-16 automatic rifles with thirty-round magazines. When he was ready, One stepped out of the van and shot out the camera over Wicker House's back door. The suppressor muffled the sound of the bullet.

Two and Three exited the van, went to the steel-reinforced rear door, and set small, directed explosive charges on the lock and the hinges. They stood back as Two remotely detonated the charges. The soft explosions were virtually unnoticeable in the area, which was largely deserted at night.

One and Two lifted the door away from the frame. Three entered the short hallway that led to the lab and started firing with his suppressed automatic rifle. Glass shattered. Blood sprayed. Once the men in the lab were down, the three men in the Windbreakers rushed the locked door to the second floor.

When the lock had been shot out, the shooters breached the door and bolted up the stairs toward the second floor.

They were met with a furious onslaught of gunfire.

Chapter 40

TWO WAS IN the lead as the blast of gunfire shattered the Sheetrock in the stairwell, showering plaster and spent brass down on him and the other guys in the crew.

The gunfire was expected.

The three men flattened themselves against the stairwell wall. One screamed, *"This is the police! Drop your weapons!"*

Two aimed his CapStun launcher and fired the military-grade pepper bomb up the stairwell.

There was a loud bang. The canister dropped onto the warehouse floor and hissed as it released the fine mist. A moment later, two men on the second floor stumbled toward the head of the stairs, hands over their watering eyes, coughing helplessly, calling out, "We don't have guns. Don't shoot."

One said, "I'm sorry, but put yourselves in my place."

He fired two short bursts with his M-16, then stepped out of the way as the bodies tumbled heavily down the stairwell.

The shooters climbed to the second floor, and One looked around the warehouse, which was just as the snitch had described it. It took up the whole second floor.

In front, against the wall facing the street, were stacks of wicker furniture. In back, around where One and his crew stood, office equipment was lined up on the various tables and shelves. There were copiers, rolls of plastic and tape, scales and money counters, cardboard cartons, and a laptop with the screen showing a quadrant security camera view of the inside and outside of the factory, including the static from the camera he'd shot out over the back door.

There was a gun safe in the corner, five by three by two, and it was open, saving them the trouble of blowing off the door with explosive charges. The safe was full of packets of heroin, and next to the safe were stacks of small cardboard cartons and a half dozen army-green duffel bags. Three unzipped the bags and announced, "A whole lot of cash, One."

One heard a racking cough coming from a closet. Gun readied, he opened the door to find a man sitting in a crouch, covering his eyes with his arms. The man looked up, his face swollen from the pepper bomb. He cried out, "I can't *see*."

One said, "Where's Donnie? Where's Rascal?"

The man in the closet hacked and wheezed. "They left."

One said, "OK. Sorry. I have to do this, bro."

He pointed his weapon at the man on the closet floor and fired. The guy screamed, then collapsed.

One called out, "You guys OK?"

After Two and Three said they were fine, One went over to the cartons stacked on the floor. He opened flaps and did a rough tally of the eight-by-six-by-four-inch parcels, neatly wrapped in glittery paper, taped and labeled BLUE WAVE, MAD FANTASY, SUNNY DRAGON.

There were hundreds of pounds of synthetic pot in these packets, the kilos of H in the gun safe.

With the duffel bags of cash already packed, they were good to go.

The three men made several trips up and down the stairs, which were littered with bodies and shell casings. They carried the bags of money, the cartons and packets of drugs, and the laptop down to the van.

When the last of the haul was safely stowed, One went back into the house, where he checked to make sure the downed men were all dead. Then he turned out the lights and locked the door.

Wicker House was out of business, but One and his crew were very damned close to early retirement.

Job well done.

Chapter 41

THE BLEEPING PHONE rang way too early.

Joe said to me in his sleep, "I'll get her."

"Stand down, pardner," I muttered. "I got this."

I grabbed my phone from the nightstand and noticed that the time was 5:51 and that my caller was Brady. As far as I knew, I was off duty. I took the phone into the bathroom. "What's wrong, Brady? Personal or business?"

"Business."

Thank God. I didn't want to hear that he or Yuki was in a jam. Once that was out of the way, I had to know, why the hell was Brady calling me at oh-dawn-hundred?

"What's up?" I said.

Martha came into the bathroom and made

circles around my legs until she successfully herded me into the kitchen. Her bowl was empty.

"I'm in your neighborhood," he said.

"You're saying you want to stop by? It's not even *six*."

"I've just come from the scene of a massacre," he said.

"I'll put the coffee on," I told him.

By the time I'd showered and dressed in whatever was on the bedroom chair, Brady was at the door. He looked blanched, and this wasn't the fault of the lighting.

"Sit," I said, indicating a stool at the kitchen island. I double-checked that both bedroom doors were closed. Then I poured coffee and set out milk and sugar. I leaned against the stove, arms crossed, and waited for him to speak.

He said, "Why did you turn down the lieutenant's job? I mean, you had it before you stepped down. Then, when Jacobi moved up, you could've had the job. But you turned it down again."

"I couldn't stand the paperwork, the meetings, the middle-management crapola," I told him. "I wanted to work cases. One at a time."

He said, "No kidding. I feel like a shit sandwich about ninety percent of the time."

He sipped coffee. The suspense was killing me.

"What happened, Jackson?"

"Narcotics had been watching this house in lower Bernal Heights for a couple of months. It's a factory disguised as a furniture showroom. They had eyes on the place, but they didn't know what was going down until it was over.

"The scene inside that house." He shook his head. "Like a freaking war zone."

"Fatalities?" I asked him.

"You bet. I think seven."

"What was it? A robbery?" I asked.

"That's what it looks like. The dead men look like employees. We think the shooters got away," Brady said. "Narco caught a nanosecond of video showing three guys in a white panel van leaving the Wicker House parking lot. At least one of them was wearing an SFPD Windbreaker."

"Come onnnn."

Brady said, "If those were our guys, they're escalating from ripping off drug slingers and mercados to major scores like this. We may have caught some kind of break."

Brady sank into thought.

"What, Brady? What kind of break?"

He snapped out of it. "We've got visuals of two punks leaving the house earlier in the morning, before the raid went down. They don't look like our shooters, but they gotta know something. And we've ID'd them. Punks. Like I said.

"You call Conklin. I'll call Swanson and Vasquez. Clapper is at the scene right now," he said, referring to my friend the forensics lab director.

Brady stared into his coffee mug and said, "Look, Lindsay. I know I've been a dick lately. I'm worried about all this renegade-cop shit going down. I don't mean to take it out on you. And I'm sorry."

His voice caught in his throat. That was Brady apologizing.

"It's OK. I totally understand."

"I'm on your side. Always."

I smiled at him. He smiled back. Sometimes I dislike Brady, and sometimes I love him. Right now, I loved him. Before someone started to tear up, he gave me the crime scene coordinates and told me to check it out and to call him every hour.

When he had gone, I texted Conklin.

He texted back.

We arrived at Wicker House within ten minutes of each other. After touring the bloodbath, my partner said, "I have a hard time believing cops did *this*."

Four of the seven dead men were unarmed, and spent brass littered the floors and stairwell.

Swanson, Vasquez, Conklin, and I were looking over the CSIs' shoulders when Clapper came over to me and said, "We've got more prints than a frame shop. As for the casings, we've got all kinds. From the position of the bodies, it looks to me like the shooters had the advantage of surprise. And they used suppressors."

Then Clapper nicely told us we were in the way.

"As soon as I know anything, I'll call you," he said.

Chapter 42

IT WAS JUST after 5 a.m. and Donnie Wolfe was parked on a free-parking residential street in the Inner Sunset neighborhood.

He was leaning against the hood of his red 2003 Camaro. There were attached houses on both sides of Twelfth Avenue, short flights of steps up to the front doors, slopes down to the garages, almost an apple-pie-and-baseball feel to it.

He'd been out all night and was talking to his girl on the phone, saying, "I was working late, Tamra. You just pack everything you need for a couple of days and don't talk to your friends. Do *not* talk to your mother, or that stupido downstairs. I got a couple of meetings and then I'm coming home to sleep. And then we're outta here."

Tamra was pregnant. Twenty weeks. Donnie didn't tell her his business, and she was cool. But obviously, she didn't like breezing out of town on the sneak, not knowing where they were going and not telling her mother, neither.

"It's going to be beautiful, Tam," he said. "Trust me. Don't talk. Pack. Chill."

The gray Ford was coming up on him, slowing and parking right behind his ass. Donnie pulled on his shirt-tails, making sure they covered the piece he'd stuck in his waistband. Then he got out of his car and walked toward the man he knew as One.

"How you make out? Everything good?" Donnie asked the stocky man wearing big shades and a ball cap pulled down low over his eyes.

"That's close enough," One said to his inside man at Wicker House. Donnie stopped walking and showed his empty hands.

One asked, "Where's your buddy?"

"Rascal's cool," Donnie said. "He's staying out of sight."

One nodded. He said, "Here's your go bag." He reached over to the passenger seat, then tossed a black nylon duffel bag through the open window to Donnie.

Donnie caught the bag, stooped to the sidewalk, and unzipped it. There was a pair of Colorado plates at the side of the bag, which was filled with stacks of banded used bills.

The kid riffled through the money. It looked good and like it added up to the agreed-upon hundred thousand, his cut and Rascal's.

He said to One, "So I guess this is bye-bye."

"As long as you keep quiet. Don't make me come looking for you."

"The big boss—"

"The last I saw of the big boss, he had a mouthful of carpeting."

"Not Mr. Royce," said Donnie. "I'm talking about *his* boss, man. The King. He has an idea who you are. So don't blame me for that."

"I know who *he* is, too," said One. "And I know where he lives."

"Not *my* boss and not *my* problem," said Donnie. "I'm good. I'm checking out. I got plans."

"Your first plan should be to ditch that flashy car," said One. "Be careful, Donnie."

Donnie said, "Back at you, Mr. One. Adios. Take care."

Donnie got into his car and watched through

his rearview mirror until One drove off. Then he took the duffel bag and walked up the block and across the street to the car repair shop on Judah Street, which didn't open for another three hours.

He went behind the garage and picked out a blue Honda Civic, not new, not old, just right. The car wasn't locked. There were no keys, but he'd been boosting cars since he could walk. This was cake.

He hot-wired the engine. Then he got out of the Civic and changed the license plates to the Colorado ones from One. Passing his Camaro on the street, Donnie waved good-bye to his flashy car and drove the Honda east toward the Bay Bridge.

Chapter 43

AFTER CHARLIE CLAPPER had shooed us out of his crime scene, Conklin and I returned to our desks in Homicide, where we spent the morning reviewing Narcotics' footage of the street in front of Wicker House.

At 2:34 a.m. precisely, before the shooting went down, two men had left Wicker House by the front door. They were wearing street clothes: jeans, a dark jacket on one, a light jacket on the other. One of the men was tall and wide, the other smallish and skinny.

The two men each had a quick smoke outside before bumping fists and getting into their cars.

The skinny one got into a red 2003 Camaro registered to Donald Francis Wolfe. The heavyset guy got into a brown 1997 Buick wagon belonging to Ralph Valdeen. Both men were in their twenties and Wolfe had an arrest record ranging from attempted home burglaries to possession to assault. He had also done time as a juvie for car theft.

As we'd been told, at 3:12 a.m., the surveillance crew had captured a split-second clip of a white panel van with three unidentifiable men inside— one of whom could be seen in the camera-side passenger seat and might have been wearing an SFPD jacket. The van was speeding past the front of Wicker House. Looked like mud had been smeared over the license plates.

We saw that clip for ourselves now, forward, backward, zoomed in, paused, and enhanced, and there was no way at all that we could ID any of the three men in the van, not in that light. SFPD Windbreakers? Maybe. I saw what looked like white letters on dark blue or gray or black.

Clapper had reported that the surveillance camera at the back of Wicker House had been shot out and that no hard drive had been found inside the store, not a computer, nothing.

At about nine thirty this morning, Donald Wolfe's red Camaro was called in for blocking a driveway on a residential street a block and a half from an auto repair shop. Then the guy who worked in that repair shop reported that a blue Honda Civic had been stolen and that the plates had been left in the backyard, which wasn't covered by a security camera.

That meant that Wolfe had abandoned the Camaro and was now likely driving a blue Honda Civic with stolen plates.

An APB for the Honda and the Buick had paid off when both cars were sighted on the 101 Freeway just after three.

Conklin and I, with the help of SFPD Traffic Control, located the two vehicles in AT&T Park's parking lot at half past three. The Giants were playing the St. Louis Cards, and it was a beautiful, sunny-streamy day. The lot was completely filled.

Conklin and I showed our badges and IDs and entered the stadium through the Willie Mays Gate. Even the worst seats in the ballpark had a view of the Bay Bridge, and from where we descended the field box steps, directly behind home plate, we could see the entire ballpark.

At the plate stood St. Louis's best hitter, Matt Holliday, with the score tied 1–1 in the bottom of the ninth. All eyes were on the pitcher, Tim Lincecum. All except mine and Conklin's. We had still photos of both Wolfe and Valdeen in our breast pockets. All we had to do was pick those two out from the other forty thousand spectators.

Lincecum dealt Holliday an inside fastball that he lined over third and into the left-field corner. The fans erupted in unison as everyone sprang to their feet. But it was the last my partner and I saw of the game.

Conklin pointed off to our right and about six rows above us to a group of men standing in front of a Tres Mexican Kitchen.

"That's Donald Wolfe. Dark jacket, Giants ball cap."

"You've got a good eye, buster."

I wasn't sure, but by the time we had trotted up the aisle, I saw that it was Wolfe, beyond a doubt.

I approached Wolfe from behind and tapped him on the shoulder. When he spun around, I said, "Donald Wolfe. I'm Sergeant Boxer, SFPD. We need to have a word with you about your recent grand theft auto."

I put Wolfe against the wall and frisked him. As I dealt with Wolfe, Valdeen threw a wild roundhouse punch at Conklin. Conklin blocked it and Valdeen threw another, putting his full weight into it. This time Conklin ducked, then landed an uppercut to Valdeen's chin that made the big guy stagger backward into the Doggie Diner stand.

Tin panels rattled. The vendor squawked. Conklin twisted Valdeen's arms around his back and clapped on the cuffs, saying, "Ralph Valdeen, you're under arrest for assault on a police officer."

No one thought either Wolfe or Valdeen was one of the Wicker House shooters, but there was every chance they knew who had executed the seven men inside. If the shooters were Windbreaker cops, we might have a clue that would help us solve the armed robberies of the check-cashing stores and the mercados, and the shakedowns and shootings of drug dealers all over the city.

I couldn't wait to get these two into the box.

"Hands behind your back," I said to Wolfe.

That was when he decided to make a break for it.

Chapter 44

RALPH VALDEEN WAS winded, cuffed, and newly docile.

But Donald Wolfe had taken a split second of opportunity, tucked his bag under his arm, and run for his life. He tore off past the Doggie Diner, the Port Walk Pizza stand, and the coffee cart, through a group of fans, knocking them over like bowling pins.

Wolfe was small and he was fast. While I stood with Valdeen and called for backup, Wolfe gave Conklin a workout, vaulting over seats, stiff-arming spectators as he wildly searched for an exit.

Wolfe had reached the lower rows of the stadium when Conklin tackled him. My partner got a cheer from all the fans in that entire section as he dragged Wolfe to his feet and shoved him back up the steps to where I stood with Valdeen at the hot dog concession.

"You have the right to remain silent," Conklin said to Wolfe. "Anything you say can be used against you, jerk-off . . ."

Wolfe said, "I gotta call my girl. You gonna hold that against me in a court a law?"

Wolfe is what's called a real smartass. There was no fear in his face at all. And there should have been. He was in trouble. I pulled his duffel bag away from him and unzipped it. There was an astonishing amount of money inside, maybe fifty thousand in neatly banded used bills.

"I'll hold this for you," I said to Wolfe, "until you can produce your pay stub."

Meanwhile, we had attracted some attention at the Doggie Diner. The fans were pumped up and buzzed, and now some of them were turning on my partner and me. Oh, I really love the sound of drunken a-holes yelling, "Hey! They didn't do anything wrong. It's a free country, isn't it? We're all just watching a ball game. What's the damn problem?"

The backup I'd called for was on the way and stadium security was trotting directly toward us.

I said to the hecklers, "Anyone feel like joining our party? Because we've got plenty of room at the jail."

"Police brutality. That's what this is," said a beefy young bruiser showing off for his girlfriend. "I saw it," he insisted. "I'm going to report you. What's your badge number?"

The girlfriend and others were pointing their phones in my face and at my badge. And you know what? I finally got mad.

I shouted to the security guards, "Cuff these people. This one. These two. And her. I'm taking you all in for interference with the police. For obstruction. For being drunk and disorderly."

Hecklers fell back, but not before we had four of them in Flex-Cuffs and were marching them out to the cruisers at the gates.

Two hours later, at half past dinnertime, the night shift was parking at their desks in the squad room. Ralph "Rascal" Valdeen was in holding, and Conklin and I were set to interrogate Donald Francis Wolfe in Interview 1.

Chapter 45

I HADN'T EATEN anything but a burger and a stack of pickle chips since Brady's surprise visit at six that morning. I was irritable and frustrated, and now Conklin and I were in the box with Donald Wolfe, who didn't act like a man who was going down for a felony.

"Do you understand you're on the hook for a felony?" Conklin asked him.

"I didn't do nothing. *You* tackled *me*. That's assault, yo. With a deadly weapon on your person. I got *witnesses*. I didn't *know* you were a cop and that's why I ran."

Conklin yawned. Then he said, "For the record, Sergeant Boxer announced that she was a police officer and showed you her badge. I'm a witness. Sergeant, I'll be back."

Conklin got out of his chair and left the interview room. Generally, Conklin took the role of "good" cop, but right now, he was keeping his powder dry for Valdeen. So I took over the interview with Wolfe.

"Donald," I said. "OK for me to call you Donnie?"

"Donnie is OK," he said. He was twenty-five. He had a sixth-grade education. He had done small time and had had a lot of experience in rooms just like this one.

"Look, Donnie. We've got you on boosting the Honda. Got you cold. I'm going to say you didn't find that big bag of money under a bench at a streetcar stop."

"Funny you say that, Sergeant. That's right. Bench outside the ferry terminal. You got a report of that money being stolen? No, right? It's all mine."

I acted like he hadn't said anything.

"Grand theft auto is going to get you twelve to fifteen."

"For that beater? It's an oh-seven, and I didn't steal it anyway."

"Found it at the ferry terminal?"

"Yes, ma'am. Man said to me, 'Take this car from me, please. I can't afford to have it fixed.' I gave one large in cash and he said, 'Thanks.'"

I picked up the rather thick file of Donald Wolfe's record of juvenile and petty crimes and slammed it down hard on the table. It made a nice loud crack.

I said, "Cut the shit. You want a break on that stolen car, you've got exactly one minute to help me out. After that, my partner is getting what we need from Valdeen. He looks soft, Donnie. I'm betting he's gonna step up to the line."

Wolfe looked down at the table and started shaking his head while muttering, "Nuh-uh-uh. No-no-no."

"No what, Donnie?"

"What is it you want to know, exactly?"

"What do you know about the armed robbery at Wicker House this morning?"

"N.O. Nothing. When I left work, everything was cool. Do you understand? Rascal and me. We're stockroom boys. We unpack the boxes. We ship boxes out. We make labels and check inventory and sometimes we bring coffee to some decorator lady. I don't know shit about shit."

"Did you know there was going to be a raid on Wicker House?"

"How would I know anything about that?"

"Seven people were shot to death. You knew those men, Donnie. You worked with them. You want whoever killed them to get away with it?"

"I hope you get whoever did that. I do."

He looked at me like I was supposed to believe him.

I said, "Do you know anything about men wearing police Windbreakers knocking over mercados? Hitting up drug dealers?"

"What? Cops taking drugs and money off dealers and keeping it for theirselves? I never heard of anything like *that*."

He laughed. Then he got serious. He leaned across the table and said, "Listen up, Sergeant. Other people will take care of this problem that happened at Wicker House, OK? They're a whole lot better at it than you."

That stopped me. "Meaning what? Who's going to take care of this? How?"

Wolfe shrugged. His flip, phony wise-ass personality was back. "Follow the money, Sergeant."

"Explain what you mean by that," I said.

He said, "I get my phone call now? My girlfriend is worried about why I'm not home. Did I say? We're having a baby."

"Who will get to kiss his daddy in twelve to fifteen?"

I left the room and walked next door. I looked through the glass into Interview 2 and watched Conklin get absolutely nowhere with Ralph Valdeen. Another stockroom boy. Didn't know nothing.

Seven men had died, and if that massacre was over wicker furniture, it was a first. More likely, big money and a lot of drugs had been boosted from that drug factory.

I thought about what Wolfe had said in that one honest-sounding statement: Someone would take care of the men responsible. Someone better at it than us. "Follow the money."

I had a shivery feeling as I thought about what kind of payback there might be for the massacre at Wicker House. A feeling the Irish might express by saying "Someone just walked over my grave."

Chapter 46

CINDY WAS BEING treated like a celebrity in a bookstore called Book Revue on Long Island, New York.

This part—the book signings, the people applauding her—she hadn't thought about this at all during the years she'd spent thinking about writing a book.

She had staked out psycho killers in sketchy areas, had spent nights in rough motels or in her car, had worked nights and weekends and pestered cops, even ones she loved, for information that would become a great story, possibly an exclusive one. She had worked the crime desk for the challenge of finding an angle that the police didn't have, for the rush of turning her hand-mined facts into dramatic prose.

It had been a nonstop thrill, and now there was this.

In a time when bookstores were going virtual, this one was what a real bookstore still looked like in her dreams. There were a blue-and-white-checked floor, thousands of linear feet of bookshelves, comfortable nooks for people to sit and read in, and an inviting performance space where writers could give readings and sign books.

The owner of Book Revue, Bob Klein, was coming over to talk to her now. Bob was a good-looking man in his fifties wearing glasses, a starched shirt, and a smart tan suit.

"Cindy, I've got open cartons under your table. I'll test the microphone for you when you're ready."

There was a rope line leading to a table with a blow-up of her picture on an easel behind it, and another easel holding a poster of her book jacket. A stack of books rested on the table with a line of pens. And people were coming into the store in response to the ad and were filling up the chairs, easily twenty women, who lit up when they recognized her from her picture.

She was talking to Bob when her phone rang.

Cindy answered the call and said, "Richie, I'm at Book Revue."

"Hey, sweetie, hang on."

She heard him say, "I'll be back in a second, Mr. Valdeen. Sit tight."

A door closed; then Richie was back.

"Sorry. Got a couple of mutts could have some information on this bloodbath in a drug lab."

"You want to speak later?" Cindy said.

"No, I'm good. So how did it go? Your speech."

"I'm going on in a couple of minutes."

Richie said, "You'll do great. I know that for a fact."

Cindy sent love and kisses out to San Francisco. And then Bob said to her, "Your fans await."

Cindy took the lectern to a nice little round of applause. There were twenty-two people there, her world record. She spoke into the microphone.

"Hello, everyone. So nice to see you all here. I'm Cindy Thomas, and I want to tell you about my book, *Fish's Girl*. Whatever you think about the love between a man and a woman, you probably never thought that serial murder could bond two people.

"But I'm here to tell you about Randy Fish and Mackie Morales, two savage killers, and their marriage—with child—which was as tight as a marriage can be."

Chapter 47

AT JUST ABOUT midnight, One drove a white panel van packed with cartons of synthetic drugs and kilos of heroin toward a meet with a man called Spat.

One had dealt with Spat before. He was a middle-aged guy, a deadly old hand, and go-between for a midwestern drug distributor.

One's sole purpose tonight was to offload a few hundred pounds of drugs and take in stacks of Andrew Jacksons and Ben Franklins. The sooner that was done, the happier he'd be.

The meeting place was a residential area in West Oakland, a dodgy part of the Bay Area known for poverty and crime.

Now One crossed the Bay Bridge to Oakland,

then followed the sign to I-980 west and downtown Oakland, obeying the speed limit and signaling for every turn. Last thing in the world he wanted was a traffic stop. He'd done enough killing for one day. His hands were actually shaking from the trauma of firing the gun.

The GPS was giving him the turns, and he easily found Sycamore Street, a desolate residential block. The houses were scabby with tar paper, the asphalt was littered and potholed, and a group of tough guys gathered on one corner, harassing one another, looking for a fight.

One parked the van, then lifted the M-16 from the foot well and put it on the seat next to him. He ran his finger under his collar, scratching the itch left by the pepper spray that had gotten under his mask.

Time dragged its ass. Spat was late. One had half decided to pull out and arrange another meeting, another venue, when he saw a black minivan rolling toward him in the oncoming lane. The minivan parked across the street from him and flashed its headlights twice before the engine was cut.

One's phone rang. He answered it, saying, "You're late."

"Yeah, but you're going to thank me," said Spat. "I'm coming to see you now."

One clicked off, watching Spat get out of his minivan with a large canvas bag in hand.

Then Spat spoke to him through the open window.

"How's this? I got two kids to unload the van for us. This should take no time. Check it out."

One took the bag of money through the open window and said, "Not that I don't trust you."

"No problem, brother. I'll be right over there," Spat said. When Spat was back in his vehicle, One undid the fasteners on the satchel and riffled through the packets of money. A lot of phony money was circulating these days, and it was common in swaps like these for fake bucks to get into the stacks.

He opened some of the bands, fanned out the bills, and turned on a UV light, looking for signs that the bills were counterfeit. At the same time, he did a first count, arrived at the agreed-upon 1.2 million.

He counted a second time, then repacked the bag and called Spat's phone. The two men exchanged a few words. The minivan started up, then did a U-turn and parked behind One's panel van.

One pulled the lock release, and Spat opened the cargo doors and checked out the drugs in the same way One had checked out the money: carefully.

When Spat was satisfied, the two young men in his employ moved the cartons efficiently to Spat's minivan, then got back inside it.

The transaction was completed quickly. Spat came around to the driver's side of the panel van and said to One, "Talk on the street about some mayhem in a furniture store."

"That right?" One said. "I haven't heard."

"OK, my friend. *Vaya con Dios.*"

"Stay in touch," said One.

It was a cool night, but One was sweating. The Wicker House drugs had reportedly been paid for and were on the way to Kingfisher. He'd expected there would be talk on the street. As long as no one knew who he was.

The gangstas on the corner shouted something at him as he drove past.

He gave them the finger before he realized they

had only shouted "Lights!" He switched on his headlights, got onto the freeway, and headed home.

He'd earned a good night's sleep.

He hoped he could get one.

Chapter 48

TWO MEN SAT in a darkened car on Texas Street, two houses in from the corner of Eighteenth, one block away from a commercial strip. Potrero Hill was a pretty area with a view of the bay from higher on the hill, but lower, in front, all you could see were the facades of the somewhat run-down Victorian houses, the intermittent trees, and the rats' nest of telephone wires overhead.

The guys in the car were watching one house in particular, a quaint, middle-class house that was light green with dark green trim, fronted with a short brick wall and a walk of cement pavers leading up to an unpainted wood-panel front door.

At about midnight, a silver Camry backed into

a spot between a couple of scruffy trees. The man who got out of the car was white and had dark hair with a balding spot at the back of his head. He was wearing a dark-blue SFPD Windbreaker. As he locked up his car, his phone rang. He leaned against his car and spoke and listened.

Then he pocketed his phone, walked up to the front door, and let himself in with his keys. Lights went on in the downstairs hallway and then the kitchen. Those two lights went out, and another went on in the second story, in a front room, probably a bedroom. Within the next half hour, the only light in the house was the blue light from the TV.

And then the TV went off, too.

One of the men in the car said to the other, "I've never liked these old houses. I look at them. All I see is maintenance."

"When you have a family, you like a deck in back. A yard. Barbecue and whatnot. Christ. How long we been waiting here?"

"Take it easy," said the first man. "After we say hello to Inspector Calhoun and his family, we can go get something to eat."

"I'm way ready," said the second man.

"You're sure you don't want to sit here and count stars?"

The second man scoffed. One of them was going to take the front door while the other went to the back.

"See you inside," said the first man.

"Don't get anything on you," said the second man. They both adjusted their guns and got out of the car.

Chapter 49

I WAS AWOKEN out of a heavy sleep by my husband saying, "Lindsay, honey. Wake up."

But why? I heard no shrieks or alarms or barks, no wails or any other emergency sounds. I was in bed and the light in the bedroom was dawnlike, so why was Joe waking me up?

Then my eyelids flew open.

"Where's Julie?"

"Julie is fine. Everything is OK, honey."

I rolled over onto my side and scanned Joe's face for whatever was behind his waking me up when I needed to sleep. He was smiling.

"What time is it?"

"Seven," he said.

"Is it Saturday?" I asked him.

"Yes. We're going for a drive: you, me, and baby makes three. And Martha makes four."

"I can't go," I said.

"The car is gassed up. I'm going to feed Julie. Coffee is on. Just get yourself up and leave the surprise part to me."

I blinked at Joe, thinking how pretty much everyone in the Southern Station was working the weekend on the helter-skelter case of the Windbreaker cops. Still, he was right. I needed a little time to recharge.

I texted Brady that I was taking a mental health day.

He got right back. *Really?*

It's just for the day.

OK. I'll buddy up with Conklin.

A half hour later, the Molinari Four were in Joe's lovely old Mercedes, heading down the coast. Highway 1 hugs the shoreline, and I was reminded once again how gorgeous California is. I'm not saying I stopped thinking about the Windbreaker cops, but I shook the case off long enough to call my sister, Cat.

We made a pit stop in Half Moon Bay, where my sister lives with her two daughters. Pretty soon, the little girls were romping with Martha on the beach and we grown-ups lagged behind them, catching up on missed chapters in each other's lives and marveling at the way the sun lit the coastline.

"You doing OK, Linds?" Cat asked me.

"Yeah. Sure. Like usual, a little preoccupied. How about you?"

"When a princely frog appears, it will all be perfect."

We grinned at each other. I for one was thinking about when Joe and I got married here in Half Moon Bay not long ago.

My sister and I held hands and the girls hugged and kissed me, after which the Molinari family piled back into the car and continued in a southerly direction. Martha sat on my lap and hung her head out the window. The baby slept in her carrier behind us. Joe sang along with the radio.

It was kind of marvelous.

We reached our lunch destination, Shadowbrook Restaurant, which is built into the side of a hill overlooking Soquel Creek. And the best part, the part that made our little kiddo squeal, was the cable car that traveled down from the parking lot to the restaurant so that you could see the tropical gardens and waterfalls outside the glass.

Joe was quite animated over lunch. He'd been working on the case he called CBM, Claire's Birthday Murders. He had mined and sieved the databases, looking for intersecting lines between stabbings of women in San Francisco on May twelfth, as well as murders, bank robberies, domestic violence, and more traffic accidents than I would have thought possible. But still, even with his giant brain and investigatory genius, plus access to law enforcement databases, he'd come up with no hard evidence connecting the incidents to an actual suspect.

But you know what?

Our minds were sharp. We had the space to talk and turn ideas over, to compare what we'd already confirmed about the five women who'd been stabbed to death in San Francisco on May twelfth in sequential years.

Namely, the women were strangers to one another. None of the crimes had been witnessed or solved, and no serious suspects had even been questioned.

We had made progress by the process of

elimination, and Joe and I were even more firmly convinced that the five CBMs on our list had all been done by the same guy.

Something had tripped off that killer five years ago and sent him on an anniversary spree. Unless his fury had run its course, he was still free and highly likely to kill again.

Chapter 50

ON THE WAY home, Joe dropped me off at Susie's Café. Susie's is the Women's Murder Club "clubhouse," where Cindy, Claire, Yuki, and I get together more or less weekly to brainstorm our cases, to bitch about the lumps life hands out, and of course to celebrate good news, both tiny and huge, over hot Caribbean food and cold beer on tap.

I blew kisses to Joe, then turned toward the bright light coming through Susie's windows and the faint plinking sound of steel drums, which got louder when I opened the front door.

Hot Tea was warming up, and regulars at the bar waved as I walked through the main room, down the narrow corridor past the kitchen, and into the back room, where Claire and Yuki were waiting at our cozy red leather booth.

Claire was telling Yuki something that required vigorous use of her hands, and Yuki was listening intently as I slid in beside her. I got and gave a couple of good hugs, and Claire said, "I'm telling Yuki about this stinkin' case I got."

"Catch me up," I said.

I signaled to Lorraine that I needed beer, and Claire said to me, "Yesterday morning, EMTs bring in this eight-year-old girl. The one in charge says Mom's story is that she gave the little girl a bath at four in the morning, went to get a fresh towel, and when she came back, the little girl had drowned."

I said, "A bath at four in the morning?"

Claire said, "Exactly. The EMT quotes the mom as saying the little girl is hyperactive and sometimes a bath calms her down. So I'm checking out this poor little girl, and damn, there's no foam in her mouth, fingers aren't wrinkled up, the lungs do not cross at the midline, but her hair is wet. I look her over. No bruises. No nothing."

Lorraine came with a glass and a pitcher of beer and said, "Lindsay, I recommend the coconut shrimp with rice."

I told her I was up for that, and Yuki and Claire said, "Me, too," in unison. Then Claire went on.

"I give her the full-body X-rays and they're fine. No broken bones, and I send her blood to the lab and it comes back negative for drugs or poison."

Yuki said, "What the hell? She had something viral? Bacterial?"

"Nope," said Claire. "I checked. But when I'm doing the internal exam, I find pizza in the little girl's stomach."

We all pondered that bit of information for a few moments. Then Lorraine brought the food We all sat back as the plates were set down, and Yuki said, "Don't stop now, Claire. Go on."

"OK, hang on," said Claire. She sampled the shrimp and rice, swallowed some beer, dabbed at her lips, and said, "So I call Wayne Euvrard. You know him, Lindsay. Vice, Northern District. He finds out that Mom's got a sheet for prostitution and now this whole four a.m. bath and pizza story is just grabbing me all wrong. And I still don't know what killed this little girl.

"So I ask Euvrard to have Mom come in for a chat. And he does and tells me she comes in to see him wearing a new outfit, has her face on and her hair done. And he says to her, 'What happened to your baby?' And he's pretty sure she's going to say, 'She drowned.'

"But instead, he tells me, 'Mom takes a deep breath and squeals the deal. She says, "I had an outcall. Steady customer, and I needed the money. Anita has a seizure disorder but hardly has seizures anymore and when she does, we just leave her on the floor and she gets over it."'

"Mom goes on to tell Euvrard that Anita must've gotten up and eaten something and then had a seizure, because she was dead on the floor when Mom came home from her call. And Mom decides if she leaves her there and calls the police, they'll take her kids away. So she put her daughter in the tub and called nine-one-one.

"And I thought, *Christ, they'd be right to take away her children. She's irresponsible. Maybe criminally negligent.* And I say to Euvrard, 'Did she say, "If only I had stayed home, my daughter would be alive"?' And Euvrard said, 'Nope. Nothing like that. I saw no remorse at all.'

"So I write Anita up as probable seizure disorder, manner of death natural."

I said, "You're going to let this lady slide?"

Claire said, "That's up to the prosecutor, but Inspector Euvrard did book her on child endangerment resulting in a homicide."

Claire stabbed a shrimp with her fork, held it up, and said, "And *that's* how we close cases in the Medical Examiner's Office."

Claire's delivery was priceless, and Yuki spat out her beer, and yes, this was a bad story, but it was good to hear Yuki's merry-bells laughter, which I hadn't heard in a while. And of course, that was when my phone rang.

"Sorry to interrupt your day off," Conklin said.

"What's up?"

"Tom Calhoun—"

"Calhoun who's working with us on the mercado shooting?"

"Yeah," said Conklin. His voice sounded terrible. "Calhoun and his whole family. They were murdered."

Chapter 51

I APOLOGIZED TO my girlfriends and tried to pick up the check, but they objected, hugged me, and watched me go.

Conklin met me at the curb in his Bronco, PDQ. I got into the passenger seat and buckled up. He turned on the siren and we sped toward Potrero Hill, revving over the slopes and slamming the undercarriage on the downhill drops.

There were only a few streaks of light left in the sky when we got to Potrero, but I knew this neighborhood in the dark. Knew it cold. I had lived a few streets over from the murder house until a few years ago, when my own house burned to the ground.

We turned off Eighteenth Street onto Texas,

which looked like a Saint's Day street festival. Lights blazed from every window on the block, and strobes flashed from dozens of law enforcement vehicles crowding the street. After parking between two CSU vans, Conklin and I badged the unis at the barricade between the street and yard, ducked under the tape, and took the short walk up to the front of the two-tone green Victorian house.

When we got to the front steps, I saw vomit on the foundation plantings and that the doorknob and lock assembly had been shotgunned out of the door.

Charlie Clapper met us on the doorstep. Even on the weekend, he dressed impeccably; his hair was freshly combed, the creases in his pants were crisp, and his jacket looked like it had just come from the cleaner's.

But Charlie looked stunned.

"This is as bad as it gets," he said.

Clapper is director of the forensics unit at Hunters Point, but before he took over the CSU, he was a homicide cop. A very good one. Top dog at a crime scene, he does a first-class job without grandstanding or getting in our way.

I was about to ask him to run the scene for us

when Ted Swanson came out of the kitchen, shaking his head and looking pale and as shocked as if one of his arms had been ripped off.

He moaned, "This is fucked up."

Conklin and I gloved up, slipped booties over our shoes, and entered the kitchen, where we saw the formerly animated robbery cop, Tom Calhoun.

Calhoun was naked, duct-taped to a kitchen chair. He'd been beaten up so badly, I wouldn't have recognized him but for his bald spot. There was no doubt in my mind. He'd been tortured for a good long time by professionals.

All of his fingers had been broken; his soft white underparts had been burned with cigarettes; his eyelids had been sliced off; and finally, probably mercifully, he'd been shot through his temple.

"He didn't go fast," said Swanson, who was standing behind us. "Those fucks cut up Marie, too, before they shot her."

Clapper said, "Marie was found lying over there by the stove. She's on her way to the morgue."

Conklin asked about the kids and Swanson said, "Butch and Davey were asleep when they were shot, looks like. I don't think they knew anything, right, Charlie?"

Clapper said, "I'd have to agree with you there. They didn't wake up."

"I knew these people," Swanson said. "I had dinner here last week. What the hell was the point of this?"

He began to cry, and I put a hand on his arm and told him how sorry I was. Swanson's partner, Vasquez, came into the kitchen, saying, "Sergeant, the second floor is off limits. CSI is dusting everything. We should all get out of here and let these people work."

Chapter 52

I TOLD VASQUEZ and Swanson we'd catch up to them later, but first I wanted to chat with Clapper.

The front door opened and closed, and Conklin and I were alone in a brightly lit living room with CSIs taking pictures, dusting for prints, and swabbing for trace.

Conklin and I had to piece all this into a narrative that made sense, something that would explain what now seemed inexplicable.

Conklin said, "What do you think happened here, Charlie?"

"My opinion? A couple of guys wanted something, and they were willing to torture and murder four people in order to get it," he said. "What did they want? Don't know. Did they get it?

Don't know that, either. It wasn't a robbery. Nothing was tossed. There's small cash and jewelry on the dresser in the bedroom."

He didn't have to tell us to be careful. We followed in his footsteps as he showed us that the lock had been shot off the back door as well as the front. That told us that at least two shooters were involved.

Dr. Germaniuk, the medical examiner on call, came back into the house and said he was taking Tom Calhoun to the ME's office now if that was OK. Clapper said, "Go ahead. We got what we need."

Then Clapper said to my partner and me, "The wife had duct tape residue on her wrists and ankles and across her mouth, so she'd also been taped to a chair. I'm guessing she was cut loose and beaten while her husband was still alive and watching."

I said, "Oh, my God" a few times, and Conklin looked like he wanted to punch the wall. I asked Clapper to go on.

"Here's how it probably went down," Clapper said. "The family was upstairs, probably asleep. The doers shot out the locks and entered. Calhoun probably came downstairs."

"He had to be armed," I said.

"His nine was found in the living room. Fully loaded. The gun is bagged and ready to go to the lab."

"So Calhoun comes down the stairs with his gun," I said. "He didn't shoot?"

"He was outgunned. Outmanned. I think he tried to negotiate. I imagine he told the perps, 'Get out. Nothing's happened yet,' something like that. The doers maybe turned it around on him."

Conklin said, "Like, 'Come into the kitchen and let's talk. We'll leave your family alone.'"

"Yeah," Clapper said. "Something like that. Then maybe the wife comes down the stairs."

Conklin said, "Right. They take the gun from Calhoun. Move him and his wife into the kitchen."

"Oh, man," I said visualizing the scene, the terror. I saw the shooters telling the Calhouns to get undressed. She has to duct-tape her husband to the chair, then one of the shooters does the same to her.

Putting the next part of it together in my mind, I figured Mrs. Calhoun was tortured to motivate Calhoun to give them what they wanted. What did they want? Did Calhoun have it?

We followed Clapper upstairs to the bedrooms and saw the blood-drenched sheets in the bunk beds where the two boys had been shot in their sleep. They were now in body bags on the way to the morgue with their parents.

My partner and I stood in the open front doorway with lights flashing red and blue behind us and thanked Charlie for the tour.

He didn't have to say, "Get these bastards," and I didn't say, "Call us if you learn anything." We all knew what we had to do. Calhoun's death was job one. Every cop in the Hall of Justice would be on this until the Calhouns' killers were found. The work would go on all night and it would continue until it was over.

But there was nothing for my partner and me to do in this house. Not tonight.

Chapter 53

WHEN I WALKED into our apartment and kicked off my shoes, Jimmy Fallon was on the tube and I no longer felt like the same woman who'd spent the day with windblown dog ears in my face, who had walked and talked with my sister and nieces, who had cuddled with my husband and baby, laughed over nouvelle cuisine, and slugged down beer with two of my best friends.

I briefed my husband on the aftermath of the torture and murder of a cop I knew, and his family, and gratefully accepted a glass of wine and a neck rub.

Then I got on the phone. My first call was to Dr. G., followed by a conference call with Brady and Conklin. After that, I called Ted Swanson, who was not only emotionally involved, but had also been part of the Robbery Division team working the Windbreaker cop case with Vasquez and Calhoun.

When I had all the available information, I called Jacobi, our chief, my dear friend and former partner, and brought him up to the minute. He already knew parts of the Calhoun tragedy, but I gave him a few details he didn't know.

"A roll of garbage bags had been left on the kitchen counter," I told Jacobi. "I think the perps changed their clothes and took their bloody ones with them, along with their cigarette butts, shell casings, and sharp instruments."

Jacobi said, "So let me guess. No prints. No DNA."

"Nothing yet," I said.

Jacobi used strings of expletives in combinations I'd never heard before. The gist of the F-bombs was that all the freaking over-the-top TV crime shows had taught the freaking criminals what not to freaking do.

"They knew a few things from experience," I said. "It was a very buttoned-up operation."

I let Jacobi rant for a while, then told him good

night, and when I finally hit the sheets, I couldn't sleep.

I was organizing the case in my mind, getting ready for the squad meeting in the morning, doing all that thinking while lying with my head on my husband's chest, listening to him sleep. My thoughts circled in and around the Calhoun house, where people had been sleeping in their beds.

I had a bad fantasy of the same guys breaking into our nest on Lake Street. I heard locks being shot off doors. In this bad fantasy, I got my hands on my gun, but it wouldn't fire. My fantasy didn't go any further, thank God.

But sleep became an impossible dream.

When Julie woke up at three, I walked her around the living room and looked out at the street below to see if anyone was lurking in an idling car. At six I took Martha for a quick run, and by seven fifteen I was at my desk in the Homicide bullpen.

Conklin arrived a few minutes later. He hung his jacket behind his chair and said, "I had a dream."

I looked up at him. He wasn't kidding.

"I woke up thinking there's a connection between what happened to Calhoun and the Wicker House shootings."

"What was the connection?" I asked.

"I'm still thinking about it."

"OK," I said. "Your subconscious is making a link. Probably from all the dead bodies. All the blood."

"Probably," my partner said. "But there is something sticky about those two things together."

Just then, Richie got a call from Cindy, and then a ragged-looking Brady dropped by our desks. He said to me, "At eight o'clock. You can brief everyone, right?"

"No problem."

The squad room filled with cops. Some sat behind their desks, others parked themselves in spare chairs, and more cops stood three deep at the back. The room was packed with the day shifts from Homicide, Narco, and Robbery.

Swanson and Vasquez stood at the front of the room with me and I introduced them. Then I told about sixty of my fellow officers what we knew about what had gone down in the green Victorian house on Texas Street.

Brady gave out assignments. And then we went to work.

Chapter 54

CONKLIN AND I brought Swanson and Vasquez into Interview 2. When we all had coffee in front of us and were settled in, I started by saying, "I can only guess at how rotten you feel. We need everything and anything that could help us with the Calhoun murders. Anything you may have heard or surmised about enemies, disagreements, contacts with informants, shady business dealings, a fight over a parking spot—it doesn't matter how unlikely it might seem to you."

Swanson stopped me from going on. He said, "We get it, Boxer. You ask, we answer. You need a handle on this, and we're counting on you."

Conklin checked that the camera was on, then

sat down next to me, saying, "We're recording this, just because."

Vasquez clenched his fists and said, "Calhoun wasn't dirty. He was a good person. He was a good cop."

I nodded. And Conklin said, "Tell us whatever you know about him. We'll ask questions as they come up."

Swanson sighed and said, "Calhoun transferred in from LA Vice about two years ago with a good reputation. He was partnered with Kyle Robertson, who joined Robbery, don't remember when offhand, but before that he was in uniform since the Flood. You should talk to Robertson. They were close."

I nodded. We were seeing Robertson in a little while.

Vasquez said, "Calhoun was a good kid. He wanted to do good in the job. If I had to fault him, I would say he was a little bit overenthusiastic."

"Meaning what?" I asked.

"He could be seen as not taking things as seriously as an older guy with more years on the job. Or maybe he wasn't hardened, yet. What-chacallit? He wasn't jaded. Either way, Calhoun had a future on the force."

Conklin asked, "How'd his mood been lately? Was anything bothering him?"

"I didn't notice anything," said Swanson.

"Did anyone have it out for him?" I asked. "Anyone he may have busted?"

Swanson said, "When I had dinner at their house last Wednesday, he was in a good mood. He was talking about Little League and how he and Marie were saving up for the boys' college in a five-two-nine fund. Regular dinner talk. With photos."

The interview went on for another half hour. By the time the empty coffee containers were in the trash, I had a few leads to follow up and no connections that would explain why Calhoun had been tortured or what anyone could have wanted from him.

Conklin and I met with the long-timer, Calhoun's partner Kyle Robertson. Along with Calhoun, we'd met Robertson during the canvass after Maya Perez had been killed.

Robertson was maybe fifty, but he looked older. His face was heavily lined and his hair was gray, thin, combed over. He was eager to help, but could only say he was torn up by the killings. That nothing Calhoun had ever said to him would lead him to think he had anything worth killing him for.

"It's a complete mystery," Robertson said. "I can't make a thing out of it."

Conklin said, "Narco has been working some street crimes, looking for some cops who might be taking money and drugs off dealers. Could Calhoun have been a part of that?"

Robertson shook his head vigorously.

"He was just a regular guy. If he hadn't become a cop, he could have been a firefighter or a high school coach. I never heard him talk about money. He smoked cigarettes, but that's the only addiction he had. Ask me, this bloodbath was entirely senseless. Maybe the killers went to the wrong house and killed the wrong people. Crazier things have happened."

Chapter 55

CONKLIN AND I went to Brady's office with our fat notepads and thin theories.

We had interviewed the Calhouns' neighbors, who had been sleeping last night when the Calhouns were being tortured and shot. They'd seen nothing and heard nothing and were completely shocked and very frightened.

We had also interviewed cops who'd worked with Calhoun, and they, too, were in utter disbelief. Calhoun was a good cop. He loved his job, maybe too much. They chalked that up to his youth and romantic nature. We told Brady that the three cops who knew him best, Swanson, Vasquez, and Robertson, had no clue as to why he and his family would have been tortured and slain.

Brady listened to what we told him, then said, "Here's where I'm at. In the last two weeks, there've been more robbery and narcotics-related homicides than in the entire last year."

He put a piece of paper on the desk and turned it so Conklin and I could see his handwritten list of the crimes that had taken place in our division in the last two weeks. Brady stabbed the list as he read it out loud.

"The first two check-cashing-store holdups, one fatality.

"A mercado robbery with a murdered shop owner.

"Another check-cashing-store holdup, and this time, there are three dead, would-be robbers in SFPD Windbreakers. Turns out, they're not cops. They're idiots, copycats who've heard about the Windbreaker cops but don't know how to pull off any kind of robbery.

"Here. A takedown of a drug factory, seven dead. Possible sighting of a Windbreaker cop.

"This is from Narcotics," Brady said. "Six drug dealers, that they know about, have been shot and robbed in crack houses and on the street. The word is that cops are doing it. It's a random pattern, but a pattern nonetheless."

Conklin and I nodded like bobbleheads.

Brady went on.

"Probably a shitload of drugs was stolen from Wicker House. Could have been worth millions. Somebody could be in a rage about that. Makes me think an organized crew has put on SFPD Windbreakers as an inside joke.

"And the joke is working. The crew disguises themselves as cops. And they're into drug house takedowns and cash-rich robbery opportunities. It's almost like this is an act of war, cops versus drug thugs. And I wonder if Kingfisher is somehow involved in this. He has his fingers in everything. He can be very violent. Read up on him. Sickening stuff. Torture for fun. Sadism. Keep Kingfisher in mind."

Kingfisher was a notorious drug lord, said to be based in Southern California, though no one knew for sure. But evidence of his manufacturing and distribution enterprise was widespread. Was this big-time player somehow involved in small-time takedowns in San Francisco?

Brady wasn't done. He pushed his fingers through his hair. He looked at his computer screen and pressed some keys.

I thought maybe he'd forgotten about us. But then he was saying, "Maybe I'm just trying to make sense of unrelated incidents by making lists, turning the pieces around, hoping they'll fit. Or maybe there's something happening here that we can't quite see.

"We don't stop until we know."

PART TWO

PART TWO

Chapter 56

COURTROOM 5A WAS small, paneled in cherry-wood with matching cherry benches, tables, and chairs. The judge had turned to speak to his clerk. Behind him was the golden seal of the State of California flanked by two flags: the Stars and Stripes and the California state flag.

The room was full, but court was not yet in session. Yuki and her second chair, Natalie Futterman, sat behind their counsel table. Yuki skimmed the notes in front of her, rehearsing her opening lines in her mind like a mantra.

Beside her, Natalie whispered, "I can't *wait*."

Yuki said, "I can. I may be a pit bull, but he's a lion, Nat. An angry one."

Natalie said, "New thought for a new day."

"Do *not* tweet that," Yuki said.

Yuki wished she felt as excited as Natalie. Her eager second chair was a forty-six-year-old recent graduate of law school. Her kids were out of the house. Her husband had left her. And Natalie finally had the degree in law she'd put off twenty-five years ago. She was sharp, bookish, organized, had passed the bar on the first try, and was ready for prime time. Or as Natalie had put it, "You can only learn so much in a classroom."

Natalie had nothing to lose but her novice status.

Yuki, on the other hand, had a pretty substantial reputation at stake, and if she lost this case, she would be known for it: Kordell v. City of San Francisco. *Yuki Castellano. She sued the SFPD and they destroyed her.*

Across the aisle, the defense looked as calm as still waters. Len Parisi, Red Dog himself, filled the chair on the aisle. Sitting next to him were two partners from Moorehouse and Rogers, one of whom was the legendary Collins Rappaport as second chair. Parisi, as co-counsel to the law firm, would be first chair, and he would be doing hand-to-hand combat with *her*.

Yuki had dressed in red today. It was a big color that required big action. You couldn't equivocate in red. You had to go for the jugular, and that was her plan.

Strike first. Strike hard.

Natalie wore almost-matching black separates, a jacket and pants that had probably come from a consignment shop twenty years before. But that was OK. The two of them were representing the victims here. They were the lawyers for the poor and the unfairly persecuted, and Natalie looked the part.

Parisi's suit was moss green and made him look like a heart attack ready to happen.

Yuki smiled to herself.

Whatever helped her through the fight.

She and Natalie had worked hard prepping for this trial and had spent two days just going over her opening statement. She knew what she had to do and what she had to say; if she rehearsed anymore, her impassioned true feelings for the Kordell family would sound overly rehearsed.

She didn't want that.

Yuki was deep in her thoughts when she felt a touch on her shoulder. She turned to see Mrs.

Kordell giving her a teary smile. Yuki squeezed her hand and smiled at the rest of the Kordell family seated behind her, about eleven people all told.

Yuki was here today for them: for Bea and Mickey Kordell and for Aaron-Rey's grandfather, cousins, and friends, who were counting on her to bring justice to Aaron-Rey's name.

She turned to the front of the room as Judge John G. Quirk finished speaking to the clerk.

She liked Judge Quirk. Despite the miserable people he'd dealt with in his twenty years on the bench, she'd found him to be kind. In chambers, he showed that he had an understanding of impulses and frailties of character.

Would that generosity of spirit work for or against her?

And now the bailiff announced that court was in session. She watched as the jury came in through a side door and took seats in the box. She wished she could have gotten more than one person of color on the jury, but it was what it was. Judge Quirk welcomed the jury and spent a little time giving them instructions and answering questions. Then he turned his bespectacled eyes on her.

"Ms. Castellano. Are you ready to begin?"

"Yes, Your Honor."

"Go get 'em," Natalie said, her voice carrying in the lull.

There was a smattering of laughter. Yuki pushed back her chair and, propelled by an adrenaline rush, walked to the lectern in the center of the well.

Chapter 57

AS YUKI STOOD behind the lectern, she felt warm all over, her heart and adrenal glands giving her a little more rush than she actually needed. But she composed herself and lifted her eyes and said to the jurors, "Good morning, everyone.

"I represent the family of Aaron-Rey Kordell, a fifteen-year-old boy with a below-average IQ who was arrested, then bullied by two very experienced police officers who deprived this young man of sleep for sixteen hours, lied to him about his right to counsel, and induced him to confess to a crime he did not commit. After being coerced into giving a false confession, Aaron-Rey was incarcerated and was murdered while awaiting trial.

"Why was Aaron-Rey coerced? Why did he have to die?

"Because the police had no witnesses, but they had a suspect, and they were going to make sure they nailed him. Which they did."

Yuki paused to make sure she had the jurors' attention. Then she continued.

"Here's what happened in February of this year.

"Aaron-Rey was hanging out at the neighborhood crack house after school. If he had lived in a different neighborhood, maybe he would have spent after-school hours in the gym or at a friend's house. But this crack house was a block from where he lived with his parents, and to him, it was where he waited until his folks came home from work.

"You will hear from witnesses who will tell you that Aaron-Rey didn't use drugs. He just liked to be around the big boys at that house, who teased him and made him laugh and sent him out for cigarettes and treated him like a mascot.

"On this particular day, Aaron-Rey was on the top floor of the drug house at 463 Dodge Place when unknown persons robbed and killed three drug dealers on the floor below, then fled the scene, along with all the other people who were in the house at that time.

"Aaron-Rey had an IQ of seventy, which is thirty points below average. He was functional, and he was also exceptionally inquisitive, trusting, and childlike.

"After this shooting occurred and the scores of people ran down the stairs, Aaron-Rey also ran. As he told the police and others, he was on his way out of the house when he found a gun on the stairs, which he stuck into the waistband of his pants, like the big boys do. He had this gun in his possession as he ran east on Turk, a very scared and freaked-out boy of fifteen.

"Two patrolmen in a cruiser witnessed Aaron-Rey running along Turk Street. They turned on their lights and sirens and ran their car up on the sidewalk, after which they tackled Aaron-Rey to the ground.

"And what did Aaron-Rey say, ladies and gentlemen?

"He said, 'I didn't do it.' You will hear these patrolmen tell you that when they asked him what he didn't do, Aaron-Rey said he didn't shoot the three men in the drug house.

"Aaron-Rey was brought into the police station for questioning, where two senior narcotics detectives seized on an opportunity to close three homicides in the easiest possible way. Aaron-Rey was slow. And he was gullible. And he was under arrest.

"Over half the day and most of the night, Aaron-Rey Kordell repeatedly denied shooting anyone. But as you will see on the video, Inspectors Whitney and Brand convinced Aaron-Rey to waive his right to counsel and to having his parents present. They bullied, cajoled, and flat-out lied until this boy, by now helplessly confused, finally said, 'I did it.'

"Once Aaron-Rey made this false admission, he was jailed pending trial and was subsequently murdered in the showers. We can only hope that he died quickly and that he wasn't in pain.

"This is Aaron-Rey," Yuki said, holding up a photo of her dead client cuddling with his baby sister. He had been a handsome young man, and the expression on his face showed his affection for his sister.

Yuki said, "Aaron-Rey was sweet. He was innocent. And he could not, did not, kill three hardened crack dealers. He didn't know how to load and shoot a gun, and the defense will not say otherwise. Furthermore, during all those hours of interrogation, the police never tested Aaron-Rey's hands or clothes for gunpowder residue. The police did not bring in any of the habitués of that drug house for questioning and did not consider any other suspects. Aaron-Rey was the only one they needed.

"At the end of this trial, you're going to be asked to decide if Aaron-Rey Kordell's confession was coerced. If it was coerced, *it wasn't a confession*, and you must hold the SFPD and the City of San Francisco accountable for this innocent boy's cruel, unwarranted, and untimely death."

Chapter 58

PARISI GOT HEAVILY to his feet and, ignoring the lectern, walked directly to the jury box. He smiled, greeted the jurors, and said a few words about how important jury duty was, adding that as the district attorney for the City of San Francisco, he could not do his job without good people deciding verdicts in trials like this one. He noted how important it was to make sure that justice was always done.

Yuki watched him perform, her mind splitting between her good feelings toward Len Parisi—based on five years of working with him, learning from him, and supporting him in her capacity as an assistant DA—and the other side of her brain, which was not yet accustomed to thinking of Len as her enemy, which he surely was.

Furthermore, Len's calm and personable demeanor made her feel that her own presentation had been borderline hysterical.

Even Natalie seemed transfixed by Red Dog.

Len put his hand on the railing and walked along it, making eye contact with the jurors as he said, "I have to commend opposing counsel for presenting such a pretty picture of Aaron-Rey Kordell, but I'm very sorry to say, that's not who he was.

"Aaron-Rey was hanging around at a crack house for the same reason anyone goes to a crack house. He used drugs. He didn't just go there after school. He went there *instead* of going to school. At least, he did most days.

"And I have to say, Ms. Castellano has no idea whether Aaron-Rey picked up the murder weapon on the stairs as he was leaving the crack house, or whether he picked up the gun inside the crack house, or whether someone gave him a few bucks and told him, 'Here's a gun, Aaron-Rey. Shoot those dudes,' so that's what he did. I think the crack house closed-circuit TV cameras were down that day."

The jurors laughed. Yes, he was winning them over.

Len continued, "No one has come forward to say that they saw what went down inside that crack house, and no one ever will. I will agree with Ms. Castellano that a gunshot residue test was not performed on Aaron-Rey. That was a mistake. But what Ms. Castellano didn't tell you is that the bullets that killed those three men came from the gun in Aaron-Rey's pants.

"We will put the gun into Mr. Kordell's hand, and there will be no question at all, no dispute, that he had the gun in his possession. He had the murder weapon on his person. He ran. And he told the officers who pulled him in that he had *not* killed three people in the drug house, and then he named them.

"The police officers asked him where he got the gun, and he said he found it. And they found three dead men and they arrested Aaron-Rey Kordell—of course they did. That was their job.

"So, you might ask, how did Aaron-Rey get that gun? Well, he's not around to tell us now, and it doesn't matter how he got it. It was the murder weapon, and when he had the chance to tell us what happened in that crack house, he told the narcotics investigators that he killed A. Biggy and Duane and Dubble D.

"But this trial is not about where the gun came from or who shot those drug dealers. It is also not about who killed Aaron-Rey Kordell.

"As Ms. Castellano said, this trial is only about one thing: Did Inspectors Stanley Whitney and William Brand from Narcotics coerce Aaron-Rey into making a false confession?

"We say they did not.

"Did they use legitimate interview techniques? Yes, they did. Did they lie? Very likely. An interview in a police station is like a lying competition where both parties lie and bluff and do whatever they can to get the other party to believe them.

"It's legal for police to lie.

"And when we show you clips from the interview, you are going to see that this young man was cool, calm, and collected and that he confessed to murdering three men.

"So when he confessed, Inspectors Brand and Whitney put him in jail, where he belonged, because killers shouldn't be loose on the street.

"Aaron-Rey was in jail awaiting his speedy trial,

as was his right as an American, when an incredibly unfortunate incident happened.

"And we're sorry for the pain of Aaron-Rey's family.

"But Aaron-Rey's death was not the fault of the San Francisco Police Department."

Chapter 59

THE FUNERAL OF the Calhoun family was held at Cypress Lawn Memorial Park in Colma. It was one of the most emotionally devastating events I'd ever attended.

Marie Calhoun's father, Tom Calhoun's father, the boys' Little League coach, and their homeroom teacher all gave eulogies. The SFPD was also represented at the service by Chief Jacobi, Sergeant Phil Pikelny from Robbery, and Inspector Ted Swanson, who choked out a few words about "what a good kid" Calhoun had been.

Hundreds of cops in dress blues packed the chapel and spilled outside, many of them crying, and they formed a thick blue wall behind the broken family at the graveside, where four caskets, two of them child-size, were slowly lowered into the ground.

The pervasive grief was cut with anger that these hideous, nauseating deaths had happened—and had happened to a cop and his family.

I'd hardly known Calhoun, but I vividly remembered his optimism that morning at the check-cashing store where three copycat Wind-breaker cops had been gunned down by passing patrolmen.

And *that* thought nagged me and wouldn't quite let me go.

Finally, the funeral was over.

Conklin and I climbed up into his Bronco and crept along with the traffic moving out of the cemetery. We slowly passed the block where my mother was buried and then the place where Yuki's hilarious mother, Keiko, had been laid to rest. Washed over by images of so many other funerals, we left Colma and took 101 back to San Francisco.

When we were within the city limits, I wanted to hit a saloon, a quiet one where old barflies would be watching a ball game and where no one knew my name. I wanted time and space to get my feelings under control before I went home to my family.

But Conklin said, "I want to look at the Calhoun house again."

"Why, Rich?"

"I just do."

I sighed. "OK. If that's what you want, that's what we'll do."

Chapter 60

CONKLIN PARKED IN front of the green house on Texas Street. We sat quietly for a moment under a telephone line loaded with blackbirds, then got out, ducked under the tape, broke the seal on the front door, and shouldered it open.

The murder house had no trace of life in it, but it smelled bad, and in the seconds before we threw on the lights, I could almost hear Marie Calhoun screaming.

Finally, I suggested we each take a room and try to look at it with fresh eyes. Conklin wanted to see the boys' room.

I took the kitchen.

The first thing I saw was the spoon and bowl in the sink with the remains of a helping of chocolate chip ice cream. I imagined that this had been someone's last meal. There were blood-spattered drawings of Easter rabbits and Little League baseball schedules stuck up on the fridge with magnets, five feet above the chalk marks on the linoleum floor where Marie Calhoun's body had come to rest.

The refrigerator door was open, and the food had gone bad. The smell of rotting meat permeated the room. I looked into the trash can, just in case it had been forgotten, but the garbage had gone to the lab and the bin was empty.

The knife block on the counter had one knife missing, presumably the paring knife, which had likely been used to slice the lids off Tom Calhoun's eyes.

I tried to take my own advice to look at this scene as if for the first time, but it was impossible to keep any distance from a multiple homicide, especially one like this.

The word that kept echoing in my mind was *why?*

Brady had wondered out loud if Calhoun was one of the Windbreaker cops, wondered if he had had knowledge about the large stash of drugs we assumed had been the reason Wicker House had been robbed and the lab rats killed.

I trusted Brady's instincts. So if Calhoun was one of those renegade cops, he wasn't alone. Could he be working with other cops? Could Swanson, Vasquez, even Robertson be part of the crew?

Conklin, too, had thoughts that Wicker House and this quadruple murder were related. I heard his footsteps and turned as he came into the kitchen.

He said, "Linds, there's nothing new upstairs. It was a straight-up execution. I don't see signs of a robbery. As Clapper said, nothing was tossed."

"Who killed them?" I asked my partner, but I was really asking myself.

"What do you think, Linds?"

"Let's say Brady is right, that Calhoun may be one of the Windbreaker cops. Calhoun was pretty excited by those dead Windbreaker-wearing copycats, remember?"

Conklin nodded.

"It was like he was saying, 'Yahoo. The case is closed.' And maybe it was because if he could convince us that the Windbreaker case was solved, there'd be no heat on him."

"Go on," said my partner.

"OK," I said, "let's take it a step further. If Calhoun was involved in the Wicker House robbery, those drugs were worth a lot to someone. And that someone, let's say it was Kingfisher. What if Kingfisher knew who robbed him?"

"Oh. OK, so you're saying maybe this wasn't torture for information," Conklin said. "Maybe the Calhoun family was the message. 'Screw with us, this happens.'"

"It's a leap," I said, staring at the blood on the kitchen floor.

Conklin said, "It's a leap. But it makes more sense than anything I've heard so far."

Chapter 61

I WAS HOME before dinner, and after showering and changing into sweats, I took Julie onto my lap and fed her strained lamb and peas while listening to Valerie June singing "Pushin' Against a Stone." After that, I put Julie in Joe's arms. I filled Martha's bowl with a premium kibble I'd been saving for a special occasion, and I told Joe I was cooking dinner.

"I have to do something that I can control and that will make me feel like I'm doing something good."

"You had me at 'I'm cooking,'" Joe said.

I laughed, first time that day, and even laughed a little too long and hard. My husband joined in, then gave me a glass of cold orange juice, which is our code for "chill."

As I chopped vegetables, I told Joe about my shitty day.

"I said I'd go with you to Colma," he told me.

"Nah, it was better I went with the troops."

I gave Joe a brief verbal tour of the after-funeral return to the Calhouns' house of horrors. And while I pounded the veal cutlets with a mallet, I told him my thoughts that Kingfisher had been involved. When the cutlets were so thin they were almost transparent, I felt Joe gently taking the mallet out of my hand.

I laughed again, which was very cathartic, I've got to say.

While I sipped my juice, Joe talked about drug kingpins he has known and about Kingfisher in particular, a brutal psychopath who earned his name by annihilating anyone who got in his way.

"He's both a legend and a myth," Joe said. "No one knows what he looks like, but it's said that he gets a piece of all the drug action in the state. Or else."

"Yeah," I sighed.

"Not to overworry, Linds, but you think Kingfisher's gang tortured a cop who may have been involved in the case you're working."

"Right, I know," I said. "I know."

The oil and the veal were sizzling in the pan, and Joe poured the wine.

"Linds, it concerns me."

"I'll be careful. I won't take any unnecessary chances."

Joe nodded. He set the security system while I dished up dinner. We ate at the dining table for a change, Martha sitting hopefully between our chairs. When the coffee was brewing, Joe changed the subject and told me he had a lead on "his" case, Claire's Birthday Murders.

"I've got a possible suspect," Joe said. "His name is Wayne Broward, and he was charged with slashing a neighbor's car tires. The judge fined him, and Broward responded by threatening to kill the judge, rape his wife, and suffocate their children."

"Whoa. A seriously crazy person."

"He was sentenced to the max for threatening a judge, which is a five-thousand-dollar fine and a year in the hoosegow. Broward got out early for good behavior. You ask—when was that? And I answer, just before Claire's birthday five years ago."

"Huh," I said. "Let's see what else you've got."

While I cleaned up, Joe brought over his laptop.

I looked at the files he had found, then tapped into the SFPD database and looked up this madman, Wayne Lawrence Broward, who lived in the Bayview neighborhood at Hollister Avenue and Hawes Street.

Apart from the attack on the neighbors' tires, Broward had a record for assault on a neighbor who had put his garbage cans too close to Broward's driveway. And in addition to these attacks, there was a domestic abuse complaint from Broward's wife.

She had dropped the charges, but her statement made interesting reading.

"Joe, listen to this. Mrs. Broward described her husband as 'ruined by his crazy-ass schizo mother and has intermittent explosive anger disorder.'"

"And she stuck with him."

"Yes, she did. If I can find a spare moment tomorrow, I'm going to check up on this guy," I said.

"Be very careful," said my dear husband.

Chapter 62

WAYNE LAWRENCE BROWARD'S house was a brown, wood-shingled shanty, the third one in from the intersection of Hollister Avenue and Hawes Street. Standing behind a chain-link fence that was hung with a dozen NO TRESPASSING signs, the house looked like a seething box of paranoia.

I parked in front of the fence and clipped my badge to my lapel so that the gold metal would glint against the navy-blue twill. I unbuttoned my jacket so that my gun was visible on my hip. Then I pushed open the short chain-link gate.

Even as I put my hand on the gate, I knew I was way off the rails here. Tina Strichler's murder was being worked by Inspectors Michaels and Wang of our department, but even though they were new, or maybe because of that, I didn't feel comfortable asking them to look into a fairly baseless hunch conceived by Joe and me.

Still, a hunch was hard to put aside. And I had to check it out. I went through the gate and up the poured-cement path to the front door, upon which was taped another NO TRESPASSING AND THAT MEANS YOU notice.

I pressed the buzzer.

I heard a dog woofing deep inside the house, and a man's voice said, "OK, Hauser. Let's see who this damned son of a bitch is."

There were sounds behind the door, a peephole sliding, a chain coming off a track, a bolt unracking. Given the modest means of residents of this neighborhood, either Wayne Broward was stashing gold bullion at home, or he was an officer in a one-man war.

Or maybe he had stabbed a woman to death on each of the past five May twelfths.

There was more barking, and then the door was pulled open. A brown-haired white man of average height and weight, in a denim shirt and jeans, holding a Winchester rifle, showed himself in the slice of open doorway.

"What the fuck do you want?" he asked.

"I'm Sergeant Lindsay Boxer," I said, showing him my badge. "I'm looking for Wayne Lawrence Broward."

The dog, a boxer as it turned out, lunged at the door, and the gent with the rifle used his leg to push the dog back from the doorway.

"I said, 'What. The fuck. Do you *want?*'"

I pushed my badge forward. "I'm the police. Put the gun down."

The man in the doorway scowled, but he lowered the muzzle.

I took a photo of Tina Strichler from my breast pocket. Her bloody death on a pedestrian crossing in front of about a hundred tourists was still vivid in my mind.

I said, "Do you know this woman?"

Broward peered at the photo, then opened the door wide and said, "Why didn't you say so? Come in."

Chapter 63

BROWARD HAD AS much as said he recognized Tina Strichler. But I wanted to hear him actually say it.

"You know this woman?" I asked.

"Come in," he said. "I don't bite. Even Hauser don't bite."

He yanked on the dog's collar, shoved the dog into a bedroom, and closed the door.

I put my hand on my gun, cautiously entered the house, and looked around. The interior of the place looked like *American Pickers* meets *Hoarding: Buried Alive*.

There wasn't one inch of clean or uncluttered surface. There were live chickens in a slatted box under a table, canned food stacked against the walls to the ceiling, boxes of ammo on countertops, and guns hanging from racks on the walls.

I scanned the room for trophies of dead women. I was looking for photos or newspaper clippings taped to the wall or signs of the abused wife. I also looked for a collection of assorted knives that might have been used to commit murder and then been taken away by the killer.

But mainly, I was so stunned by the chaos that I lost sight of Broward—until I felt a cold gun muzzle against the back of my neck.

Wayne Broward said, "Why don't you take off your gun and stay awhile."

"Love to," I said, fear and shame flooding my body to my fingertips and out through my eyes. I was a jerk. I'd walked right into this, and I might die in this very room.

"I'm taking my gun out very slowly," I said, my back to him. "Just using my fingertips."

As I was trained to do, I spun around fast, knocked the barrel of Broward's rifle away from me, grabbed the rifle with both hands, and wrenched it out of Broward's grip, throwing him off balance. I flung the rifle far from where I stood. As it clattered against a wall hung with hubcaps,

I pulled my Glock and leveled it at Broward's nose.

From the chill at the back of my neck to the Glock in my hand took about ten seconds, but it felt like the last ten seconds of my life. Hauser was barking his head off, and I wondered at my luck, that Broward had underestimated me and had put the dog behind a door.

"Bitch," Broward spat at me. "I shoulda shot you. I coulda done anything to you. No one would ever know what happened to you."

"Turn around. Put your hands on your head," I said.

He did it.

"I coulda given you a real good ride first," he said mournfully. "I haven't had a blond in a while."

"Shut the hell up," I said.

I holstered my gun, wrenched Broward's arms down, and cuffed him behind his back.

"You're under arrest for assault on a police officer," I said. And then I read him his rights.

Chapter 64

I HAD BROWARD in the back of my vehicle, behind the Plexiglas and in cuffs.

As for me, I was still twitching with adrenaline because he could have killed me. That would have been my fault entirely for having made such a dumb-ass, rookie mistake.

I couldn't stop flicking my eyes to the rearview mirror to look at him. He was wild-eyed crazy, for sure, but whatever kind of psycho he was, he didn't seem to know or care that he was on his way to jail.

Broward said loudly, "Remember when we were living with my mama?"

"Yep. It was a trip, Wayne."

"You used to call me Honey-boy. I just loved when you did that."

"That was then, Wayne," I said, playing along. "I'm over you now."

Wayne Broward began to sing "Jesus Loves Me."

I turned up the squawk box and kept my eyes on the road. I didn't like what I was going to have to say to a judge about why I had been inside the house of a man who hadn't been under suspicion of anything; my probable cause was a hunch. Thank God Broward had invited me to come in. Perhaps that and his history of threatening a judge would help me sound a little less stupid.

Twenty minutes later, I parked in the all-day lot on Bryant and tossed the keys to the guy who worked days in the shed. Broward gave me no trouble as I escorted him across the street and into the building in cuffs. I walked him through the metal detector and up the stairs to the desk sergeant on the third floor.

I said, "Sergeant, we need to book Mr. Broward for assault with a deadly weapon on a police officer. Make sure he gets a psych eval."

Sergeant Brooks asked questions and filled out a form, and a uniformed cop came up and took Broward to booking. My rifle-wielding collar would be kept busy for the next twenty-four to thirty-six hours while being processed: There would be a body search, fingerprints, a shower, and examinations by a nurse and a shrink. Then he'd be given a jumpsuit and locked in a holding cell until I could get back to him.

After leaving the front desk, I went down the hall and through the door to Homicide. I found Conklin in the bullpen with files on drug dealers fanned out all over his desktop.

"Rich. I'm very sorry. I got hung up." I fully planned to tell my partner about Wayne Broward, but he cut in with a news flash.

"Ralph Valdeen was hit."

Ralph Valdeen, aka Rascal, was one of the two former stockroom boys at Wicker House. Valdeen had been charged with assault on a police officer for that punch he'd thrown at Conklin at the ballpark. But he'd been released on bail. Unlike Donnie Wolfe, who had stolen a car, we had had nothing else on Valdeen. There was no evidence that he knew the Wicker House shooters or that he knew what happened to the drugs that had been stolen from that lab.

"What happened?" I asked my partner.

"His mom went over to his place and found him

dead in the bedroom," Conklin said. "Two shots to the chest, one to the head. Makes me think someone was cleaning up after themselves. Maybe he could've ID'd the Wicker House shooters."

"Another dead witness," I said.

"And he's all ours," said Conklin.

Chapter 65

BRADY HELD AN impromptu standing-room-only meeting at the end of the shift. We were a ragged-looking crew but highly motivated to stop the growing body count and rescue our reputation, which was getting trashed by the media daily, nightly, and on weekends.

Brady is a hard-ass, but he wasn't saying "you guys."

He said, "We have a big problem. All of us. More than a dozen people are dead, including one of our own and his family. Some of the dead are victims of crimes, some are witnesses, and some are perps. I'll be frank. I'm not sure we always know who is who.

"This is what I see.

"The nature of the war between the drug dealers and us has changed. Cops may be involved in drug-related crime, and drug dealers are firing back. No one can say with certainty who is doing what to whom, and that makes it even more, I don't know, disgusting.

"This cannot go on.

"Everyone here, you are all working a piece of this war. Talk to your CIs. Think about things that have been said or done and you looked the other way. I don't want any crap about never ratting out a brother. One of our brothers was tortured before he and his family were murdered.

"This was a first in my experience, and I don't have to tell you that this can never happen again. My door is open to all of you. If you have a clue, even if it involves someone we know and trust, you tell me in private."

Brady paced a little in front of the room, then asked if there were any questions. There were none. There were no strangers in our bullpen, just people who'd had our backs for years.

One of them had left an anonymous note on my desk saying WATCH YOUR BACK.

Brady went on.

"Boxer and Conklin are primaries on Wicker House and the homicides of Tom Calhoun and his family. If you're assigned to those cases, report to them.

"Swanson and Vasquez are responsible for the mercado and check-cashing robbery homicides, past, present, and future.

"Whitney and Brand are point men on cases where drug dealers have been shot. Any information about dealers being ripped off or killed by cops, report immediately to me.

"My cell phone number and private e-mail address are posted in the break room. We're smart enough to put this trouble down, so let's do that. Vacations are canceled.

"That's all."

The meeting broke up, and Brady made his way through the roomful of cops to his office. When Conklin and I reached our desks, I picked up the phone. I called the men's jail and in just a few minutes had set up a room for a conference with a car thief and former Wicker House stockroom boy by the name of Donald Wolfe.

Chapter 66

DONNIE WOLFE LOOKED to be in a pretty good mood when he was brought into the interview room in orange jumpsuit and cuffs.

"Wassup?" he said, sliding into a chair as the guard left the room. He angled around in his seat, getting comfortable, enjoying the attention or maybe just happy to have company. "You making me miss my dinner."

Conklin said, "I've got some bad news for you, Donnie."

"Oh, yeah?"

"Someone took out your friend Rascal."

"Nuh-uh, no, they didn't."

Conklin took his phone out of his pocket and found the photo of Ralph Valdeen lying facedown on his narrow bed, his blood soaking through the baby-blue covers. Conklin put the phone on the table and turned it so that Donnie Wolfe could see the picture.

For a moment, you could see the young kid in Wolfe. His eyes got big, he drew back—and then, only a moment later, he disguised his shock and took on the cocky scowl of a criminal with aspirations to become a bigger, better criminal.

"You faked that picture," he said. "Trying to scare me."

"Really," Conklin said. "You really think we staged this blood and brains on the headboard to shake you up?"

"Sure. Why not?"

"Because, Donnie, we don't need to scare you. You're in a cell. You've got a trial coming up and you'll be convicted of grand theft and you will go to prison for a long time. You might get out in time to see your unborn baby get married."

A long minute passed as Donnie seemed to picture that. Then he said, "Or what?"

This is one of the things I love about Conklin. He's a trustworthy dude. His goodness comes through, even to punks like Donnie.

"Look, we need to know about Valdeen," my partner said. "Why was he shot and who do you think did it? Help us and we'll tell the DA you cooperated. That will count at sentencing. I promise you that."

A lot of quiet time gathered in the small interview room. I did my best not to fidget as Donnie thought over his options. Then he said, "How am I supposed to help you? I wasn't there. I don't know why anyone would do that to Rascal."

I had to step in.

"Donnie. Your friend Rascal Valdeen was *executed*. You see that, don't you? He wasn't shot while holding up a store or stealing a car or screwing someone else's woman. He was shot in his bed. While he was asleep."

"No, nuh-uh, no, no."

"*Yes*. And this is what I'm thinking, Donnie. Ralph *knew* something and someone didn't want him to *talk*."

After a long pause, Donnie said, "He might have known something that I don't know."

I pressed on. "Did he know who shot up Wicker House? Do you?"

Wolfe looked up at the camera, then back at Conklin. He said to Conklin, "Not with that."

Conklin left the room and when he came back, the red camera light was off.

"Go ahead, Donnie," Conklin said.

"Cops did that Wicker House deal."

"What cops?" I asked.

"They was *cops*. Rascal and me, we told this one of them when the drugs were moving out for distribution. It was just supposed to be a heist. We didn't know they were going to shoot. They didn't tell us that, I swear on my baby's soul. I just needed money to go away and that's all."

Real tears were filling his eyes. He wiped them away, and again I saw the kid in him.

"How do you know they were cops?"

"They wearing jackets saying police."

"That's all? Did you see a badge? Were they cops you knew?"

"They talk like cops. They walk like cops. They cops," Donnie said.

"How many?" I asked.

"I only met the one that made the deal with me and Rascal. I hear on the street could be, like, five more in the crew. I told the one that paid me. I say,

'Watch your ass.' I say to him, 'Those drugs belong to the King.'"

"Kingfisher? And what did he say?"

"He say, 'No problem.' Like, 'I got this.'"

Conklin said, "What's this cop's name? We need his name."

The silence went on for long seconds as Donnie Wolfe thought about his odds if he gave us a name, and his odds if he didn't. I think it came out as a draw.

"What does he look like?" Conklin said.

Donnie shook his head again, then made a decision.

He said, "Both times I see him, he sitting in a car. White guy, wears a police cap and big shades. You can only see, like, his nose. And it's just a regular nose."

Conklin asked again in his kind, steady voice, "What's his name, Donnie?"

"One. That's what he said. That's what I call him. Mr. One."

Chapter 67

I'D JUST GOTTEN home when I got a call from Cindy. She was at the airport, just back from her book tour, so I invited her and Richie to come on over to our house for Joe's sausage lasagna.

A half hour later, Julie was in bed and two of my very favorite people were standing around the kitchen with me and Joe, all of us sampling the fine wine Cindy had picked up at our neighborhood liquor store.

Cindy was wearing a butter-yellow pullover and jeans and had glittery clips in her curly blond hair. She stood hip-to-hip against Richie, and he had his arm around her. They both looked radiant. I loved to see this. Loved it.

While I tossed the salad, Cindy told a story

about her last stop, at the Mysterious Galaxy Bookstore in San Diego. A woman had hung back until every one of the thirty people who'd wanted Cindy to sign their books had moved on. Then, said Cindy, "This woman whispered, 'I have a story I think you'll want to write.'"

"Really," Joe said. "A true story?"

"That's what she said."

Cindy relayed the woman's fairly intense tale of a serial polygamist with five wives, each unknown to the other four. The guy posed as a traveling salesman, but in fact was a con man.

Cindy said, "This woman, Nikki, told me, 'Benny was the sweetest man you'd ever want to meet. Super-kind. Always attentive. He always made me feel like I was the most important person in the world—Oh. I forgot to say Benny was my father.'" Cindy laughed at the shocked expressions all around her. Then she said, "Nikki said her father disappeared ten years ago and is presumed dead, but his body has never been found. She wants me to write an exposé of her own father and his mysterious disappearance. She wants me to find him, dead or alive, and if he was killed, to find the killer. She's not asking much, right? But I *am* thinking about it."

Dinner was hot, tasty, and served with plenty of laughs, which I needed. But I was still feeling crappy about my set-to with Wayne L. Broward and couldn't wait to tell Joe about it.

I found everything that had happened from the moment I knocked on Broward's door so embarrassing, I hadn't even told Conklin. Luckily, Cindy and Rich were eager to take their party home right after dinner. As soon as we'd all hugged and kissed good-bye and I'd checked on Julie, I said to Joe, "I did a tremendously stupid thing today."

I told him about my lunchtime visit to Wayne Broward and how I'd let the guy get his gun on me. Joe scowled, and I could feel him winding up to remind me that I had a child now.

I said, "Please don't scold me, Joe. I've already had some strong words with myself."

"I haven't said anything."

"I know. But you'd be within your rights. The guy is wacko. And by that I mean, his mind hardly tracks at all. He could be demented. I can't see him making a note to kill a woman every year on May twelfth and then doing it and after that, getting away with it."

I shook my head, thinking about the house piled high with junk, the way Broward's mind veered from past to present, and why I was pretty sure he'd never even focused on my badge.

I said, "I turned my back on him. He had a gun."

"Come here," said Joe.

I went into my husband's arms, took a few deep breaths, then pulled him to the sofa and leaned against his shoulder.

"I'm gonna have to tell Brady and Richie about this guy, and after the arraignment the story is gonna get out. And I'm gonna take some crap for going into the guy's house on a hunch."

"It was a dead end. The wrong tree," Joe said. "But Tina Strichler's killer is still out there."

"True," I said. "But I wonder if there really is a pattern to these killings, Joe. Or if linking five separate stabbings to one killer with a mind like a clock is all in our minds. It could just as easily be that there are five different killers with minds of their own."

Chapter 68

IT WAS DAY two of the trial.

Yuki had had a rough night. She and Brady were at opposite sides of the justice system, and the so-called Chinese Wall was in play. She couldn't talk to him about her case, he couldn't talk to her about his, and that made conversation forced and sleep barely possible.

She was at her desk at quarter to eight, and Natalie arrived a few minutes later with coffee. They picked apart Parisi's opening statement, guessed about what he might be planning to do with their witnesses. Natalie told Yuki not to worry.

Zac arrived and stopped in the doorway.

"About a dozen people texted me about your

opening yesterday," he said to Yuki. "Mazel tov. And thanks to both of you."

Yuki's mood lifted and, feeling freshly caffeinated, she drove with Natalie to McAllister Street and parked the car in the underground garage.

Once in the courtroom, Natalie gave the videodisc to the clerk and joined Yuki at the counsel table. They spoke softly to each other as the courtroom filled. The proceedings were called to order.

When it was time to present the plaintiff's case, Yuki rose from her seat, walked past the lectern, and approached the jury box. Today, everything depended on the video.

She said to the jurors, "Good morning, everyone. When I made my opening statement yesterday, I said you would see portions of the police department's sixteen-hour interrogation of Aaron-Rey Kordell.

"I also said that this case is about one thing: whether or not Aaron-Rey was coerced into making a confession. Because if a confession is coerced, it's not a confession. And if Aaron-Rey didn't confess, then he should not have been jailed, and if he had not been jailed, he would not have died.

"I've selected portions of the interview to show you, but you'll be able to read the transcript of the interrogation in its entirety."

Yuki told the clerk to play the videodisc. The lights dimmed and the video came up on the flatscreen. Aaron-Rey, heavily built and easily six feet tall, sat across a scarred wooden table from two police officers who introduced themselves as William Brand and Stan Whitney.

Whitney was in his thirties; he had a close-cropped beard and round, wire-rimmed glasses. He looked more like a science teacher than a narc. From his posture and tone of voice, he appeared to be sympathetic to Aaron-Rey's distress.

He said, "Is this how it happened, A-Rey? You got scared? Those dealers. Freakin' lethal dudes. Armed and dangerous, right? They threatened you and you surprised them, right? You shot them and ran. Because if that's what happened, you were protecting yourself, and anyone would understand that."

Aaron-Rey said, "I *didn't* shoot them. I didn't even know they was *shot*. I found the gun on the stairs and I thought I could make fifty dollars.

That's wrong because it wasn't my gun. I'm sorry about that."

Whitney said, "Aaron, listen. You don't have to lie anymore. What you did is all gonna come out. But if you tell us, we can protect you. That's what you need to do, son."

Yuki showed five minutes of Whitney befriending Aaron-Rey, telling him it was safe to confess. "Don't you want to go home, Aaron-Rey? Don't you want this to be over?"

"I want to go home."

Whitney passed a piece of paper across the table. He said, "This paper says that we told you what your rights are and that you're waiving them because you don't want a lawyer. You don't want to complicate this, do you, A-Rey?"

"I didn't shoot anyone," Aaron-Rey said.

Brand said, "Good for you, A-Rey."

He handed the boy a pen, and Aaron-Rey signed his name on the line where the detective put his finger. Brand hardly waited for Aaron-Rey to lift his pen before he whipped the paper away and took it out of the room.

Whitney said, "Feel better now?"

"No," said Aaron-Rey.

Yuki used the remote to fast-forward to hour six, which was the point where Inspector Brand took the lead.

Chapter 69

THE FOOTAGE ROLLED and the jurors' eyes focused on Inspector William Brand's interrogation of Aaron-Rey.

Brand was on his feet.

He stalked around the narrow confines of the interview room. He made angry gestures with his arms. At some angles you could see the tattoo on his neck, under his left ear, at the collar line. The tattoo was only an inch square and looked like a cow brand of his initials, *WB*.

Brand said to his suspect, "You signed this *waiver*, A-Rey, saying you didn't need a lawyer, so now *you have to tell the truth*. That's what it *means*. And if you keep lying, you are going to drown in your own crap. Under*stand*?"

"I *told* you the truth," Aaron-Rey said. He was crying. He put his head down on the table and sobbed into his folded arms.

"You're a liar, Kordell," said Brand. "You make me *sick*. You're a big man when you have a gun, but look at you now. A lying sack of shit, the worst kind of person, can't stand up for what he did. And you should get an award for what you did. Taking out those dirtbags. That's what you did, didn't you?"

"Nooooo," said Aaron-Rey.

"You dumb piece of crap," said Brand. He leaned over and shouted in Aaron-Rey's face. "I'm trying to help you. Don't you understand? Tell the goddamned truth and end this. Don't you want your parents to be proud that you stood up like a man?"

"I didn't shoot that gun," Aaron-Rey sobbed.

Yuki forwarded the video again. She said to the jury, "This is hour fifteen and forty-five minutes. Aaron-Rey has had three sodas and a bag of chips. He has waived his rights so that he can go home—that's his understanding, and he has told the truth. But Inspectors Whitney and Brand aren't buying it."

Parisi objected. "Your Honor, the video speaks for itself."

"I'll allow it anyway," said Judge Quirk.

Yuki hit Play. The placement of the individuals in the room was the same. Brand had his hands in his pockets. He was pacing, and his anger was undisguised.

He said, "Last chance I'm giving you to get ahead of this, A-Rey, and then we're done. You're going to jail for the rest of your life, or maybe you'll get the death penalty. Either way, you're never gonna hug your mama again. Or . . . you can tell us what happened. You were high. You were confused. You felt threatened. And so you had to defend yourself and shoot those three violent, dangerous men."

Brand sat down, pulled his chair right up to Aaron-Rey, and put his hand on the back of the boy's neck.

Brand said, "It's safe to tell us, A-Rey. It's now or we're done. I have a family, and I gotta go home. Tell the truth, or the next time I see you, it will be as a witness at your execution. Your moms and pops will be crying, but I'm gonna be saying to them, 'I told him to tell the truth, but he told me to piss off.' Is that how you want this to go?"

Aaron-Rey picked his head up off the table.

"I can go home after?"

"Yes. What did I say? Start talking," said Brand. "Or I'm walking out of here and going home. Unlike you."

Aaron-Rey sighed. "Awright. I did it," he said. "I was scared and so I shot them, awright?"

"Shot who?" said Whitney.

"A. Biggy. Duane. Dubble D."

Aaron-Rey was crying again.

"Good man," said Whitney.

He looked at the two-way mirror, gave a thumbs-up. Brand opened the door and uniformed officers came into the room and pulled Aaron-Rey Kordell to his feet.

Whitney and Brand high-fived and low-fived and the video went black.

Yuki submitted the transcript into evidence and returned to the counsel table.

Judge Quirk said, "Ms. Castellano, you have a witness?"

She was getting a jump on Parisi by calling two witnesses who might normally have been called by the defense. In legal terms, they were "adverse witnesses," and she could deal with them as if she were cross-examining the opposition witnesses.

She hoped she could pull it off.

"Plaintiff calls Inspector Stanley Whitney to the stand."

Chapter 70

NARCOTICS INSPECTOR STAN Whitney wore jeans, a denim shirt, and a striped tie under a navy-blue jacket. He looked very respectable and trustworthy, and the wire-rimmed glasses just frosted the cake.

He swore on the Bible to tell the whole truth and nothing but, and then he took his seat in the witness box.

Yuki spent a few minutes establishing that Whitney had been with the SFPD for eight years, the first five in uniform, the last three in Narcotics.

She asked him to describe his interview with Aaron-Rey.

Whitney said, "Well, he was like a lot of people who are pinched for committing a crime. Young, old, first-time offender or career criminal, no one sits down and says 'I did it,' even if you catch them standing over a body with a gun in their hand and blood all over them."

"I see," said Yuki. "But since this was a presumed triple homicide, why were detectives from Narcotics interrogating the subject?"

"Mr. Kordell was pulled in for running from a crack house with a gun in his hand. We've run into Mr. Kordell before. At first, we figured him to be a witness."

"While you've run into Mr. Kordell before, you never arrested him, correct?"

"Correct."

"And he's never before been suspected in a crime, isn't that true?"

"Yes."

"So what was the context for previously running into Mr. Kordell?"

"He was a hanger-on in the neighborhood. We'd do a bust and sometimes he'd be on the scene."

"OK. And so you've never known him to be violent, have you?"

"Well, he was violent when he took out three men."

"You don't have any proof that he shot anyone, do you, Inspector?"

"He had the murder weapon in his possession."

"And did you test Mr. Kordell's hands or clothing for gunpowder residue that would show that he'd actually discharged that weapon?"

"No, we did not."

"And that's because you knew you wouldn't find any gunpowder residue, isn't that right, Inspector?"

"The interview was going well. We were involved in getting answers and we were confident that we would turn up a witness to the shooting."

Yuki was sweating under her black suit, but she thought she was giving Stan Whitney better than she was taking. She stood at a distance from the witness stand and asked, "The fact is, you didn't turn up any witnesses to the shooting of those three men, did you?"

"No."

"And Mr. Kordell maintained for more than fifteen straight hours that he didn't shoot anyone, didn't he?"

"I suppose. Yes."

"But you didn't accept that."

"It seemed clear to me that he did it."

"It's not clear to *me*, Inspector. You didn't have a witness. You didn't have a gunshot residue test. You had no forensic evidence, and for almost sixteen hours, you didn't have a confession, either. Isn't that right?"

"Right."

Yuki said, "One of the functions of a police officer is to elicit an incriminating response, isn't that right, Inspector Whitney? Yes or no?"

"Yes."

"And isn't it true that a teenager, especially one with mental challenges, would try to please the authority in the room who told him he could go home? Isn't that exactly what you told him, Inspector? Isn't that how you obtained Mr. Kordell's false confession?"

Parisi stood up and said, "Objection. Which of those questions does Ms. Castellano want the witness to answer?"

"I withdraw the questions, Your Honor."

There was a low rumble in the room: people in the gallery whispering to their neighbors. The jury looked at the judge.

Judge Quirk said, "Do you want to cross-examine the witness, Mr. Parisi?"

Chapter 71

LEN PARISI, DA of San Francisco and co-counsel with Moorehouse and Rogers, who were paid to defend the City against lawsuits, got up from his seat and walked across the well to the witness, Inspector Stan Whitney.

"Inspector Whitney," Parisi said. "Did you believe you had grounds to arrest Aaron-Rey Kordell for shooting the three drug dealers?"

"Absolutely."

"Did you believe Mr. Kordell killed three men?"

"He's innocent until proven guilty. But he was our number one suspect and I believed he did shoot them. He not only named the dead men, but he was carrying a weapon when he was arrested fleeing from the scene of the crime."

"Did you hit Mr. Kordell in order to get him to confess?"

"No, I did not."

"Did you physically intimidate him?"

"No."

"Did you read him his rights?"

"Yes."

"Then why did you get him to sign a waiver of his right to an attorney?"

"Because we just wanted to make it absolutely clear that we gave him every opportunity to have an attorney and he decided he didn't want a lawyer. His decision."

"And what about access to his parents?"

"There was a note on the arresting officers' report not to call the parents."

"Do you know why?" Parisi asked.

"He told the arresting officers he was eighteen. It's common for kids not to want their parents to know whatever it is they've done."

"Did you know Aaron-Rey's age?"

"No. He had no priors and no ID."

Parisi turned so that he was facing the jurors and asked, "Why do you think this was a properly obtained confession, Inspector Whitney?"

Whitney said, "Because we used the tools at our disposal. We wanted a confession, yes, but we didn't do anything outside the law. Mr. Kordell said he killed those three scumbags, and in my opinion, that was the truth."

"Thank you, Inspector. I have nothing else for this witness," said Parisi.

There was some shifting in seats and some murmured conversation as Parisi returned to the defense table.

The judge said, "Quiet." He banged his gavel, and when the room settled down, he said, "Redirect, Ms. Castellano?"

"Yes, Your Honor."

Yuki stepped out from behind the table, passing Parisi without looking at him on the way to the witness box.

She faced Whitney square on and said, "Inspector Whitney, will you agree that before Aaron-Rey said he shot those 'scumbags,' he said he didn't shoot anyone?"

"Like everyone else we ever had in the box."

"Please answer the question. In fact, Mr. Kordell said he didn't shoot anyone, isn't that correct?"

Whitney said, "Yes, that's true."

"And would it surprise you to know that during the course of your interrogation of him, Mr. Kordell said he didn't shoot anyone on sixty-seven different occasions?"

"I didn't know that."

"Well, we counted."

"OK."

"And would it also surprise you to know that during the course of your interrogation, he denied owning the gun on twenty-two different occasions?"

"Again, I wasn't counting."

"Again, Inspector, we counted. So, adding this up, on sixty-seven different occasions Mr. Kordell denied shooting the gun, and on twenty-two different occasions he denied owning the gun. And Inspector Whitney, how many times did he say he shot these three drug dealers?"

"Once, I guess."

"Once. And that was after more than fifteen hours in the box, wasn't it?"

"Yes," Whitney said, showing no emotion at all.

"And you had no witness or evidence to impeach this boy's statement, did you?"

"No."

"And so you wore this boy down until he finally said, 'I did it,' isn't that right?" Yuki asked.

Whitney just looked at her.

Yuki said, "You can't answer, can you?"

She let her question hang in the air, then said, "Nothing further, Your Honor. I have no more questions for this witness."

Chapter 72

NATALIE FUTTERMAN PUSHED her tablet toward Yuki so that she could read the word *Awesome* in giant letters. Yuki smiled, then got to her feet and called Inspector William Brand.

Brand came in through the swinging doors at the back of the room, walked across the hardwood floor, and pushed through the bar to the witness stand. He put his hand on the Bible, said his name and that he agreed to tell the truth, then sat in the chair in the witness box.

Yuki approached him, seeing the anger coming off his square face, the tension in his muscular form, his collar denting the flesh around his neck.

She got right to it.

"Mr. Brand, were you familiar with Aaron-Rey Kordell before he was your suspect in the murders of three drug dealers?"

"Yes."

"How did you know him?"

"I've seen him in that crack house at Turk and Dodge when we made busts there a couple of times."

Yuki asked, "And did you ever search him for drugs or weapons?"

"Yes."

"How many times?"

"Twice, I think."

"And you never found drugs or weapons on his person, isn't that right?"

"That's right."

"Was he belligerent?"

"No."

"How would you characterize his personality?"

"He was a big dumb kid in a crack house. I didn't give him a personality evaluation. And I didn't think about him too much."

"He had no criminal record prior to his arrest for carrying a weapon, isn't that right?"

"Correct."

"Was he belligerent when you interrogated him in conjunction with the shootings on February sixteenth of this year?"

"Not really."

"Could you describe his demeanor in a few words?"

Brand sighed, shrugged, and then said, "He cried. He denied having anything to do with the crimes."

Yuki said, "So just to make sure I understand this: You'd seen Mr. Kordell before. You didn't know him to be a drug user or to carry a weapon, and he had no prior record, isn't that right?"

"Right."

"But in this instance, you pushed him to confess to a crime that he denied committing, isn't that true?"

"He had the smoking gun, miss. Those guys were shot in the chest at close range. Only a dummy could get close enough with a gun to kill A. Biggy and his crew. Understand what I'm saying? They weren't afraid of the shooter, of A-Rey. Anyone else, they woulda defended themselves."

Brand had just told Yuki something she hadn't heard before. If he had made a mistake, she might be able to capitalize on it and destroy his credibility.

On the other hand, she could be about to make a big mistake of her own.

Chapter 73

THE FIRST RULE of cross-examination was never to ask a witness a question if you didn't know the answer.

Sometimes, though, you had to gamble.

"Inspector Brand, you just stated that Aaron-Rey Kordell, a 'dummy,' was the only person who could have gotten close enough to the drug dealers to shoot them at close range, isn't that right?"

"That's right."

"But you didn't know that the shots that killed those three men were fired at close range, did you?"

"I don't understand the question."

"I'll rephrase it. Mr. Kordell was arrested for carrying a gun at around noon on February sixteenth. He was brought to your station, and almost immediately thereafter, you interrogated him until the morning of the seventeenth. When did you see the bodies of the dead drug dealers?"

"Couple days after," said Brand.

"Couple of days after you interrogated Mr. Kordell?"

"That's right."

"So, just to make sure I understand: When you saw their bodies, they were in the *morgue*, isn't that right?"

Brand looked confused. Like he was double-thinking what he'd said, trying to follow her, maybe realizing his mistake. "Right."

"And so, to be clear, your testimony a few moments ago was *untrue*, wasn't it? You only saw the bodies several days *after* you'd extracted a confession from Mr. Kordell, correct?"

"I got mixed up about the times, that's all."

"So you didn't know how close or how far away the shooter was to the victims when you interrogated Mr. Kordell, right?"

"I said, I got my timeline wrong."

Yuki pushed on.

"And so, as I understand it, you were interrogating a 'dummy' without representation and you decided to make a case against him without a witness, without forensic evidence, without even a *theory*—you came up with that later. But first, you *sweated* this poor kid until you finally got a confession, which is all you wanted, isn't that right, Inspector Brand?"

"That's your way of putting it," said Brand.

"Yes, it is," said Yuki. "I have no other questions, Your Honor."

"Mr. Parisi?" the judge asked. "Do you want to cross-examine this witness?"

Parisi spoke from his seat behind the defense table. He looked unfazed, like a man with all the right answers.

"Inspector Brand, did you have friendships with or loyalty to the drug dealers who were killed?"

"What? No."

"Did you have anything against Mr. Kordell?"

"No. Not at all."

"So, regarding your vigorous interrogation of Mr. Kordell: That's what you do when you have a primary suspect, isn't that right?"

"Correct."

"Do you stand by the confession you obtained from this suspect?"

"Absolutely," said Brand. "He said he did it. We saw him say it. We believed him."

Parisi said, "Thank you, Inspector Brand. I have nothing else for this witness."

"If Ms. Castellano has no further questions," said the judge, "the witness may stand down."

Chapter 74

COURT HAD BEEN adjourned for the day when Yuki got a text from Brady saying, *Tony Willis was beaten. He's in the prison ward at SF Gen. Asked for you.*

Yuki ran to her car, got into the crush of traffic, and headed toward San Francisco General, where inmates requiring hospitalization were housed.

Tony Willis, aka Li'l Tony, had been a suspect in the jailhouse murder of Aaron-Rey Kordell. He'd denied that he'd been the doer, but when she'd talked to him last, he'd given her a sense that he knew who *had* killed Aaron-Rey.

Maybe he would tell her now.

If he lived.

The traffic was thick, and Yuki was determined

not to have an accident or even a fit of temper. Leaving the parking garage, she took a left on Polk and crossed through the Mission. It took close to half an hour to drive two and a half miles to reach Twenty-Third Street and another twenty minutes to park the car and gain access to the hospital.

When she arrived at ward 7D, the surgical unit, Tony Willis was alive and breathing oxygen through a cannula. Leads came off his chest, and fluids were dripping through tubes to his veins.

The doctor told Yuki, "That young man lost a lot of blood. He has several puncture wounds in major organs. He's on pain medication. I can't promise he'll know who you are."

"He asked for me."

"I understand. Keep it to five minutes, OK?"

Yuki walked down the aisle running the length of the ward. All of the eleven beds were occupied. Willis was at the far end on the left. She reached the bed, pulled the stall curtain around it, and moved a chair up to the bed.

Five-foot-tall Tony Willis had looked young before. Now he looked smaller and younger, with his defiant little hair twists and his thin cotton blanket pulled up to his underarms, monitors reporting on his vital signs.

"Tony? It's me. Ms. Castellano."

Tony Willis cracked open his eyes, winced, and put a bandaged hand on his blanketed chest. "Yo," he said. "You came."

"How're you feeling?"

"Like a lotta white dudes beat the crap out of me and then stuck me with shanks everywhere."

"That's what I heard. You stay strong, OK?"

"Right," he said. "I have something to say."

"OK."

"I need you to be my lawyer so I got confidentiality."

"You want me to represent you, Tony? There's more to it than that. I have to look at your case. I don't know what charges there are against you. And it's not my decision. I don't work for myself."

"Mrs. Cassielandro, you got to listen. I need lawyer-patient confidentiality. Right now. You hear me?"

He was wheezing. He was clearly in pain. He could die.

"OK. OK, Tony. I'll be your lawyer. What do you have to tell me?"

"Officially?"

She picked up his bandaged hand and shook it gently.

"It's official," she said.

"OK. I got a confession. I killed A-Rey."

Yuki gasped. "*You* killed him?"

"I was told 'Put Kordell down quick.' After that, I was supposed get a transfer to Corcoran, and you can see, that didn't happen."

"I'm not getting this," Yuki said.

She was *trying* to get it, but the pieces had very weird shapes and didn't totally fit. Whoever got Li'l Tony to kill Aaron-Rey had also promised him protection. Who the hell would do that? Furthermore, as he said, they clearly hadn't delivered it.

"Who told you to do this, Tony?" Yuki asked him.

"Listen to me, lady, before I fuckin' die. It was a *cop* who told me to whack A-Rey."

"What cop? Give me a *name*."

"On the street, he called One. Like Numero Uno."

"Tony. That's not a name. What else can you give me? I can't make a deal for you if all you've got

303

to bargain with is that you killed Aaron-Rey. No one is looking for his killer anymore."

Tony was straining to breathe. Any second now a nurse was going to chase her out. She touched his hand.

"You've got to give me something I can run with, Tony. You understand. Numero Uno isn't going to cut it."

"You don't look it, but you are a tough lady." He swallowed hard. Then he said, "Arturo. Mendez. Find him. He's A-Rey's fren'. He saw who shot those pushers."

"How do I find him?"

Tony closed his eyes. His breathing was ragged.

"*F-u-u-u-u-u-ck*," he said. "I got to do everything? Ask A-Rey's mom."

"Hang in," Yuki said. "I'll do what I can."

Chapter 75

YUKI CALLED AARON-REY'S mother, Bea Kordell, who had her son's phone, which showed a contact listing for "Arturo." Yuki sent Arturo a text, replied to his response, then sent another.

An hour later, at nearly 8 p.m., she parked on Turk near Dodge, the bad-news block directly across the street from the peeling three-story crack house on the corner.

She didn't have to wait long.

A kid came out of the Chinese restaurant next door to the crack house. He looked about five eight, one forty. He was wearing jeans hanging below his hip bones, striped boxer shorts, and a dark hoodie, and had iPod cords dangling from his ears.

He stood on the corner for a while, looking every which way, his eyes resting for a moment every time he swept his gaze across her bronze-colored Acura two-door sedan.

When the traffic thinned, the kid ambled across the street, nodding his head in time to music. Then he walked over to her window.

"Yuki?"

"Arturo. Get in the car," she said.

Yuki thought if Brady could see her inviting a crack dealer into her car, he would go bug-nuts.

Arturo got in and pulled the door closed, saying, "I got one minute."

"Mrs. Kordell told you? I need to know what happened that day in the crack house."

"And what I get?"

"A chance to do the right thing."

"And a free lawyer if I ever need one?"

"Yes. Free lawyer. Deal."

They shook on that. She fished a card out of her bag and handed it to Arturo. *Christ.* She'd tripled her client base today. Meanwhile, Arturo's eyes were working the streets from under his hood. The sidewalks were empty. He started talking.

"Aaron didn't shoot no one. It was three men

that did that. They looked like cops. They wore police jackets. They showed up on the second floor and everyone scattered— but I was coming out the bathroom and I saw it going down."

Yuki was startled. More than that. She was shocked.

"The men who shot those dealers—were cops?"

"I don't know if they were cops. They were wearing cop *jackets*. They had guns. They said 'SFPD.' But they were wearing plastic masks. They pushed Duane, A. Biggy, and Dubble D up against the *wall*. They kicked their legs apart, patted them down. They took they money, they drugs, they guns, they phones, naked pictures of they girlfriends for all I know.

"Then A. Biggy and his crew turns around and A. Biggy says, 'You done?'"

"And one of them cops, seemed like the head dude, said, 'I'm sorry. Put yourself in my shoes,' something like that, and he just blew them away."

Arturo's expression drooped, like he was seeing it all over again. He shook his head like he couldn't stop the images.

Yuki said, "Arturo. Why haven't I heard this before?"

"'Cause I was the only living one that saw it go down. And then I see the three of them men go down the stairs like nothing happened."

"Then what?" Yuki asked.

"I wait a couple of minutes, make sure the coast is clear, and then I'm ready to run out and A-Rey comes charging upstairs. He missed the shooting and he's looking for his homies like always. They treat him OK. He doesn't see anything yet. He says to me, 'Lookit what I found on the stairs, 'Turo.'

"He had a thirty-eight in his hand that belong to the shooter.

"And I say, 'A-Rey, get out of here, man.' He sees the dead guys and he starts to go over to them. He loves them, man, and he's crying and I just yell, 'Let's go!'

"And then we run down the stairs. Aaron-Rey is first. And by the time I get to the street, he's running and a patrol car sees that big boy and they chase him in the car. Then they get out and throw him to the ground."

Arturo went on.

"I see that, but what I'm supposed to do, huh? It was cops who shoot those boys. I just fade out of sight."

Yuki said, "You know what happened to A-Rey in jail?"

"I heard, yeah. He thought everyone was his friend."

"Arturo. Could you ID those men in the police jackets?"

"Not really. Definitely not the head dude. One of the other two, maybe. He had a little tat on his neck. I might have seen a tat like that on a narc."

Yuki felt the adrenaline shoot straight through her, but she kept her expression as neutral as possible. She said, "I'm suing the City on behalf of A-Rey's family. I need you, Arturo. I need you to testify for Aaron-Rey."

"And then what? I'll be dead, too."

"Let me see what I can do," said Yuki.

"Oh, yeah. Right," said Arturo. He started to get out of the car, but Yuki reached over and gripped his forearm.

She said, "I'm your lawyer. I've got pull. If I call you, take my call. It means I can get you whatever you need."

Arturo got out of the car and didn't look back.

Yuki sat in the car and watched him cross the street the way he'd come. Then she did the unthinkable. She called her former boss and current opponent, Red Dog Parisi. When he answered, she said, "Len. It's Yuki. I've got two new witnesses who can turn this case upside down. We need to meet right away."

Chapter 76

ON THE WAY home from another fruitless day of interviewing the Calhoun family's friends and neighbors, I found myself thinking about Tina Strichler.

Taking a chance, I phoned Mr. and Mrs. Nathan Gosselin from the car.

The Gosselins had been on Balmy Alley when Dr. Tina Strichler had been knifed in the crosswalk, and Mrs. Gosselin had actually seen the killer, although from behind and with several people between her and the man with the knife.

Conklin had interviewed Nathan and Allyson Gosselin on the scene, and Inspectors Michaels and Wang, the two homicide cops in charge of the case, had also spoken to them that day.

But because the Gosselins had said they couldn't make an ID, they'd been written off. In fact, I was pretty sure the entire case had been shelved now that every cop in the Hall of Justice was working some portion of the Windbreaker cop case.

The Gosselins sounded glad I'd called and told me they hadn't thought about much other than the woman who'd been killed on the street since it had happened. Mr. Gosselin gave me their address, which turned out to be a well-kept apartment building at Elizabeth and Diamond Streets. Mrs. Gosselin buzzed me in, answered the door, and welcomed me into her home.

"Thanks for making time for me," I said. "I just want to go over the events of that day one more time."

After my brush with death at Wayne Broward's house, I was cautious when entering, keeping my eyes on Mrs. Gosselin, walking practically sideways to the kitchen, where Mr. Gosselin was sitting at the table with the remains of his chicken dinner.

"No, please don't get up," I said.

"Have a seat," said Nathan Gosselin. "What can I get you?"

"Nothing, thanks," I said. "I only need a few

minutes of your time." I said that, but I hoped the few minutes would be full of newly recollected information that would give me a toehold on the case.

I sat at the table and asked the basic questions: *What did you see? Are you sure you didn't see the killer's face? Can you think of any detail that may have seemed insignificant at the time?*

Allyson Gosselin sighed.

She said, "I've thought about this night and day. You have to understand, not only did it happen fast, the street was jam-packed and people were trying to make the light, and I wasn't looking directly at the man who did that wretched thing."

"I understand."

"So, as I said at the time, I'm pretty sure he was white. He had brown hair, a black baseball-type jacket. He looked to be normal height. He never turned to face me. When Dr. Strichler dropped, most people panicked and ran. Me, too. I just wanted to find Nate and call nine-one-one, so when I finally did look for that man, he was just gone."

I said, "Allyson, you are obviously a very astute woman, the kind of person who notices small details. And frankly, that's the best kind of witness.

Using your mind's eye to search for detail, is there anything else, no matter how small it might seem?"

Allyson Gosselin said, "I have had a thought and didn't say anything about it."

"Well, it's not too late," I said, scooching my chair closer to the table.

"Well. I saw a lot of threes that day."

"Threes?"

"Yes. There were three people between me and the man who killed Dr. Strichler. There were three squad cars that arrived first, and three policemen spoke with me. And I saw three blackbirds sitting on the telephone line."

I did my best not to explode with *For God's sake!* I channeled my good-natured partner and said, "Allyson —"

But she wasn't done.

"And there were three EMTs around her body. And the date itself. The twelfth of May. One and two equals three," she concluded triumphantly.

"OK," I said. "So what does that mean to you?"

Mrs. Gosselin laughed. "I don't know. You're the detective, aren't you, Sergeant?"

How much deader could a dead end be?

I thanked the Gosselins, left them my card, and left their apartment.

I called Joe.

"I'm going back to work, Joe. Save me some leftovers. I know. I'm sorry. I swear I'll be home in two hours. I promise."

Chapter 77

TINA STRICHLER'S CRUEL death disturbed me above and beyond Joe's fixation on the possible sequential string of Claire's Birthday Murders. The Strichler case wasn't *cold*. It was active, and I knew Michaels and Wang weren't working it.

It pissed me off, but I understood. They had no witnesses, no leads, and no time to dig into the case, which had fallen directly to the bottom of the list.

But the case was very real and present to me. I'd seen Strichler's blood running into the street. I'd gone through her wallet and had seen that she'd had a psychiatric practice. She'd had a well-put-together appearance and, very likely, a full life, which had been terminated by a madman with a knife, an unknown killer who might never be known.

After talking with Joe, I drove to the Hall and took the elevator to the sixth-floor jail, where I asked to see Wayne Broward.

Broward was in jail because I'd breached his chain-link-barking-dog-no-trespassing-and-that-means-you security system, and I was going to be at his arraignment in the morning. However, he'd never answered my question.

I pulled rank on the desk sergeant, applying a little pressure, and Wayne was taken from his cell past visiting hours and shown into an interview room. When he saw me, he called out, "Sweetheart. Give me a kiss."

"Against the rules, Wayne."

His guard sat him down in the chair and locked his handcuffs to a hook in the table. The guard knew why Broward was in lockup, and he asked me, "Do you want me to hang in with you here, Sergeant?"

"Thanks, Santino, but I'll be OK."

It was embarrassing to be reminded, but it was true. The man sitting across from me might have killed me.

"Wayne, I have a question for you."

"Isn't my lawyer supposed to be here?"

"This has nothing to do with your case. You're being charged for assaulting me with a deadly weapon."

He laughed. "Assault. That's an overstatement, don't you think?"

I kept going. "I'm sure that's the position your lawyer will take tomorrow. Meanwhile, remember why I came to see you at your house?"

"Nope. Remind me."

I took Tina Strichler's picture out of my jacket pocket. It was creased but still recognizable. "This woman. Have you ever seen her?"

"Not that I recall. Refresh my memory."

"Do you know her, Wayne? Have you ever seen her?"

"She looks familiar."

Really? I felt a little spark of hope.

"Wait," he said. "Didn't you show me her picture before?"

I nodded. "Yep. I showed you the picture before."

Was Wayne Broward really this loony? Or was his crazy-guy persona a well-honed act? I'd dealt with crazy killers before. And actually, Wayne Broward wasn't as crazy as some of them.

I told Wayne I'd see him around and called the guard.

I left the Hall around 8:30 p.m. and made the drive home, the whole time trying to shake Dr. Tina Strichler out of my head, and not managing it at all.

Chapter 78

JOE WAS NOT in a good mood.

"You said you'd be home at seven, Lindsay."

"I'm sorry."

"OK."

His face was stiff, like he'd been fuming for a while. Embracing him was like hugging a tree.

"I'm *sorry*. Did something happen?"

"No," he said. "Just your average single-parent day. I cleaned up the kitchen. I vacuumed. I did the laundry. I put together a bag of stuff for Goodwill. Julie, Martha, and I went to Whole Foods. I peeled, chopped, parboiled, and roasted dinner. I bathed Julie. I put her to bed. I trimmed Martha's nails and I ate dinner. Alone. I cleaned up the kitchen. I took out the garbage. I made the bed. I applied for three consulting jobs in DC. Oh. I got a phone call from Evan Monroe, who was looking for you."

"Who is Evan Monroe?"

"He's Tina Strichler's brother."

Tina Strichler's brother had called me? Why? I put that newsbreak on a back burner for the moment.

I said to Joe, "Would you have been this mad at me if I'd been home at seven?"

"I doubt it. You're taking advantage, Linds."

I did get it. While I was out doing my job all day, he was holding the home team together without benefit of stimulation or adult conversation. I got that he wasn't just steamed up about today. It was an accumulation of days like this, added to the fact that I was working a very dangerous job that might follow me home—if I even *got* home.

I told Joe all of that, and I did my best to make amends. I said I would be more mindful of late hours and that I owed him a lot. And that tomorrow I would get Mrs. Rose to come in and that we could go out to dinner. "Anywhere."

I stopped short of groveling.

"OK, OK, forget it. So. Where were you?" he asked.

"I went to see Wayne Broward."

"In jail? How'd that go?"

"He's nuts. He needs to stay locked up. I hope he gets a shitty lawyer."

Joe hadn't totally forgiven me, but he laughed. Then he took a plate of food out of the fridge. I got up and took it out of his hand.

"I can heat that up. You sit," I said.

I put the plate of chicken and green beans in the microwave, and I poured wine for both of us. While my dinner revolved, I took off my shoes, put my gun away, and went in to see Julie, who was sleeping deeply.

I heard the microwave beeping.

Joe worked on his computer while I ate, which was OK. My mind was focused on the message from Evan Monroe, wondering if it was too late to call him back and if my returning that call would irritate my husband even more.

I cleaned up the kitchen, and after a quick shower and a change of clothes, I said, "Joe, what did Evan Monroe want?"

Joe said, "Wang gave him your name. I think because you were first officer. So Monroe's calling you because there hasn't been any movement on the case. He told me he had an idea about who could have killed Tina."

"He told you that?" I said.

"He was messed up, Lindsay. I told him you'd call, but he wouldn't let me off the phone. He said that when Tina was in graduate school, she was raped. She identified the guy and he was put away for twenty-five years. She saw him when he was up for parole a while back, and she told Evan afterward that she was no longer sure he was the person who raped her."

"Is the guy out?"

"Yep. His time was up five years ago. Beginning of May."

"Holy crap. Evan Monroe told you the guy's name?"

"Clement Hubbell. I looked him up on ViCAP."

Joe went to the living room and sat on the sofa. I sat next to him, and he put his arm around me. That felt good.

Joe said, "Hubbell was let out on May fifth five years ago. If Tina wrongly identified him, he's had a lot of time to make a plan. But it might have been hard to find her from lockup. She was Bettina

Monroe when she was raped. She got married and divorced and kept her married name."

"Let's see what Hubbell looks like," I said, putting my hand on my husband's thigh.

Joe leaned forward, opened his laptop, and called up Hubbell's mug shot. He was white. His hair was brown. He was five ten, which made him average height.

And as of May fifth five years ago, he was a free man.

Chapter 79

IT HADN'T TAKEN Joe long to locate Clement Hubbell, the man who'd been convicted of rape, had done twenty years in Chino, and had been released two weeks before the first of what Joe saw as five linked murders, one a year on the twelfth of May.

After lunch with Julie and her sitter, and under a sunny sky, Joe drove toward Edgehill Mountain and the home of Denise and Clement Hubbell.

Edgehill Mountain was an old, remote development with winding roads and small, widely spaced houses that had views of the Pacific and Ocean Beach. His car's GPS told Joe that he was coming up on his destination, and then he saw it up ahead on his left, a tidy tan house with red doors, standing alone at the side of the road.

Joe slowed the car to get a look at the picket-fenced vegetable garden beside the house, where an older woman in red checkered pants and a pink cardigan was weeding the beds.

He checked the number on the mailbox, then pulled his Mercedes into the driveway next to a dinged-up Toyota wagon. He took his Glock out of the glove box and slipped it into his shoulder holster, then pulled on his leather bomber jacket and got out of the car.

Putting his hands in his jacket pockets, Joe walked over to the gate and peered into the garden. The woman who was working the soil had sweet, doll-like features and white hair; she looked to be in her midseventies. Probably Hubbell's mother.

"Mrs. Hubbell?" Joe said.

The woman looked up, shielding her eyes from the sun. "Oh, hi, Jerry," she said. "Where's Clem?"

"No, ma'am. My name is Joe Molinari. We've never met. You're Clem's mom?"

"Yes, I'm Denise, but Clem isn't home. I thought he was with you." The woman laughed, got to her feet, and dusted off her knees. "Come on in," she said. "I've got blueberry muffins in the oven and a jar I just cannot open by myself."

Joe said, "Sure." He opened the gate for Denise Hubbell, who chattered away as she led him to the house about planting different types of peppers. Joe weighed whether or not to go into the house before deciding *What the hell?* Clement Hubbell wasn't home, and his mother might help him fill in some blanks.

Joe followed Mrs. Hubbell as she opened the back door, which led directly into the kitchen.

She said, "Have a seat."

Joe sat down at the red Formica table, and Mrs. Hubbell handed him the screw-top jar of sliced peaches, then fussed around the kitchen.

Joe opened the jar and said, "It's so beautiful out here, Denise. How's Clem doing?"

"Oh, still crazy after all these years." She laughed. "He spends most of his time in the hole."

Denise Hubbell used oven mitts to take the muffin pan out of the oven and put it down heavily on the stovetop. Joe saw immediately that the batter was still unbaked, but she didn't seem to realize it.

"Let's let them cool for a minute, Jerry."

"I'm sorry," Joe said. "What do you mean, 'the hole'?"

Denise removed her mitts, fluffed her hair, and said, "That's what he calls his room. Any space too big or too bright makes him dizzy. To think how the two of you used to run around all the time to all hours. I had to bait Clem with dinner and once he was in, bolt the door."

She laughed again. She had a very nice laugh.

"You think he'd mind if I saw his room?" Joe said. "I've got a note for him that I'll leave on his dresser."

"You go ahead," said Clement Hubbell's mom. "End of the hall. You know where it is. When you get back, we'll have coffee and sweets."

Joe said, "Good deal," and walked through the kitchen and into a hallway. He passed the living room on his right, then a pink-floral-papered bedroom to the left. Beyond that was a door centered at the end of the hallway.

Joe turned the knob expecting to see Clem Hubbell's "hole," but rather than a bedroom at the back of the house, there was a flight of stairs heading down. Joe found a light switch and flicked it on. He saw that the wooden stairs led to a basement room, which was another way of saying "the hole."

Joe left the hallway door open and started down.

Chapter 80

WHEN HE REACHED the bottom of the stairs, Joe saw that the basement was a typical subterranean cinder-block room. It had a washer, a dryer, a water heater, a furnace, stacks of boxes, and a pile of lawn furniture. Four small, high windows let in some light.

There was no bed or sofa or anything that suggested a living space. But under the staircase was a narrow door with a gleaming brass doorknob that suggested use and might be the entrance to Clement Hubbell's "hole."

Joe considered again what he was doing and was sure he was not breaking any laws. He'd been invited into the house, had gotten permission to go to Hubbell's room. He turned the knob and the door opened, letting him into another hallway, this one totally devoid of light.

He left the door open behind him, and after letting his eyes acclimate, he noticed that the floor of this hallway was made of poured concrete and that it was on a fifteen-degree downward angle. Calculating the turns he'd made, he was heading under the vegetable garden, but about twenty feet down.

He cupped his hands and called out "Hellooooo." Not hearing an answer or any sound, he kept one hand on the cinder-block wall and walked down the incline until it terminated in an empty twelve-by-twelve room that was dimly lit by a pale-blue light.

Centered in the floor of that room was a hatch door flipped back into the open position. There was an attic-type folding ladder attached to the hatch frame by a spring-loaded hinge, and the ladder extended straight down into a pale pool of bluish light.

Joe called "Hellooooo" again, and as before, there was no answer. He had too much curiosity to walk away, but climbing down that ladder was a big commitment to the unknown.

He would need both his hands on the ladder,

meaning his gun would be holstered and he would be backing down virtually blind into whatever lay below. Although Hubbell wasn't home, Joe still had a queasy feeling that this hole could be a bear trap.

He put his hands on his knees and peered down into the opening; he looked down from another side of the hole and saw nothing but the long length of ladder and the dim blue light. He decided to retrace his steps and tell Denise Hubbell of the unbaked muffins that he'd visit again some other time.

But instead, he found himself getting a grip on the ladder, making sure it was steady, placing one foot on the top rung. And after that step proved to be stable, Joe began the descent to the bottom of the ladder.

When both of his feet were on solid concrete, Joe found the source of the light: a couple of open laptops on a roughly made desk. He was moving toward the desk, hoping to find a lamp, when a muscular arm snaked across his chest from behind and a sharp, cold blade stung the tight skin of his throat.

"Who the hell are you?" said the man with the knife.

Chapter 81

JOE FROZE.

He considered kicking back at the man's knees, but since that action could get his throat cut, he held up his hands and said, "Nothing to be concerned about, Clement. You certainly don't need the knife, man. Your mom asked me to come down and check on you, that's all. She was worried. Didn't you hear me calling you?"

Joe had kept his voice steady, but he couldn't control either his heart's sudden drumbeat or the sweat beading his upper lip.

The arm around his chest loosened slightly, but the knife tightened. Joe felt it cut into his skin; at the same time, he felt the man's hand lift the gun from his shoulder holster.

"Nice piece," said the man's voice. "Government grade. What are you? FBI?"

"I worked for the Feds," Joe said. "I'm a civilian now. Retired."

"So what are you doing here?"

Joe said, "I drive this road sometimes, and when I see your mom in the garden, I talk to her. She gave me some chives one time." Joe was making it up as he went along, but he sounded convincing to his own ears. At the same time, adrenaline was coursing through his veins like a river over its banks in the rainy season.

He forced himself to slow his breathing and focused on his surroundings.

The room was about twelve by eight feet, the dimensions of a roomy two-person jail cell. There was a metal-framed bunk bed against one of the long sides of the room. On the short side to his right was that desk, made of a couple of ten-inch boards resting on two cinder-block pedestals.

To his left, on the other short wall, were a toilet, a washstand with no mirror, and a four-cubic-foot refrigerator. Joe had no sense of what was behind him on the opposite long wall.

"Have a seat, G-man," said the ex-con who lived

in the hole. He moved the knife away and shoved Joe against the lower berth of the bunk bed, which moved a couple of inches back toward the wall when he struck it.

Joe righted himself and got his first good look at Clement Hubbell. Hubbell was lanky, leaner than when his mug shot had been taken. His hair was close-shaven. He wore a wife-beater and a pair of cotton pants; he was barefoot. His arms were tattooed from fingers to collarbones in prison art: skulls, snakes, naked women, the word MOM inside a heart on his right biceps. The heart pulsed when Hubbell flexed his arm.

Joe watched as Hubbell set the knife down within reach on the desk and checked to see if Joe's gun was loaded. It was. He pointed it at Joe and at the same time lifted the ladder, which was weighted so that it easily rose up to rest parallel to the ceiling. As the ladder rose, the ceiling hatch closed.

Joe's hammering heart picked up its tempo. He was twenty years older than Hubbell. With the ladder up and the hatch closed, there was no way out.

Hubbell pointed to a pair of handcuffs beside Joe's feet, and Joe saw that the cuffs were linked to a length of chain that ran under the bed. The other end of the chain was likely looped around the bed leg closest to the wall.

"Cuff yourself," Hubbell said. "Then we can talk."

"This is unnecessary," Joe said. "I have nothing against you, Clem."

Hubbell pointed the gun at the wall next to where Joe sat and fired it. The sound was loud, and it reverberated for long seconds.

Hubbell said, "Next shot's for you."

Joe picked up the cuffs and clasped one, then the other around his wrists. He moved the chain to get a sense of how long it was. About five feet. He could get to the toilet, but it was too short for him to reach Hubbell, who sat facing him in a swivel chair.

"What's your name?" a relaxed Clement Hubbell asked Joe.

"Joe."

"Joe what?"

"Hogan."

"OK, Joe Hogan. Get comfortable. I feel like I've been waiting to meet you for a very long time."

Chapter 82

THE DOOR TO Leonard Parisi's office was closed when Yuki arrived for the meeting. She checked the time, confirming that she was six minutes late. She explained to Parisi's assistant that she'd been stopped at the security desk downstairs, but before Darlene could speak, Parisi opened his door.

"I thought I heard your voice," he said. "We're waiting."

Parisi's office took up a big corner section of the second floor. It was huge for offices in the Hall, but whatever it gained in size, it lost in its proximity to the sounds of the heavy traffic on Bryant Street.

Chief of Detectives Warren Jacobi was at the round oak conference table with his back to the windows. Parisi, Yuki's former boss and mentor, took the seat closest to his desk, and Yuki sat between the two men, not far from the door.

Darlene passed bottled water around, and Parisi asked her to hold his calls, then said to Yuki, "You're on first."

Yuki took a pull from her water bottle. After five years of being Parisi's protégée, she felt that the table had turned one hundred and eighty degrees.

This was her meeting. And she hoped she could pull it off

"I've got a meeting with the mayor in fifteen minutes," Jacobi said.

Yuki said, "I'll get right to the point. I met with two new witnesses yesterday. They are reluctantly willing to cooperate if they get protection.

"If they tell what they know, we'll have a strong lead on the identities of the parties who killed the dope dealers on Turk and Dodge. We'll also know who killed Aaron-Rey Kordell."

Parisi said, "This is what subpoenas are for, Counselor. Let's hear their testimonies."

"Only with protection, Len. Both witnesses are in fear for their lives, with good reason. I'm going to tell you what each of these men said, and if we can reach an agreement, I'll set up meetings. I think you'll want to settle the Kordell case out of court."

"Doubtful," Parisi said. "But go ahead and convince me."

"Will do," Yuki said. "My first witness will admit under oath that he killed Aaron-Rey Kordell."

"Where are you going with this?" Parisi asked. "We don't contest that Kordell was murdered in jail. Why would we protect his murderer? We should charge him."

Yuki said, "This man was hired to—and I quote—'Put Kordell down quick,' in exchange for being moved to a different penal facility."

"Who promised him that?" Parisi asked.

Yuki said, "A police officer did that, Len."

"Why?" Jacobi asked. "Why would a cop want Kordell dead?"

"That brings me to witness number two," said Yuki.

Neither man at the table spoke. She had their undivided attention.

She said, "The cop who commissioned the hit on Kordell is one of the three who killed the drug dealers."

Parisi said, "You're saying that a cop who

participated in the murder of the dope dealers had Kordell put down to cover his tracks?"

"That's right," said Yuki. "Witness number two was in the crack house on Turk and Dodge and can corroborate that. He saw the shooting. With protection, he'll testify that Aaron-Rey Kordell didn't do it, and he may be able to identify one or more of the men who did."

Chapter 83

JUDGE QUIRK CLOSED the door to his chambers. He picked the Bible up from his desk and went to the seating area where several people were assembled: Yuki Castellano, Leonard Parisi, Warren Jacobi, and a jittery young man in jeans and a hoodie who sat in a side chair, jouncing his feet.

The judge settled into a wing chair beside the witness and said, "Please tell us your name, young man."

"Arturo Mendez."

"Place your hand on this Bible, Mr. Mendez. Now, I need you to swear before me and everyone here that you will tell the truth, the whole truth, and nothing but the truth, so help you God."

"I do. I swear."

Judge Quirk said to him, "The nice lady sitting behind you, that's Ms. Pearson, and she's going to record what we all say. Ms. Castellano is going to ask you questions, and then Mr. Parisi, the district attorney, may have some questions.

"Mr. Parisi is the one who authorized an order of protection for you. The gray-haired man sitting next to Mr. Parisi is Chief of Police Jacobi. His interest is also in getting to the truth, Mr. Mendez. But only the truth. Not what you think. Not what you were told. Not what you think we want to hear. Just what you saw and heard. Any questions so far?"

"No, sir. I used to watch *Law & Order*."

"Fine," said the judge. "But that's a TV show, and this is real. If you lie, that's perjury, and that means jail time. Understand?"

"Yes, Your Honor. I get it."

"Ms. Castellano, your witness."

Yuki sat across from Arturo Mendez. She said, "Arturo, when did I meet you?"

"Yesterday."

"And how did I come to meet you?"

"You got my name from Aaron-Rey's mom. She has my number 'cause I was friends with A-Rey."

"That's right," said Yuki. "And did I meet you on the corner of Turk and Dodge within view of the three-story house where the drug dealers were killed?"

"That's right."

"And do you know who shot the drug dealers inside that drug house?"

"Yes, ma'am. Because I was there and I watched it happen," said Arturo Mendez.

"Were you under any drug influence when you witnessed the shooting?" Yuki asked.

"Nah. I never got a chance to score."

"Are you straight now?"

"Yes, ma'am. I ain't no junkie, anyway. I can pee in a cup if you want."

"Not now, Arturo. Can you please tell us the events that took place in the crack house when the dealers were killed?"

Arturo Mendez told the story exactly as he had told it to Yuki the day before. He'd been in the house when three men wearing SFPD Windbreakers came in and ordered the dope dealers to "grab the wall."

Mendez was hiding, but he watched those men frisk the dealers and take their money and guns and drugs. Then they turned the dealers back around. That was when he heard one of the "cops" make a comment: "Put yourself in my shoes."

Arturo Mendez told the people in the judge's office that that was the man who shot all three of the drug dealers, after which "the whole crew of guys wearing the Windbreakers left by the stairs."

Mendez said further that he waited until they were gone, then was making to leave when Aaron-Rey Kordell came up the stairs, excited because he'd found a gun in the stairwell.

Mendez said A-Rey hadn't seen the shootings and that he, Mendez, had told A-Rey to run.

Yuki said, "Can you describe the shooters?"

"Yes, sorta. They was wearing masks."

"What kind of masks?"

"Rubberlike, the kind that almost look like real faces, and like I said, they wore the blue SFPD Windbreakers and caps, you know. And cop shoes."

"Anything else you think we should know, Mr. Mendez?"

"One of those men, he had a tattoo on his neck, right about here." Mendez indicated a spot under his left ear, just above the collar line. Yuki saw Parisi's eyes widen.

"Could you identify that tattoo?" Yuki asked.

Tears spontaneously sprang from Mendez's eyes.

He said, "You gotta move me to another state, no lie. When I was coming into the building just now, I think I see that cop with a tattoo on his neck. He mighta seen me, too."

Chapter 84

WHEN JOE WASN'T telling himself he was an ass-hole, he tried to figure out how he was going to get out of this crypt alive. He sat in the lower bunk of the double-decker bed, his cuffed hands hanging loosely between his knees, the chain trailing under the bed. Off to his left, and way out of range, Clement Hubbell tapped the keys on his laptop.

Hubbell said, "There's a whole lot of Joe Hogans in San Fran. Some's retired. One of them has a deli and one is in auto parts. Here's one who works in an insurance company. He's closest to your age. Several Joe Hogans are dead. Which one are you?"

"Clem. May I call you Clem?"

"That's my name," said Hubbell. He closed out

the search engine and scooted his wheeled chair so that he was opposite Joe. A stale smell of sweat and garlic came off him.

"Clem," Joe said. "What's going on here?"

On the wall behind Hubbell was a map of San Francisco. Five points had been starred on the map with a marking pen. Were these the locations of the five dead women, including the latest, Tina Strichler?

"What's going on? This is what I call my life. Imagine how surprised I was to find you coming into my cell," Hubbell said. "This is the first time that's ever happened, and you know what? It's kind of an invasion of privacy."

"Open the cuffs and I'll get out of here. I'll pretend I never met you," Joe said.

"Where's the fun in that?" Hubbell said. "I haven't had a chance to get to know you. And you know, I'd really like to."

Hubbell opened and closed his Buck knife as he swiveled in his chair. The hunting knife had a bone handle and a six-inch blade. From where Joe sat, the blade looked as sharp as a razor.

Joe said, "You said you felt like you were waiting for me. What did you mean?"

"I like solitary. But every now and then, a man likes to have someone to talk to."

As Hubbell bent his head to his knife, Joe saw the tattoo on the top of his head, just visible under a quarter-inch carpet of hair. It was a vulture with its bill open, talons outstretched.

Joe said, "What do you want to tell me?"

Hubbell grinned. "I'm going to tell you about murders I've committed in, like, the middle of the day," he said. "And I got away with every one of them. They're right here on my map of the stars." He half turned, pointing to the map on the wall behind him. "This has been my get-out-of-jail celebration, right?"

Joe flicked his eyes to the map, this time picking out the star on the corner of Balmy Alley and Twenty-Fourth, where Tina Strichler had been gored within a crowd of tourists.

The man wanted a response. And Joe wanted him to keep talking.

"Oh. You were in jail."

"Oh, yes. You could even say I grew up there. I'm going to tell you things I've never told anyone, Joe," Hubbell said, flicking his eyes from the map to where Joe sat cuffed and chained and stooped on the lower bunk. "But you have to promise to take what I tell you to your grave. Promise? Say you promise."

"I promise," said Joe.

"Shake?" said Hubbell.

It was an opportunity Joe couldn't pass up.

"Shake," he said. He put out his linked hands, and Hubbell reached out his right one—then, before he touched Joe's hands, he pulled his away.

"Hah! Got you."

Hubbell laughed and walked a few steps to the little refrigerator near the toilet. He took out a gallon jug of water. He guzzled some down, then offered the jug to Joe, who said, "No, thanks."

The twelve-by-eight cell was soundproof at thirty feet underground. Joe was thinking he was never going to leave this place on his own two feet. After Hubbell finished telling him in loving detail about his life of crime, he would slice and dice him and take his body up the ladder one piece at a time.

Chapter 85

JOE KNEW THAT serial killers fell into two broad categories. Those in the first category were psychotic killers, criminally insane. They heard voices. They had visions. They didn't know right from wrong.

And then there were the pathological killers, who were not insane. They were conscienceless. They killed because they liked to do it. Murder gave them an incredible high, and the only way to stop them was to kill them. Or lock them up.

Clement Hubbell was in the latter category.

Joe blocked the wave of fearful thoughts pouring into his mind, images of the people he loved and would never see again, things he would never get to do, pictures of his body hacked into bloody chunks. He took a breath, then looked up at his captor.

Hubbell was younger and stronger than Joe. He was armed, and he got off on playing cat and mouse. The smart money was on the cat.

Joe had one iffy idea on how to get out of this box. But there would be no do-over if he got it wrong.

"I want to hear all about the people you killed," Joe said. "I want to hear it all. I'm a student of murder. I was never a profiler. Just your paper-pushing variety of Fed. So I feel lucky to have met you, Clem. I can't wait for you to tell me your stories."

"Oh, I will," said Hubbell. "We have all the time in the world. Maybe you noticed. I don't have clocks down here. It's what we call long time."

Joe said, "You mind if I take a leak before you begin? I had to go before I even got here."

"Be my guest," Hubbell said.

Joe got to his feet. Hubbell was still in the swivel chair opposite the bed. The toilet was just to Joe's right. He unzipped his fly and took a step toward the stainless steel can.

As soon as he cleared the end of the bed, Joe whipped around and, using his foot as a fulcrum, jammed it against the bed leg closest to him. At the same time, he gripped one of the bed's upright supports with his cuffed hands and pulled down on it, hard.

Hubbell jumped to his feet and yelled, "Hey!"

But he had nowhere to go. The desk was to his right, Joe was to his left, and as Joe kept up the pressure, the bed began teetering, then falling toward Hubbell.

Hubbell put up his hands, but the weight of the iron-framed bed had passed the tipping point. The top mattress slid, getting in Hubbell's way, and the crashing bed pinned him.

Joe was still cuffed, but the chain that had been looped around the rear leg of the bed was now free. He stepped over and around the bed frame, wrapped the chain around Hubbell's neck, and, grabbing him by the shoulders, slammed the man's ugly head against the concrete floor.

Hubbell screamed, "*Stop that!* Noooo! Stop!"

Joe let up and said, "Where's the key?"

Hubbell said, "Key to what?"

Joe slammed Hubbell's head against the floor again. He didn't want to kill him.

But he wanted to hurt him, badly.

Chapter 86

JOE SHOUTED DIRECTLY into Hubbell's grinning face.

"Where is the *key*? Where is the *fucking* key?"

"It's up my *ass*."

Joe grabbed the knife off the floor and said, "Have it your way. You've got a nice edge on this thing."

Hubbell said, "No, no. *It's in the ice cube tray.*"

Keeping the chain pulled tightly around Hubbell's neck, Joe could just reach the fridge. He snagged the small ice cube tray with the ends of his fingers. He dumped the tray on the floor, identified the cube with the key inside it, and crushed the ice with his heel.

Joe picked up the small key. "On your stomach," he said.

Hubbell rolled over, and Joe put his foot on the man's neck. He maneuvered the key with his shaking hands until he had unlocked his cuffs. When his hands were free, he zipped up his fly.

Then he pulled Hubbell's arms around his back and cuffed his wrists with the man's own cuffs. He wrestled the bed to a standing position, scooped his gun up off the desk, and holstered it.

When he jerked Hubbell to his feet, the man didn't kick out, squirm, or in any way fight him. He almost seemed accepting. Maybe twenty years of hard time did that to a person.

"You didn't need to go bug-fuck," Hubbell said to Joe.

"Yeah. Well, please accept my sincere apologies."

"I wasn't going to hurt you," said Hubbell. "I just wanted to tell you about the things I've done and how I did them."

"Don't worry. A lot of people are going to want to know all about you, Clem. You'll get to tell your story many, many times."

Wrapping the chain around his left hand, keeping his cuffed prisoner tightly in front of him,

Joe pulled the weighted ladder down from the ceiling. The hatch door opened smoothly above them.

Joe said, "What do you say, Clem? Let's get out of here."

After the two men climbed the ladder and surfaced in the basement, Joe chained Clement Hubbell to the furnace and locked the basement door behind him. He called Lindsay from the kitchen, and then he called the sitter to say he was sorry he was late getting back, and to please hang in with Julie.

When he hung up, Joe washed his hands, turned on the oven to 375, and set the timer for thirty minutes.

Joe and Denise Hubbell were eating warm blueberry muffins when Lindsay, along with a fully armed tactical team, arrived at 355 Edgehill Way, where they proceeded to batter down the red-painted kitchen door.

Chapter 87

I HAD SOME explaining to do when Joe, the SWAT team, and I got back to the Hall with a confessed killer in cuffs: a killer no one in Homicide had on their radar or even knew existed.

I filled Brady in while Joe waited at my desk.

Brady gave me a very cold stare as I told him that Joe had merely followed up a hunch, that he had been invited into the Hubbell house by the owner, and that she'd given him carte blanche to go into her son's room.

"Is this something like the hunch that took you into a house where the homeowner put a loaded Winchester rifle to your head?" Brady asked me.

"Yes. It's exactly like that."

"Personal feelings aside," Brady said, "I should write you up for that. It was procedurally unsafe, to say the least. What if you'd gotten shot? What if you'd shot someone? And now Joe does the same dumb-ass thing? Are you running some sort of private police department out of your garage? Don't you have enough work to do, Boxer?"

That was a rhetorical question, so I didn't answer, but I flushed down to my toes. It was humiliating to have Brady kick my ass. Factually, Joe was in the clear. He was nobody, as far as the SFPD was concerned. He hadn't messed up a case against Hubbell. But now it was official and I had to color strictly within the lines.

I waited a second or two, then said, "Lieutenant, while Hubbell had Joe cuffed and confined, he confessed to killing five people. I'm going to try to get him to say that again."

Brady tipped so far back in his chair, I thought it would go over. He put his hands over his eyes and threw a sigh so deep and so long, I actually felt sorry for him.

He said, "Get Wang and Michaels. Strichler is their case. They should be in the interrogation. No mistakes, Lindsay. Video everything. From this point on, do it strictly by the book."

"I get it. And I'm sorry, Brady. I'll make it up to you."

Chapter 88

HUBBELL HAD BEEN processed and was slouching in a small gray chair at a matching metal table in the small gray room we call Interview 2. Inspectors Michaels, Wang, and I took seats at the table, and Joe stood outside the two-way mirror with Brady. Brady wore a mic so that he could wirelessly fire comments and questions directly into my ear.

I was up to speed on Hubbell's arrest for raping Tina Strichler twenty-five years before and his sterling record of good behavior while incarcerated at Pelican Bay and, later, at Corcoran. Hubbell's personally inked "star map" of his homicides was now spread out on the table.

He'd even thoughtfully provided a key to the

murders on the back of it: names, locations, and the date of each.

Wang and Michaels were there to watch and share in the glory—if there was any glory—and I would be happy to hand off this serial killer collar to them.

I formally introduced myself to Hubbell, introduced him to the other cops in the room, and told him I appreciated his coming in to talk to us. I said that without a trace of sarcasm.

But still, he laughed.

"That was a hell of an escort I got."

"First-class treatment, Mr. Hubbell. Nothing but the best for you. You're kind of a superstar, aren't you?"

He laughed again. Oh, man. He was enjoying himself.

"Mr. Hubbell, you've told us that you killed five women in locations you've starred on your map of San Francisco. This is that map, right?"

Hubbell said, "You mind getting me something to drink?"

Wang took Hubbell's order. "What can I get you?"

"Got any Mountain Dew?"

"One frosty-cold Mountain Dew coming right up."

I was sitting directly across the table from Hubbell, and after he slugged down his soda, I said, "Are we ready now?"

"I have one other request."

I said sweetly, "Tell me."

"I want to go back to Pelican Bay. If you promise me that, I'll tell you every single thing."

"Why Pelican Bay?"

"I want to go home."

Brady spoke in my ear. "Tell him that your CO gives you his word, and that we'll get a commitment from the DA in the morning."

I repeated that to Hubbell. I expected him to say, "Well, I guess this can wait until I hear from the DA."

But he said, "OK. Just promise to do your best."

"I promise," I said, and that was all Hubbell needed. He was eager to talk about his attenuated five-year killing spree, and I've got to give it to Joe. He had been right from the beginning. Clement Hubbell killed on the anniversary of his conviction for rape. He called it a celebration of the start of his wonderful life in prison.

As for the murders themselves, with the exception of Tina Strichler, Hubbell said they were killings of opportunity.

"It was a test of my skill," he told me, leaning over the table, really wanting me to understand.

"I selected a knife from my collection. I looked for a woman who was in a good place to be killed. Sometimes they were alone. Sometimes I'd see one in the thick of a crowd. Like the one I killed at the race last year. I gave myself twelve hours to do the job and earn another star for my map. And then, once I was back home, I would wait for news of my perfect crime." He grinned. "And I'd think about it for another year."

"But you couldn't tell anyone? That must've hurt," I said.

"Sure. That's true," Hubbell said. "I missed having a cell mate."

"So Tina Strichler was the only victim you knew?" I asked.

"Bettina Monroe. The only girl I ever loved. Raping her, well, she was my first. I held a knife on her, but it was just a turn-on. I wasn't going to kill her. I didn't even *think* of killing her. I thought she might be willing to date me. I know you want to laugh, Sergeant—"

"No, no. I'm just surprised that you cared for her."

"Yes. Until I raped her, she didn't know I was alive."

"And so why *did* you kill her?"

"I was leaving the police a clue," he said.

"Because?"

"It was time."

At the end of an hour, Clement Hubbell had told us in great detail about each of the murders he had committed. He never asked for a lawyer. After a while, he put his head down on the table and nodded off. Wang woke him up, and Michaels charged him with five homicides. Before he was taken out of the room, Hubbell thanked me. That was a first.

"You're very welcome," I told him.

I left the box and found Joe and Brady waiting for me.

"Good job, the two of you," Brady said. "All is forgiven. Don't ever put me in this position again."

He shook Joe's hand. He shook mine. He squeezed my arm.

All in all, it was a good day to be a cop.

Chapter 89

YUKI WAS HIGH from the thrill of it.

She had just faced off with Red Dog Parisi across his leather-topped desk and negotiated a three-point-five-million-dollar settlement and a public apology for the Kordell family, which, during two intense phone calls, they had accepted.

She texted Brady before she left the Hall, again from the street, and another time from the parking lot at Whole Foods on Fourth Street. No reply.

During her drive home to Telegraph Hill, she revisited highlights of her meeting with Parisi, especially the part when he'd said, "I think two million is the right number." And she had said, "No, it's not, Len. No freaking way."

Yuki hardly remembered arriving home, but

after putting away the groceries, she checked her landline and saw that Brady still hadn't called. And now she was getting annoyed about that.

She took a bottle of coconut water from the fridge, got into her comfy chair, and was opening her e-mail when the doorbell rang. She bounced up, looked through the peep-hole, and saw a teenager standing in the hallway with a clipboard and a gigantic bouquet of flowers.

This was more like it.

She exchanged her signature for the flowers and read the note on her way to the kitchen. *Damn, Yuki. Hiring you was the best thing I ever did in my life. Congratulations. Zac.*

Yuki liberated the flowers from the wrapping and carried the vase to the console table behind the sofa. Then she returned to her laptop and opened her mailbox.

There was an e-mail from Chief Jacobi.

Yuki, thought you'd like to know that Inspector Brand is on suspension pending an investigation. I've got your young Arturo Mendez in protective custody until I can park him someplace safe.

Sorry to tell you Li'l Tony Willis passed. As for you,
young lady, hell of a job. Hell of a job.

Yuki's eyes stung.

She palmed them and tried to hold back the
tears. She thought about Li'l Tony, with tubes in his
nose and his arms, asking her to get him moved to
another prison. That was all he'd wanted. When
she opened her eyes again, she had a new e-mail.

Yuki, we're moving as soon as we can to a better
place for our child. I am sorry Aaron-Rey never
met you. He would have loved you like we do. We
will never forget you,

Love, Bea Kordell

That was when Yuki really started to cry. She
went to the bedroom, undressed, and got into bed.
She was sleeping deeply when she was awoken by
a kiss on the cheek.

Brady was sitting next to her, looking at her in

a way he hadn't looked at her since before she took the job at the Defense League. She backed up to the headboard and sat up.

"I'm a dumb dick," he said.

"Uh-huh."

"I'm dumb, I've been a dick, and I'm sorry."

She was still mad. She reached for a tissue and blew her nose. She said, "It wasn't anyone's fault that we weren't allowed to talk about our cases."

"I could have made tea. We could have watched movies together. Had pillow fights. Something."

"I'm not that mad at you," she said.

"You *are*. You *should* be. You know why I couldn't take your calls today? Because I was in nonstop meetings. Because you cracked this dirty-cop murder case that I've been working—me and the entire Southern Station—"

"I didn't do all that."

"You kicked the door down, darlin'. We've got a chance now of closing this whole nasty thing. Thanks to you."

"I'm glad." She liked his voice. That southern thang. She couldn't take her eyes away from him, either.

Brady put his hand along her cheek, under her

chin. She looked up at him.

"I was a dick," he said, "but it was killing me. I've really missed you."

"Me, too." Her voice cracked.

Brady got up and closed the blinds. He took off his tie, then his jacket, threw them onto the chair, unstrapped his holster, kicked off his shoes, and opened his shirt. He went for the button at his waistband.

Yuki said, "Wait, Brady. I have to be somewhere."

"Really?" he said.

Yuki laughed. "No."

Brady stepped out of his pants and she gazed at him adoringly. He opened the envelope of blankets and sheets and got into bed. Yuki put her arms around his neck, fitted herself against him, and let him take it from there.

He always knew just what to do.

Chapter 90

JOE AND I were in bed. It was early, ten something o'clock, but I was too tired to go for a run, too edgy to sleep. Joe yawned and stretched beside me. He was feeling wonderful. In fact, the last time he'd been in this kind of mood was when he'd first seen the face of his baby girl.

My version of Joe's day had been terrifying.

I could still hear his breathless voice over the phone saying I had to come quick—he had Clement Hubbell in custody.

I had moved like there was a bomb tied to my tail. I got hold of the SWAT commander and said I'd get authorization later. I hoped to hell I could. I'd jumped into the lead SUV for the warp-speed race to Edgehill Mountain, the whole way hoping we would get there in time.

Now that it was behind us, I pictured SWAT battering down the red door, the hinges popping, the door lying down like a big red tongue on the floor as a dozen men with shields up and guns drawn stormed the kitchen. Joe was at the table with a muffin in his hand, sitting beside a shocked old woman, who'd huffed, "You could have *knocked*."

Joe had started grinning like a kid who'd unlocked the parental controls on the adult entertainment channels—and that was *before* Hubbell had been booked.

I was still in post-adrenaline shock and kept thinking about how badly it could have gone. My husband could have died.

"You're so tense," Joe said, stretching out an arm, pulling me toward him.

"Pretty happy with yourself, aren't you, hon?"

He laughed. "You bet I am. After all these years as a desk jockey, I still have the goods."

He wrapped both arms around me, and I lifted my face for his kiss. His mouth and hands felt so good, I tried to let my thoughts go, but I couldn't.

I was wired: flashing from the Calhoun family

massacre, to the Windbreaker cops, to the notes from anonymous cowards accusing me of crossing the thin blue line.

"Lindsay?"

"I'm sorry, Joe. My mind's still cranking. How about in the morning?" I said. "OK?"

He stroked my hair with his big paw.

"Course it's OK. Talk to me," he said.

I snuggled up to him and said the cases involving the dirty cops were still making me crazy. "I no longer know who to trust in the SFPD, not even in our own department."

I hadn't been talking long when I realized that Joe's breathing had deepened and he'd dropped into sleep.

I got out of bed quietly and went to look in on Julie.

Little Miss Precious saw me peering into her crib. She burbled and raised her arms. I picked her up and took her to the chair by the window. I held her against my chest and rocked, all the while watching the traffic on Lake Street.

I saw no suspicious activity.

No men loitering or sitting in dark cars.

I rocked my sweetie until she fell asleep, and

soothed by the motion of the chair and her breathing, I finally relaxed. I put her down in her crib and covered her up. Then I checked the locks on the front door and made sure the security system was on.

When all the hatches were battened down, I returned to bed, where my dear husband was alive and well, and maybe dreaming about his ten-star megaday.

I must have slept, because I woke up and looked at the clock. It was quarter after three. After what seemed like a minute, I looked at the clock again.

It was 7:45 a.m.

I had a meeting at eight. I was going to be late.

Chapter 91

I CALLED JACOBI from my car and told him I was on the way. He barked, "Damn it, Boxer. Get your ass moving. We're holding the meeting for *you*."

He wasn't kidding.

I said, "I'm ten minutes out," and clicked off before I could bark back at him out of pure hurt-feelings reflex.

Of course my feelings were hurt.

Five years ago, when Jacobi and I were partners, we were both shot down in a dark alley in the Mission and almost died. I called in the "officers down" with what I thought would be my next-to-last breath. After that, Jacobi and I were bonded for life.

Yesterday, in a completely unrelated event, I'd interrogated a serial killer, which had been a lot like walking barefoot on the edge of a knife. I'd gotten the confession on video. All corners had been squared. Our solved cases rate shot up. Big day for the SFPD!

Today, I was late for a meeting with three men I trusted with my life, who trusted me with theirs. And Jacobi had chewed me out for being *late*.

I heard my dead father saying, *Toughen up, Princess.*

I have little love for my father, but this was right.

I had to toughen up. I applied the brakes about twelve inches before I rear-ended a minivan full of kids and dogs at the red light up ahead. I took a breath. A few of them.

I sat there and got my brains together, and when the light changed, I didn't flip on the siren. I proceeded toward the Hall within the speed limit. I got to 850 Bryant at 8:46.

I parked in the all-day lot, tossed the keys to Carl, and crossed the street against the light. I badged security and took an elevator to the fifth floor.

When I walked into Jacobi's office, three grim-faced men were sitting in "antiqued" leather furniture around a glass coffee table. The framed photos on the wall were of Jacobi with various politicos, and there was a shot of the two of us in our dress blues, receiving commendations from our former chief.

I stepped around Brady's legs and took the seat next to Conklin. I felt better now. I was surrounded by friends, and I had myself back.

I said, "Sorry I'm late."

Conklin passed me a container of coffee, no longer hot, but I knew he'd stirred in three sugars.

Brady said, "Chief, you want to tell her?"

I was saying, "Tell me what?" when Conklin said to me, "Robertson is dead."

"Robertson?"

For a moment I didn't know who the hell he was talking about, and then I got it. Kyle Robertson, Tom Calhoun's partner, the fifty-something former beat cop looking for an early retirement as soon as possible.

"How did he die?" I asked the room.

Jacobi said, "He left his dog tied to the neighbor's fence and stuck a note between the chain links. He put his badge on the dining table and then he sat down and ate his gun."

"Aw, shit. What did the note say?" I asked.

"The note said, 'I'm sorry. Please take care of Bruno. He's a good boy.' There was a check for the neighbor, a thousand bucks. Robertson signed and dated the note midnight last night. The neighbor called it in a couple hours ago."

"What now?" I asked.

Jacobi said, "Deciding that is the job at hand."

Chapter 92

WHEN JACOBI SAID, "Deciding that is the job at hand," he meant it was *our* job, the four of us, to connect the sketchy evidence and bring the bad cops down.

Brady is a list maker. He had a yellow pad, and he wrote names down on the left-hand side of the page with a red Sharpie.

Calhoun's name was first on the list, and Robertson's name followed. The two had been partners; now both were dead.

Brady said, "For the sake of argument, let's say that Robertson killed himself because whatever had closed in on Calhoun was knocking on his door."

I said, "When I interviewed Robertson, he

vouched for Calhoun, said he was a good kid who'd had no dirty dealings of any kind. I didn't pick up that he was covering for his partner—or himself. Maybe I got that wrong." I went on, "Robertson and Calhoun reported to Ted Swanson."

Jacobi said, "I called Swanson. He's going through Robertson's house now, looking for something that could explain this. He and Vasquez are talking to the neighbors."

Conklin brought up Donnie Wolfe, the inside man at Wicker House who had informed the holdup team when the drugs and money would be in the house.

Conklin said, "Wolfe told us the robbers were cops, that the head dude's tag was One, and that he was the boss of a six-man Windbreaker crew."

Brady wrote *One* +5 on the top of his pad.

Jacobi said, "A witness to the crack house shootings saw a tattoo on the neck of one of the Windbreaker cops. It sounds a lot like Bill Brand's tattoo."

I'd seen that tattoo. *WB*. Like a Western cow brand.

Conklin said, "We were working with these guys. Every day. So it comes down to this: Brand,

Calhoun, and Robertson are Windbreaker cops, and there may be a couple more we don't know about. Whitney's on the radar, too, by association with Brand."

Brady said, "It's a working theory. Brand is on suspension pending investigation. Jacobi and I are meeting with him in an hour. Boxer, you and Conklin talk to Whitney. Lean on him, hard. Whoever talks first gets a deal. The other guy gets the jackpot."

Back at my desk, I called Whitney's cell and left a message, the first of three. Conklin said, "Maybe this has to be done in person. I'll be right back."

And ten minutes later he was.

"Whitney isn't in and hasn't called in," Conklin said. "But I'm gonna say he already got the message."

We headed over to Brady's see-through office. He looked up and said, "Brand didn't show."

Conklin said, "Likewise, Whitney hasn't punched in. Hasn't returned our calls."

It was a good bet that Whitney and Brand had split. And without them, we might never find out who had killed Calhoun, who had ripped off Wicker House and killed seven people and a snitch called Rascal Valdeen. We might never know who had killed the dope slingers in the crack house, another half dozen pushers, or the innocent owners of a couple of check-cashing stores. And there was the matter of that mercado shooting. Maya Perez had died along with her unborn child.

I felt like we were on the verge of everything or nothing. And suddenly, my refried brain kicked up the obvious candidate for the job of "One."

I'd thought of him before, but his all-American good looks and kind manner had thrown me off my guard. Currently, he wasn't on our radar at all.

I sat down across from Brady so I didn't have to speak from the open doorway. "What about Swanson?"

"What are you saying? You think he's in on this?"

"Swanson's a distinguished cop. He was sold to us as a superstar. Calhoun and Robertson reported to him. How could he not be involved?"

"Trust your gut," said Brady.

Chapter 93

MY GUT SAID we shouldn't go Rambo on Swanson.

Conklin agreed. "You talk to him. I'll work on locating Whitney."

The Swanson family lived in the Parkmerced apartment development, twenty minutes from the city center in a 150-acre private village with both high-rise flats and town-homes. It was twilight as I drove down the lush, tree-lined streets, passing charming small parks and playgrounds.

It was easy to think that nothing bad could happen here. Swanson lived in a two-tone burnt-orange-and-dark-brown stucco-faced building that looked to be a three-family unit. I'd just braked at the curb when he came out of his front door and down the walk to meet me at the car.

"Sorry to drop in unannounced," I told him. "But we have to talk."

Swanson said, "Come in, Boxer. Glad to see you, actually."

Ted Swanson was disarmingly likable. His whole clean-cut, easygoing manner made my theory of him as the boss of a dirty-cop crew seem ridiculous.

Once inside his living room, Swanson introduced me to his wife, Nancy, who said, "Come meet the kids."

She walked me to the door of the den and I saw three little ones, each under ten years old, lying on beanbag chairs, watching a movie in their pajamas.

I was introduced to Maeve, Joey, and Pat as "Daddy's friend from work," after which Nancy stayed with the kids and I went to the wood-paneled living room furnished in plaid-covered sofas with dense pile carpet underfoot.

I sat on one of the sofas and turned down Swanson's offer of "coffee or whatever." And I was struck by how much he had aged in the last few weeks.

His face was ashen. His shoulders slumped. He looked like a man who was headed for a heart attack. And that it could happen any minute.

"I spent the day at Robertson's house," Swanson said. "I saw the chair where he shot himself. Thought about what a decent guy he was. Asked myself why he had done it."

"What did you make of that?" I asked him.

I don't think Swanson heard me.

He said, "I went through his checkbook. He wasn't loaded and he wasn't hurting. I rummaged through the files in his desk. Found the results of his last physical. No diabetes or cancer or heart disease. His blood pressure was a touch high. So is mine.

"I looked in the medicine chest. Advil. Tums. Something for athlete's foot."

Swanson shook his head.

I said, "What else?"

"Vasquez spoke to the neighbor who inherited the dog. Guy's name is Murray. Murray was Robertson's drinking buddy. They watched ball games together. Murray didn't see it coming. He said Kyle had been moody but not overtly depressed. But I gotta tell you, Boxer, none of us saw this coming. CSI has Robertson's laptop. Maybe that'll tell us something."

"Ted. Can we get real, here? Kyle Robertson

didn't kill himself on a whim. Was he involved with the robberies we've been working? Had he been threatened? Did he have information he wished he didn't have? I think you know."

Swanson's face sagged. He said, "I could be a target. What happened to Tommy Calhoun's family could happen to mine. What would you do if you were in my shoes?"

"I would talk to someone who can help you."

"What are you suggesting, Boxer?"

"You know what I'm getting at. Give me something to work with. Chief Jacobi was my partner. We've been tight for more than a dozen years. He'll listen to me."

"I've got nothing to say."

Swanson was crouching in his seat, leaning over his knees as he talked. "We were working our jobs. Just like you. Maybe Calhoun got too close to something and maybe Robertson knew what it was."

"That's the story you're going with? You don't know anything?"

"I'm going to bed now, Boxer," he said. "It's been another rotten day."

He was saying he didn't want to talk to me, but

the look on his face told me otherwise. I swear he wanted to confide in me. But we both stood and he walked away from me. I showed myself to the door, and as I passed the den, I heard the children laughing. I was crazy scared for those little kids and for Nancy and Ted Swanson, too.

Honest to God, I found him believable, even though I didn't believe him at all.

Chapter 94

I CAME AWAY from my visit with Ted Swanson thinking he'd been lying, and that was not only disturbing, but it added to my doubts about him.

He said he was worried about being attacked, but he wouldn't tell me what he knew. I was frustrated and angry and I couldn't help thinking about the murder scene at Tom Calhoun's house, knowing that Swanson was thinking about it, too.

My hand was on my car door when Nancy Swanson called my name. She was walking quickly across the lawn, and when she reached me, she got right into my face.

She said, "You listen to me, Sergeant. It's hard to keep the job out of this house, but I try. If it were up to me, I wouldn't have let you through the door."

I said, "Nancy, I want to protect your family, but I can't help if Ted won't talk to me. If you know something, for God's sake tell me."

"Nice meeting you," she said.

My hands shot out and I grabbed her by the shoulders before she could turn away. I said, "Listen to me. I know what I'm talking about. You can't take care of your family by yourself."

She threw my hands off her shoulders, saying, "Goodbye. Don't come back."

I watched Mrs. Swanson march up the walk to her doorway. She turned and shot me an angry look before sweeping into the house and slamming the door.

I was inside my car, reporting back to Brady, when Ted Swanson came boiling out of his house wearing an SFPD Windbreaker. *Christ. What now?*

He knocked on my car window and I buzzed it down.

Swanson said, "Vasquez called me. Strange cars are coming into his neighborhood. Parking near his house. Something's going down. Call it in."

He got into my vehicle and gave me Vasquez's

address, which I relayed to Brady; I asked him to send all available units. We were between shifts. I didn't know how many people Brady could round up.

I pulled out onto the street, and Swanson shouted directions over the wail of my siren.

Chapter 95

MY CAR RADIO was crackling and screeching under the blare of my siren. The dispatcher was calling all cars to Vasquez's address, and cars were responding that they were on their way.

Swanson stared ahead through the windshield. He looked mesmerized, seemingly lost in his own world as I pitched my Explorer toward Naglee Avenue in the working-class neighborhood known as Cayuga Park.

As we approached Naglee from the southwest on Cayuga Avenue, I heard rapid gunfire, and then I saw the cars parked at angles on both sides of the street.

There were police cruisers, their flashers painting the houses with vivid splashes of red and blue light. The cops in the cruisers were exchanging fire with shooters in the three late-model American-made sedans, probably the strange cars Vasquez had reported rolling up to his house.

Naglee Avenue runs west from the 280 Freeway, adjacent to an overhead BART track. The homes on this block were a long bank of multifamily attached dwellings, the driveways marked by short hedges.

The playground across the street from these homes was empty at this time of night.

The firefight was centered on a house in midblock, a nondescript beige wood house with a rock wall at the garage level.

"That's Vasquez's house," said Swanson.

"Does he have a family?"

"No. He's divorced, no kids."

I parked outside the firestorm but within view of it. I had two Kevlar vests in the trunk of my car. I told Swanson to stay put.

I got out of my vehicle, ducked down, and crept along the car on the far side of the gunfire. I popped the trunk, retrieved my vest, and put it on over my jacket. The spare vest was in my hand and I was creeping back to my car door when Swanson opened his door and bolted toward Vasquez's house.

I yelled, *"Swanson! Get down!"*

Swanson was running along the short hedge that separated Vasquez's driveway from his neighbor's when I saw his body jerk twice, then, drop.

I climbed back into my seat, grabbed the microphone, and yelled into it, *"Officer down! Officer down!"* I gave my location, even though I knew that an ambulance couldn't enter this block until the firing stopped. That was protocol.

I didn't know what Swanson had been trying to do, but if he was alive, I had to get to him. With my lights and siren off, and keeping my head down, I drove over the sidewalk until I saw Swanson lying alongside the hedge.

I braked the car, slid on my belly across the front seat, and wrenched the door open. I was looking directly down at Swanson.

He was bleeding, but he was breathing.

I shouted, "You're a stupid *fuck,* Swanson. You know that?"

Blood was spreading across his Windbreaker. Still, he grinned.

"Look who's talking," he said.

Chapter 96

MY CAR WAS a reasonable barricade against the fusillade of gunfire to my left, but I wouldn't call it safe. I heard the banshee cry of an ambulance siren, then a second one, the sounds cutting out as the EMTs parked under the freeway.

I sat cross-legged on the ground next to Swanson. He was humming "The Star-Spangled Banner," breaking into words now and then. "Mmm-mmm. Rockets' red glare. Mmm-mmm, bursting in air."

I folded the vest and put it under his head. He seemed peaceful. Maybe he was going into shock. Maybe he'd taken a hit to his spine. Maybe he was bleeding out.

He said, "It's been good knowing you."

"Not so fast," I said. "You're tougher than this. We're cops, right?"

"I want you to do something for Nancy. The kids."

"That's *your* job, buster."

"Say that I died . . . on the job. That's the truth."

"Talk to me, Swanson. It's the least you can do."

". . . that our flag was still there."

"Swanson, are you known to some people as One?"

I heard an engine start up, tires squeal. There was renewed gunfire. From the sound of it, a vehicle was making for the freeway exit at the far end of the street.

Swanson said, "Numero Uno. That's me."

Did he understand me? Did he know what I was asking him?

"You were the number one guy in the Windbreaker cop crew?" I asked.

He laughed.

"What's funny?"

"The way it sounds. Numero Uno and the Windbreaker Crew."

"Why did you fucking *do* it?"

He sighed. "*If* I did it, it was a victimless crime."

"What the hell do you mean by that? Over a dozen people are dead."

"Stealing drugs from dirtbags. That's victimless."

How did a man become a cop—a superstar—and think like that? But I knew the answer. They were called public-service homicides. In other words, he figured, justifiable.

"What about Calhoun?" I asked him.

He lifted a hand and pointed in the general direction of the gunfire that was still raging.

"Poor Tommy."

Swanson's voice slurred. His hand dropped.

"Ted. Ted, don't you dare leave me."

He coughed up blood. I gripped his hand.

I heard a cop shouting from afar.

"*Get out of the car with your hands up!* Get out of the car *now!*"

A voice shouted back, "*You're a dead man!*"

There were loud bursts of automatic gunfire. Then an echoey silence. I heard Brady's voice coming over my car radio asking for the buses to come in.

I stood up and shouted his name over the roof of my car. A moment later, Brady, our homicide lieutenant with the shining blond hair, was standing with me.

"You OK?" he asked me.

"Yes. Are you?"

"I'm good."

He bent at the waist and said "Swanson" to the downed man in the SFPD Windbreaker. "Swanson, speak to me."

"Yo," Swanson said. His eyes were closed. His breathing was shallow.

"He's losing blood," I said. "Where the hell's the bus?"

Brady left to direct the ambulance, and I stayed with Swanson until the paramedics got to us. I watched as they loaded him onto the board, strapped him down, and lifted the board into the bus.

Unlike Robertson, Swanson had a family, and the only way they'd get benefits was if he died on the job. And there Swanson was, with holes in his SFPD Windbreaker. He'd seen his chance and he had taken it.

I grabbed one of the EMTs, pulled him to the side of the bus, and asked, "Is he going to make it?"

First the EMT shrugged; then he shook his head; and then he climbed into the bus and closed the doors.

I had wanted Swanson to tell me who else was in his "crew." But I had a strong feeling that even if he'd lived, he wouldn't have given his people away.

Chapter 97

AMBULANCES WERE COMING in, taking away the injured. The ME's van had arrived, and Claire was talking to Clapper. CSU had barricaded all but one slim lane of the road. Techs were setting up lights and an evidence tent, and investigators were working the scene as best they could under the circumstances.

According to Brady, the body count was four, and all of the dead were unidentified shooters. One car had gotten away, and the number and identities of the people inside were unknown.

I sat in my car, and after I'd checked in with Joe and with Conklin, I called Nancy Swanson.

"I have to see you," I said when she answered.

"What happened? Did something happen to Ted?"

"He's hurt, but he's alive."

"What happened? *Tell me—now.*"

"I'll be at your house in fifteen minutes. I'm driving you to the hospital. Get someone to watch your kids."

Her phone clunked to the floor. I called her name, but she was screaming and calling to her children.

I took the quickest, fastest route to the Swanson house, thinking that now, maybe, Nancy would tell me what she knew.

She was standing at the curb in a man's white shirt, jeans, and bedroom slippers when I pulled up.

"Which hospital?" she asked me, getting into the passenger seat. "What's his condition? Is it serious?"

"Buckle up," I said.

The car shot off the curb and I set my course for Metropolitan Hospital. Nancy clenched her fists and beat her thighs as I told her about the standoff at Oswaldo Vasquez's house.

I told her Vasquez had called her husband in a panic, saying that a number of cars had driven up to his house and that he perceived them to be a threat. I said that by the time Ted and I arrived, a full-scale shootout between the police and the men in those cars was in progress.

"He was safe in the car with me," I told Nancy. "Then—he jumped out of the car and ran toward Vasquez's house."

"Oh, my God. That's when he got shot?"

I nodded. "He was down but not out when the EMTs arrived."

"This is all your fault," she hissed at me. "Damn you, Sergeant."

"I understand what you're going through, Nancy, and I feel terrible for you."

"I don't care how you spin it. You've been crowding Ted for weeks now and he's never done anything wrong. Anything he did, he did it for us. His family."

"Do you understand the truth? Your husband is a criminal."

She scoffed and said, "The real criminal is Kingfisher."

"I don't understand what you mean."

"He's the one who had the Calhoun family killed, or didn't you know?"

"Do you know this for a fact?" I asked her.

Nancy Swanson covered her face with her hands. Her neck and arms were red with welts. She sobbed, "I don't know. I don't know. I have three kids. We can't lose Ted. He has to live, do you understand?"

I said, "Nancy, can you tell me anything that might help us get the shooters?"

She turned her burning eyes to me and said, "Are you out of your mind? I'm a cop's *wife*. Don't you think I know what you're trying to do?"

I stopped the car outside the emergency room and Nancy unbuckled her seat belt, opened the door, and took off at a run.

My phone began buzzing before I could close the door.

It was Brady.

"Vasquez is missing," Brady said. "He doesn't answer his phone. His house is empty, Boxer. He's just gone."

Chapter 98

THE NEXT MORNING at ten, Conklin and I took the drive to Parkmerced with two uniformed officers following behind.

Nancy Swanson opened the door. She was wearing the same big shirt and jeans she'd been wearing yesterday, and from the look of her eyes, she'd been crying since then, too.

I introduced Conklin, but she didn't look at him. I handed her the search warrant and she stepped aside, snapping, "What do you have against Ted? Do you even know how he's doing?"

"Have you heard from Vasquez?" I asked her.

"If I had, you'd be the last person I'd tell."

Conklin and I went through the house, which looked cheerful now with daylight coming through the many windows facing the greenery of Villa Merced Park. We gloved up, and with Nancy watching, Conklin and I searched the den. We found a trick panel in a bookcase. There were innumerable banded stacks of twenty-dollar bills inside.

One of the uniformed officers uncovered more cash under the frozen food in the basement freezer, and Conklin uncovered a cache of guns in the bedroom closet, under the carpet, below a trapdoor. I turned up more stacks of money in the dishwasher.

Nancy had stashed it there in a hurry.

Swanson's car was included in the warrant, and I turned up five passports and some cash in a trap inside the dash. We bagged and tagged everything. While we packed up, I called Jacobi. He sighed loudly and said, "I love you, Lindsay."

I had to laugh. And so did he.

Once we were back at the Hall, we went straight to Jacobi's office with our cartons of Swanson's stuff. Jacobi picked up the phone, punched in a number, and said, "We're ready for you, Sergeant."

A few minutes later, we were comfortably seated on Jacobi's leather furniture, telling Phil Pikelny what we had found at Ted Swanson's house.

Pikelny was lean, maybe thirty-five, an East Coast cop from New York or Boston. He had no discernible accent, and he had a good haircut, handsome clothes, and nice shoes. Swanson, Vasquez, Calhoun, and Robertson had reported to him.

"This is unbelievable," he said. "How much money was there?"

"Looks to be like a million or so," I told him. "Between that, the guns, and the passports, I'm guessing that Swanson was leaving soon."

Phil said, "I completely trusted Ted."

Jacobi asked Phil what he knew about Vasquez and he said, "I liked him. A lot. And I would say that my opinion of Vasquez now means absolutely nothing. I have no idea where he might be, and he certainly hasn't called me."

Conklin and I stopped off at the property room and signed in a million two in US currency and a half dozen assorted guns.

After that, we briefed Brady on the Swanson house haul.

Brady had just gotten off the phone with the hospital. He said, "From what I could determine, Swanson is hanging on by a frayed thread."

404

He also told us that Brand and Whitney were in the wind. Not answering phone calls. Not going home.

"Vasquez is still missing," Brady said. "The car that got away from Naglee was found in a ditch off Highway Ninety-Two with about a hundred bullet holes in the chassis. There was blood in the backseat. The lab is working it up."

Had Vasquez been murdered or abducted, or had he just gotten a ride out of town?

"Why don't you two take the rest of the day off," said Brady. It was five in the afternoon. I don't remember the last time I'd gone home at five, but this was good.

I had plans for the evening.

Chapter 99

I HAD A terrific red dress hanging in my closet. I'd bought it before I got pregnant, without an event in mind. It still had tags on it.

Joe was still out with Martha and Julie when I got home, so I showered and put on my makeup, including eyeliner and mascara.

The red crepe dress had an asymmetrical neckline and hem and a fitted waist. I slipped it on, stepped into a pair of low heels, and looked at myself in the mirror.

I didn't look like the same woman who wore chinos and a blue blazer every day.

Wow. This was me, too.

The Women's Murder Club was meeting at a bar and restaurant called Local Edition. It was officially a Women's Murder Club "Welcome Home Cindy" event, and we were also celebrating *Fish's Girl* getting a mention in the LA *Times*. These were fine reasons for the four of us to spend some quality time together.

I left Joe a note and headed out toward the restaurant. One block later, while I was negotiating traffic, my phone rang. I glanced down and saw UNKNOWN CALLER on the faceplate. I was stuck between a Porsche and a panel van, so I took the call.

The voice was muffled, but the message was clear.

"You break the blue line, you get what you deserve. You and your family aren't safe, Boxer. They'll never be safe."

My blood stopped flowing through my veins and dropped to my feet. "Who is this?" I said.

The line was open. I could hear static, but there was no answer.

I stared at the rear end of the Porsche, but I wasn't seeing it. I *was* picturing the face of a cop. One cop in particular.

"And you're not safe from *me*, Vasquez."

There was a click as the call was disconnected,

and at just about the same instant, the driver of the panel van behind me blew his horn.

I put my foot on the gas, wondering if I'd been right when I said "Vasquez."

But whether my caller was Vasquez or some other vicious hater, I wasn't going to let this call ruin my evening. That was what I told myself, but I felt a tremor, an internal earthquake, a shifting of my sense of security in my own home. It was almost intolerable.

So what was I going to do about it?

Chapter 100

YUKI HAD PICKED the perfect venue to toast our crime reporter friend on her return from her triumphal book tour.

I parked the car at a metered spot on Market and walked a couple of blocks to the historic Hearst Building.

The doorman escorted me down the stairs to the subterranean room that once housed the *San Francisco Examiner*'s printing presses and was now a dark and glamorous club.

The ceilings were high; typewriters lined the walls; the long bar was of polished wood, with rows and rows of wineglasses hanging on overhead racks by their stems. Looking around the perimeter of the room, I saw red leather booths facing white leather swivel chairs across white marble tables, and a number of huge presses were still on the floor, adding to the 1950s feel of the place.

I released a long sigh.

I was going to drink and laugh tonight, that was for sure.

The doorman showed me to our table, and I was about to sit down when Yuki appeared and fairly danced across the floor.

I was reaching for Yuki when Claire called out "Hey, you two," and joined us in a three-way hug.

When we were seated, we said "Phones off " in unison, and when we had done it, Claire said to Yuki, "I heard you've got big news."

Yuki had already called me about her settlement for her client, but it was a great pleasure to hear her telling the story to Claire, using her hands, imitating Parisi's voice.

"When he signed the agreement, he said to me, 'You really are a little shit, Yuki.' And I said, 'I learned from the biggest and the best.'"

And then Yuki laughed her joyous, infectious chortle, and we laughed with her, loud and long. When she got her breath, she said, "Then he winked at me."

"Did he?" I asked.

"He did. He winked. He smiled. He passed the document across the table and said, 'Have a good day. I think you will.'"

"He adores you," Claire said. "He still totally adores you."

Feeling her presence before we saw her, we looked up to see Cindy wearing slinky black, smelling of lilies of the valley as she leaned down, hugging and kissing all of us.

"*Who* still adores you?" she asked Yuki, sliding in beside her.

Yuki got to tell the story again, and as Cindy had been out of the loop, she heard the long version. She laughed and asked for more detailed explanations, which broke up the dramatic flow, but hell, Cindy is a reporter and facts are her thing.

Then Cindy said, "I've got a little news of my own."

"We know your book got great reviews," Claire said. "What else you got?"

Cindy said, "I found this next to my clock this morning."

She pulled a black velvet box from her handbag and put it on the table. There was a collective gasp.

411

We'd seen this movie before. The first time, Richie had gotten down on one knee in the nave of Grace Cathedral. He had proposed and had given Cindy his mother's ring. In her telling at the time, the angels sang and doves flew through the church and she knew she was blessed.

Then, after the pre-honeymoon period, when the conversation turned to children, she and Richie had hit a thick brick wall.

What had changed?

Cindy opened the box and pulled out a fine gold chain with a sizable diamond pendant.

"This *was* the ring," she said. "Richie had it made into something different. Just for me."

Cindy fastened the chain around her neck, then held the stone in its simple setting and slid it back and forth on the chain. That stone was a gasper then, and it was a gasper now.

"So you're *not* engaged?" Yuki asked Cindy, the only one of our group who was still single.

"There was a note with the necklace," said Cindy. "Richie wrote, 'When we're ready to get married, we'll pick out a ring together.'"

"Beautiful," said Claire. "The diamond and the note."

"That calls for a drink," said Yuki.

The waiter appeared and recommended several house special cocktails named for people, places, and headline events in the newspaper business.

We toasted everything: Cindy and Richie's renewed commitment, Yuki's settlement for the Kordells, Claire's baby girl's admission to first grade—and as for me, we toasted the fact that nine months after Julie was born, I could pull off a skinny red dress—"fabulously."

It was customary for the four of us to discuss our cases, but I just wasn't up for sharing Numero Uno and the Windbreaker Crew. Not tonight. I held up my phone.

"I'm just calling my husband to say I'm on my way."

I punched in Joe's number, and when he answered, I said, "Hey. I'll be home by nine."

Chapter 101

RICH CONKLIN WAS waiting in a patrol car, parked in front of a row of three-story wood-frame buildings on Stockton Street in Chinatown. All the buildings were occupied by ground-floor retail businesses, while the top floors were mostly residential.

From where Conklin was parked, he had a full view of the downstairs deli-type greengrocer and the door next to it, which was the entrance to the lobby of the Sylvestrie Hotel, a rent-by-the-hour flophouse.

Conklin knew this place pretty well, having busted drug dealers and prostitutes there when he was a beat cop, before Lindsay got him moved up to Homicide.

What he remembered most about the Sylvestrie was that the rooms were pitifully furnished, with dirty sheets in the windows instead of curtains, and that the place vibrated nonstop from the air conditioning in the market downstairs.

This evening, Conklin had been on his way home when he'd gotten a tip from one K. J. Herkus, a CI and a small-time dope dealer. Herk lived and worked the streets in Chinatown, and he had recognized the narc with a short beard and John Lennon–type glasses who'd checked into the Sylvestrie.

Herk was hoping Conklin could hook him up with the narc with the glasses, that maybe he could make himself useful from time to time.

Conklin said, "Don't approach him unless I say so, OK, Herk? He's undercover. I'll look for some work for you."

Conklin had been watching the hotel for about two hours before Inspector Stan Whitney came out. Whitney went to the market, came out ten minutes later with a plastic bag of something, then reentered the hotel.

Conklin thought there was a good chance that Whitney had gotten take-out for dinner and wouldn't be going out again. He thought about going into the hotel, getting Whitney's room number, and knocking on the door.

But he quickly quashed the idea.

Whitney was likely desperate enough to introduce a loaded gun into the conversation. Conklin knew the best thing for him to do was continue to keep an eye on the door and be ready to tail the cop.

Conklin called Brady. He described Whitney's denim shirt, jeans, and blue cap partially hiding his face, and asked for backup in an unmarked.

Brady took down the details and said, "Don't lose him."

Conklin resumed watching the door, and damn if Whitney didn't walk out and take a right, then a tight left toward Vallejo.

Conklin let a car get in front of him, then pulled into traffic, in time for the light to turn red. When it changed to green, he could see Whitney, still proceeding south on Stockton through Chinatown, passing shops and bakeries, hands in his pockets, as if he had just gone out for a stroll.

Conklin tailed Whitney without incident, watched him take a left on Clay and another left on

Kearny. He followed Whitney for another two blocks and was just behind him when the man in denim disappeared into Portsmouth Square Garage across from the Hilton.

Conklin parked in a no-parking zone with a view of the garage. A silver Chevy crawled past Conklin. The man in the driver's seat was Officer Allen Benjamin, a cop Conklin knew. Conklin made radio contact with Brady, who said he was keeping a channel open and restricted to the three of them: Benjamin, Brady, and Conklin.

Benjamin drove ahead, parked his unmarked in front of a hydrant up the block, and waited there. At 8:15 p.m., ten minutes after entering the garage, a blue pickup with Texas plates rolled up out of the garage and took a right.

It was Whitney.

Conklin pulled ahead of Benjamin, and they took turns staying on the pickup's tail. Whitney took a left on Washington, then another left on Stockton, the main drag through Chinatown, which was still congested with trucks making deliveries, as well as pedestrians and tourists in cabs taking in the evening lights.

Without warning, the truck Whitney was

driving stopped at the intersection of Stockton and Bush just long enough for a thickly muscled guy to leave the sidewalk and get into the truck's passenger seat.

Conklin recognized this passenger. It was Bill Brand, Whitney's partner.

Neither Whitney nor Brand was in violation of the law, and stopping them would only tip them off. With two police cars shadowing it, the blue truck turned right on Sutter, went half a mile to Polk, and parked in an empty spot outside a nail salon.

When they got out of the truck, Whitney and Brand were wearing blue SFPD Windbreakers. They crossed the street to a gray stucco building with awnings and neon signs in the windows reading PAYDAY LOANS, CHECKS CHECKED, WESTERN UNION.

The check-cashing store was lit up inside and open for business. As Whitney and Brand reached the door, they removed masks from their pockets and pulled them on over their faces. The entry bell over the door jingled as the cops went inside.

Chapter 102

I CAME INTO our apartment and heard music coming from the bedroom. Joe was sitting up in bed in a T-shirt and boxers, his fingers on his laptop and an urban blues channel on the TV.

He looked up and saw me in my slinky red dress. He whistled and I grinned and did a little pirouette. I said, "After all these years in chinos and a blazer, I've still got it. No?"

He said, "Yes, you certainly do, Blondie."

I said, "Be right back," and turned to go in to see Julie.

Joe said, "She's across the hall with Mrs. Rose. Martha's there, too."

"Oh? Why?"

"I told Mrs. Rose I needed a few hours off to get

some work done and she said, 'It would be lovely to have some company,'" Joe said, doing a pretty good version of Mrs. Rose's English accent.

I laughed. He did Mrs. Rose so well.

He patted the bed next to him and I sat down.

He asked, "How was your dinner?"

"No kidding, it was the best time we've all had together in months," I said. "We were all there, all in great moods. Richie gave Cindy his mother's diamond in a new form." I described the pendant.

I was facing away from Joe as I talked, and I lifted my hair. He zipped down my dress really slowly. I gasped. I was surprised at the heat that came over me from nowhere.

"Stand up," he said. "You don't want to wrinkle your dress."

I did what he said and watched him close the lid on the computer without taking his eyes from me. I let down the asymmetrical neckline of my dress, and when my arms were free, the red silk dropped into a puddle around my feet.

He reached out his arms. I kicked off my shoes, and in the next second, by way of some deft maneuver of Joe's, I was flat on my back in my underthings, looking up into his blue, blue eyes.

Yes, I heard my phone buzz in the other room.

No, I didn't take the call. I knew it was that freaking phone terrorist, and I wasn't going to let him steal this time with Joe away from me. It had been a long time since we'd been in bed without listening to the baby monitor, but we had that time now.

And we took full advantage of it.

His clothes flew over the side of the bed, and the blankets were shoved to the footboard. I closed my eyes and reveled in the feel of his whiskers and lips and hands on my skin and the delicious smell of him.

And I loved him back.

We romped and played like newlyweds, and at one point, Joe reached a hand down and helped me off the floor and back into the bed. The laughter was wonderful, and when we kissed deeply and connected completely, it felt as true as it had when we first fell in love.

Afterward, sweating and panting and still entwined with Joe, I rested my cheek against his shoulder and held him tightly.

I told him how much I loved him, and he said he'd never loved me more. Exhausted in the best

421

possible way, I drifted off, telling myself that it was OK. Joe was in charge. I didn't have to worry about anything. He would get the baby and her furry pal when it was time.

I was sleeping and maybe having a beautiful dream when Joe said, "Lindsay, your phone has been ringing every minute or two."

He handed it to me.

I took it reluctantly. I said, "I've been getting hangups," but when I looked at the caller ID, it read CONKLIN.

"Christ. Where've you been?" Conklin said. "OK. Never mind. Brand and Whitney tried to hold up a check-cashing store. We've got dead people. We've got hostages. They're in there now."

I heard a voice over a bullhorn, saying, "Put your hands up and come out. You don't want anyone else to die, do you?"

Conklin gave me an address on Polk, which was about three miles and five minutes away. Four if I pushed it. I started scrambling around for something to wear, and Joe turned on the lights.

"Lindsay, be safe," he said. "We want you back here. Your family loves you."

I went into his arms and we held each other tightly.

I needed to go. But I knew Joe and I were thinking the same thing. We had a lot to live for.

Chapter 103

A PATROLMAN LET me and my Explorer through the cordon on Polk. I drove to midblock and saw Conklin and Brady standing together in front of a nail salon on the south side of the street. Their eyes were fixed on the north side, on the Checks Cashed store directly across from them.

I parked in a no-parking zone a few yards down the street from Brady and Conklin, right behind a blue Ford pickup with Texas plates. I got out of my vehicle and heard sirens from cars coming in from all points.

I walked up to my partner and asked, "What happened?"

He pushed his hair out of his eyes, cleared his throat, and said, "I had a tip that Whitney was staying at the Sylvestrie, so I staked it out. He left the hotel around eight p.m. and I tailed him with backup. He walked to a garage on Kearny and got that truck." He pointed at it with his chin. Then he went on.

"He picked Brand up on the corner of Stockton and Bush, both of them in street clothes. When they got out of the truck, here, they were in PD Windbreakers."

Car doors were slamming and cops were getting out, standing on the sidewalk, looking over the roofs of their vehicles. Radios set up a cacophony of blare and static along the street. I was wearing my vest, carrying my gun—but still, I felt naked and vulnerable.

I looked more closely at the check-cashing store. The signs were still lit up over the storefront, but it was dark inside the shop.

Conklin said, "One of them flipped the sign on the door to closed. The lights were on, and I saw them corral the two customers, both women, over to the left side of the store. They made them lie down and Brand cuffed them.

"While Brand did that, Whitney put his gun on the security guard and walked him back to the tellers' cages. I'm guessing Whitney told them, 'Open up or I'll kill him.'"

"Shit," I said. "So they let him in."

"Right," Conklin said. "By then, someone hit the alarm."

Beside me, Brady lifted his bullhorn and said, "Whitney. Brand. I'm calling the store. Pick up the phone." Brady was sweating in sixty degrees. You could see it on his forehead, his upper lip, but you couldn't tell he was stressing from his voice or his actions. I was glad Brady was in charge.

"Keep going," I said to my partner.

Conklin said, "So I can see the teller open the security door, and *blam*. Whitney shoots the guard, puts that threat down. Now the tellers run for the back door and I see muzzle flare. I guess Whitney panicked or no longer cared. I think he nailed a couple of them. I didn't see them again."

Guns were everywhere on this short block. Soon SWAT would launch smoke bombs and storm Checks Cashed.

Brady spoke through the bullhorn: "Listen to me. This is going to end badly if you don't do exactly what I say. The store is surrounded. We've got snipers on the roof. Put the guns down and come out with your hands in the air."

A moment later, the front door opened a few inches and Whitney called, "*Don't shoot.* We're coming out with hostages."

Brady called out over the megaphone, "Hold your fire!"

The door swung open and two terrified women with their hands behind their backs were muscled out of the store. Whitney was behind one of them, Brand behind the other.

I saw the glint of their handguns and that both rotten cops had duffel bags with the shoulder straps crossing their chests, probably containing their latest and final score.

I was standing with Conklin when Whitney and Brand, still wearing their creepy masks, awkwardly bumped and dragged their hostages between parked cars and toward the truck. It was only a fifty-foot walk—but they were encumbered and had to pass through a shooting gallery, including right past where Brady, Conklin, and I were standing.

I don't know what came over Richie. Maybe he just couldn't take what was happening. He shouted at Whitney and Brand, "You're *filth!* Both of you. Fucking *scum!*"

Whitney lifted his gun and pointed it at Conklin. I saw my partner lift his arm, and by the time I heard the report of Whitney's gun, my own gun was in my hand. I knew Conklin was hit. But I couldn't stop what I was doing.

I didn't have a clean head or chest shot, so I dropped to one knee and fired at Whitney's hip. Before his leg buckled, a few hundred bullets pinged into the sidewalk from above.

Whitney dropped. The hostages ran, screaming. One of them fell on the asphalt, bleeding.

Brady reached Brand in terrifying slow motion and put his gun to the back of his neck. Brand dropped his gun and put up his hands.

"I give up," Brand said. "Don't shoot."

Two shots rang out, but I didn't see where they landed. My whole mind was on Conklin. He was on the ground, motionless. I stooped down next to my partner and shook his shoulder.

"Richie. Speak to me."

Chapter 104

THE SMALL WAITING room outside the ER was dull beige, and the light from the overhead fixture was flat white and glaring.

Richie was in surgery. Cindy and I sat together and she was so afraid for him, trying to hold it together, but the tears just streamed down her face. I held her hand, told her the things you say in a situation when you don't know what the fuck is going to happen. "He's going to be OK. I promise."

Yuki was pacing, and Claire was in the hallway waiting for word of the outcome. Claire had checked out the surgeon and assured all of us that Dr. Starr was the best.

Joe was off getting coffee, and Brady had waited

with us for hours but had gone back to the Hall to tell the story again, this time to Internal Affairs.

The last hours were running through my mind on a closed loop.

I kept hearing the sharp sounds of rapid gunfire and the shrill screams of the hostages. I saw the bodies of Brand and Whitney and thought their plan had been a Hail Mary pass. That they hadn't truly expected to survive.

I recalled handing my gun to Brady, then climbing into the ambulance that was taking Rich to the hospital. I was supposed to stay at the scene, but there was no way that could happen. No way. Neck injuries were serious, mostly fatal. Richie. My dear friend, my partner, my brother. He could die.

I remembered calling Cindy from the ambulance and hearing her panicked screams. And I remembered calling Joe, saying "I'm OK." Now, in the hospital waiting room, he put a tray of coffee containers down on a table, sat down next to me, and held my hand.

A moment after that, we were all on our feet as the doctor entered the room. He was a small man with a goatee and long fingers.

He said, "Inspector Conklin is out of surgery.

And I have good news. The bullet hit his left forearm, breaking it and deflecting the bullet, slowing it down. That was a lucky thing for Inspector Conklin.

"Because the bullet was deflected, instead of severing his arteries or spine, it grazed his neck. He had a ragged wound that caused him to collapse and bleed like crazy, but he's all stitched up and his arm has been set. He's going to be fine.

"Who is Cindy?" Dr. Starr asked.

Cindy stood up, her face pink and gleaming with tears. "That's me."

Dr. Starr said, "He's really going to be OK, my dear. He said to tell you he loves you."

Cindy said, "Thank God," and she sat back down from the weight of relief and emotion. We were all emoting, thanking both God and Dr. Starr, and tears were springing from all eyes.

When my phone rang, I said to Joe, "It's probably Brady."

But when I looked at the caller ID, I was shocked to see who was calling me.

It was *Vasquez*.

Where was he?

Did he know that his partner, Ted Swanson, was

in the ICU? That Kyle Robertson was dead? That Brand's and Whitney's bodies were at the morgue? I fumbled the phone, then stabbed the Talk button.

"Boxer," I said.

The voice that came over Vasquez's phone did not belong to Vasquez. It was male, unaccented, unfamiliar.

"There's been a terrible accident, Sergeant Boxer, and Vasquez himself couldn't place the call."

"Who is this?"

"Just listen. Vasquez can't contact anyone, you understand what I'm saying? He's lying in the Wicker House parking lot. But Vasquez is not important. Here's what is. I want what was taken from me. Three million in cash. Two hundred pounds of synthetic marijuana and a hundred kilos of high-grade heroin."

I said, "I don't know what you're talking about."

"Yes, you do. It's your case. You're in charge. I hope you know who you're dealing with."

"Who *is* this?" I asked again.

"I'm called Kingfisher. Ask around. You'll be hearing from me again soon, Lindsay Boxer. You can count on it."

The phone went dead in my hand.

Joe said, "Linds? Who was that?"

I stuttered, "S-some dirtbag who has been harassing me."

If only Kingfisher were your ordinary dirtbag. But he was anything but ordinary. He topped the list of the most ruthless drug lords in the country: wanted for drug trafficking, torture, murder, and organized crime up and down the length of California and many points east.

And now the King was here.

His investment at Wicker House had been stolen by cops—and he wasn't writing it off as "the cost of doing business." He'd been unable to recover his property from Calhoun or Vasquez. Robertson, Brand, and Whitney were also dead.

The only living person who might know the whereabouts of the Wicker House haul was a dirty cop known as One, real name Edward "Ted" Swanson, who'd been hospitalized with multiple gunshot wounds and wasn't expected to live.

So Kingfisher was targeting *me*.

ACKNOWLEDGMENTS

Many thanks to these top professionals for their guidance and wise counsel in the writing of this book: attorney Philip R. Hoffman of New York, Captain Richard Conklin of the Stamford, Connecticut, Police Department, and Humphrey Germaniuk, medical examiner and coroner for Trumbull County, Ohio.

We also wish to thank our fantastic researchers Ingrid Taylar and Lynn Colomello. Thanks also to Mary Jordan, who keeps it all together.

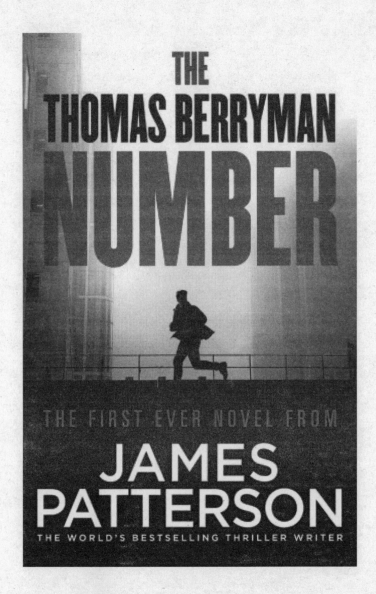

THE
THOMAS BERRYMAN
NUMBER

THE FIRST EVER NOVEL FROM

JAMES
PATTERSON

THE WORLD'S BESTSELLING THRILLER WRITER

Turn the page for an extract

MY PARENTS, WALTER and Edna Linda Jones, didn't want me to be a doctor, or a lawyer, or even successful; they just wanted me to be refined . . . I disappointed them badly, however; I went out and became a newspaperman.

———

SIGN OVER THE DESK OF OCHS JONES:

> Steve McQueen is a killer you have to cheer
> on and root for.
> > *NEWSPAPER MOVIE REVIEW*

ZEBULON, KENTUCKY, 1974

In November of this year I came back to my hometown (Zebulon) in Poland County, Kentucky; I came home to write about the deaths of men named Bertram Poole, Lieutenant Martin Weesner, and especially my friend Jimmie Lee Horn of Nashville, Tennessee . . . but most of all I came home to write about something an editor at the *Nashville Citizen-Reporter* had named the Thomas Berryman Number.

This book is mostly for my nine-year-old daughter Cat, I think.

It's a Sam Peckinpah kind of story: all in all there are six murders in it. It's about a young Texas man who decided to become a professional killer at the age of eighteen. So far as I can make out, he decided by virtue of executing several beautiful pronghorn antelopes and one Mexican priest, a bishop actually.

Random observation: A story in a Houston paper reports that *"Not less than five men in the United States are making over two hundred thousand dollars a year as independent (non-mob) assassins."* What the hell is the point of view over in Houston I wondered when I cut out the clipping and folded it for my wallet.

Random observation: Very few people have understood the character of men who do evil . . . Most people who've written about them just make everything too black for me. Either that, or they're trying to make some sugar and spice "Bonnie & Clyde" movie . . . Anyway, movie stars withstanding, I don't believe your bad man can be obtuse, and I don't believe he'd necessarily be morose . . . In fact, Thomas Berryman was neither of these.

Random observation: The other day, I showed Cat something Berryman's girlfriend had given me: it was a Crossman air pistol. To demonstrate how it could put someone to sleep, I callously (stupidly) wounded Mrs. Mullhouse's calico. It was too much for the old kitty, however, and she died.

Random observation: Even Doc Fiddler's Paradise Lounge, one of the top redneck gin mills in the state of Tennessee, has a fresh print of Jimmie Horn over the liquor these days. Horn's strictly moral drama now, and people are partial to moral drama, no matter what.

One last observation: In 1962, Thomas John Berryman graduated from Plains High School with one of the highest grade point averages ever recorded in Potter County, Texas. Some teachers said he had a photographic memory, and he had a measured I.Q. of one hundred sixty-six.

A little more digging revealed that he was known as the "Pleasure King," and nicknamed "Pleasure."

The women who'd been his girlfriends would only say that he made them feel inferior. Even the ones who'd liked him best never felt totally comfortable with him.

Most people around Clyde, Texas, thought he was a successful lawyer in the East now. At first I'd thought someone in the Berryman family started the rumor; later on, I'd learned it had been Berryman himself.

Berryman's father was a retired circuit judge. Three weeks after he learned what his son had done in Tennessee, he died of a cerebrovascular accident.

Thomas Berryman is 6'1", one hundred ninety-five pounds. He has black hair, hazel eyes. And extremely good concentration for a young man. He's also charming. In fact, he just about says it all for American charm.

Background: Four months ago, the thirty-seven-year-old mayor of our city, Jimmie Horn, was shot down under the saddest and most bizarre circumstances I can imagine.

Because of that, the *Nashville Citizen-Reporter*s of last July 4th, 5th, and 6th are the three largest-selling editions the paper has ever had.

Maybe it's because people are naturally curious when public figures are shot. They know casual facts out of their lives, and they regard these men almost as acquaintances. They want to know how, and where, and what time, and why it happened.

I believe it's usually the same: *madman Bert Poole shoots Mayor Jimmie Horn, late in the day for no good reason.*

That's what I wrote, but only in pencil on foolscap. In the *Citizen,* I wrote a long filler about the state trooper who'd subsequently shot Poole.

It was real shit, and also crass . . . It was also incorrect.

Three days after the shooting, a story in the *Washington Post* reported that the man who'd shot Bert Poole hadn't been a Tennessee state trooper as my story, and our other feature stories, had reported several times.

The man was an expensive professional killer from Philadelphia. His name was Joe Cubbah. Cubbah had been spotted in photographs of the Horn shooting; then he'd been picked up in Philadelphia.

The real Tennessee trooper, Martin Weesner, was finally found in the trunk of his own squad car. The car had been in a trooper barracks parking lot since July 3rd. Cubbah was called "an imaginative gunman" by the *Memphis Times-Scimitar.*

Needless to say, this matter of a professional killer shooting down an assassin confused the hell out of everybody. It also depressed a good number of people, myself included. And it scared a lot of families into locking their doors at night.

Coincidentally, during the wake of the *Washington Post* story, the *Citizen-Reporter* received an hour-long phone call from a resident psychiatrist working at a Long Island, N.Y., hospital. The doctor explained to one of our editors how a patient of his had been talking about the Jimmie Horn shooting nearly a week before it happened. He gave out the patient's name as Ben Toy, and he said it was fine if we wanted to send someone around to talk with him.

We wanted to send me, and that's how I fit into the story.

As a consequence of that decision, I'm now sequestered away in a Victorian farmhouse outside of Zebulon, in Poland County. It's November now as I mentioned.

I'd thought that I would enjoy hunting down the murderer of a friend—delicious revenge, they say—but I was wrong.

From 4 a.m. until around eleven each day I try to collate, then make sense out of the over two thousand pages of notes, scraps, and interview transcripts that recreate the days leading up to the Horn shooting this past July.

I've already made an indecent amount of money from advances, magazine sales, and newspaper serials on Thomas Berryman stories. This is the book.

WEST HAMPTON, JULY 9

IN NINETEEN SIXTY-NINE I won a George Polk prize for some life-style articles about black Mayor Jimmie Lee Horn of Nashville. The series was called "A Walker's Guide to Shantytown," but it ran in the *Citizen-Reporter* as "Black Lives."

It wasn't a bad writing job, but it was more a case of being in the right place at the right time: I'd written life-affirming stories about a black man in Tennessee, just a year after Martin Luther King had died there.

It felt right to people who judged things somewhere. They said the series was "vital."

So I was lucky in '69.

—

I figured things were beginning to even out the day I drove into the William Pound Institute in West Hampton, Long Island. On account of my assignment there I wouldn't be writing any of the article about Horn's murder. The good Horn assignments had already gone elsewhere. Higher up.

I parked my rent-a-car in a crowded yard marked ALL HOSPITAL VISITORS. Then, armed with tape recorder, suit-coat over my arm too, I made my way along a broken flagstone path tunneling through bent old oak trees.

I didn't really notice a lot about the hospital at first. I was busy feeling sorry for myself.

Random Observation: The man looking most obviously lost and disturbed at the William Pound Institute—baggy white suit, torn panama hat, Monkey Ward dress shirt—must have been me.

Here was Ochs Jones, thirty-one-year-old

cornpone savant, never before having been north of Washington D.C.

But the Brooks Brothers doctors, the nurses, the fire-haired patients walking around the hospital paid no attention.

Which isn't easy—even at 9:30 on a drizzly, unfriendly morning.

Generally I'm noticed most places.

My blond hair is close-cropped, just a little seedy on the sides, already falling out on top—so that my head resembles a Franciscan monk's. I'm slightly cross-eyed without my glasses (and because of the rain I had them off). Moreover, I'm 6'7", and I stand out quite nicely without the aid of quirky clothes.

No one noticed, though. One doctory-looking woman said, "Hello, Michael." "Ochs," I told her. That was about it for introductions.

Less than 1% believing Ben Toy might have a story for me, I dutifully followed all the blue-arrowed signs marked BOWDITCH.

The grounds of the Pound Institute were clean and fresh-smelling and green as a state park. The hospital reminded me of an eastern university campus, someplace with a name like Ithaca, or Swarthmore, or Hobart.

It was nearly ten as I walked past huge red-brick houses along an equally red cobblestone road.

Occasionally a Cadillac or Mercedes crept by at the posted ten m.p.h. speed limit.

The federalist-style houses I passed were the different wards of the hospital.

One was for the elderly bedridden. Another was for the elderly who could still putter around—predominantly lobotomies.

One four-story building housed nothing but children aged over ten years. A little girl sat rocking in the window of one of the downstairs rooms. She reminded me of Anthony Perkins at the end of *Psycho*.

I jotted down a few observations and felt silly making them. I kept one wandering eye peeled for Ben Toy's ward: Bowditch: male maximum security.

—

A curious thing happened to me in front of the ward for young girls.

A round-shouldered girl was sitting on the wet front lawn close to the road where I was walking.

She was playing a blond-wood guitar and singing *Ballad of a Thin Man*, the Bob Dylan song, just about talking the lyrics.

I was Ochs Jones, thirty-one, father of two daughters . . . The only violent act I could recall in my life, was *hearing*—as a boy—that my great-uncle Ochs Jones had been hanged in Moon, Kentucky, as a horsethief . . . and *no*, I didn't know what was going on.

As a matter of fact, I knew considerably less than I thought I did.

The last of the Federal-style houses was more rambling, less formal and kept-up than any of the others: It bordered on scrub pine woods with very green waist-high underbrush running through it. A high stockade fence had been built up as the ward's backyard.

BOWDITCH a fancy gold plaque by the front door said.

The man who'd contacted the *Citizen-Reporter*, Dr. Alan Shulman, met me on the front porch. Right off, Shulman informed me that this was an unusual and delicate situation for him. The hospital, he said, had only divulged information about patients a few times before—and that invariably had to do with court cases. "But an assassination," he said, "is somewhat extraordinary. We *want* to help."

Shulman was very New Yorkerish, with curly, scraggly black hair. He wore the kind of black-frame eyeglasses with little silver arrows in the corners. He was probably in his mid-thirties, with some kind of Brooklyn or Queens accent that was odd to my ear.

Some men slouching inside behind steel-screened windows seemed to be finding us quite a curious combination to observe.

A steady flow of collected rainwater rattled the drainpipe on the porch.

It made it a little harder for Shulman and myself to hear one another's side of the argument that was developing.

"I left my home around five, five-fifteen this morning," I said in a quick, agitated bluegrass drawl.

"I took an awful Southern Airways flight up to Kennedy Airport . . . awful flight . . . stopped at places like Dohren, Alabama . . . Then I drove an

Econo-Car out to God-knows-where-but-I-don't, Long Island. And now, you're not going to let me in to see Toy . . . Is that right Doctor Shulman? That's right, isn't it?"

Shulman just nodded the curly black head.

Then he said something like this to me: "Ben Toy had a very bad, piss-poor night last night. He's been up and down since he got in here . . . I think he *wants* to get better now . . . I don't think he wants to kill himself right now . . . So maybe you can talk with him tomorrow. Maybe even tonight. Not now, though."

"Aw shit," I shook my head. I loosened up my tie and a laugh snorted out through my nose. The laugh is a big flaw in my business style. I can't really take myself too seriously, and it shows.

When Shulman laughed too I started to like him. He had a good way of laughing that was hard to stay pissed off at. I imagined he used it on all his patients.

"Well, at least invite me in for some damn coffee," I grinned.

The doctor took me into a back door through Bowditch's nurse's station.

I caught a glimpse of nurses, some patients, and a lot of Plexiglas surrounding the station. We entered another room, a wood-paneled conference room, and Shulman personally mixed me some Sanka.

After some general small talk, he told me why he'd started to feel that Ben Toy was somehow involved in the murders of Jimmie Horn, Bert Poole, and Lieutenant Mart Weesner.

I told him why most of the people at the *Citizen* doubted it.

Our reasons had to do with motion pictures of the Horn shooting. The films clearly showed young Poole shooting Horn in the chest and face.

Alan Shulman's reasons had to do with gut feelings. (And also with the nagging fact that the police would probably never remove Ben Toy from an institution to face trial.)

Like the man or not, I was not overly impressed with his theories.

"Don't you worry," he assured me, "this story will be worth your time and air fare . . . if you handle it right."

As part of the idea of getting my money's worth out

of the trip, I drove about six miles south after leaving the hospital.

I slipped into a pair of cut-offs in my rent-a-car, then went for my first swim in an ocean.

If I'd known how little time I'd be having for the next five months, I would have squeezed even more out of the free afternoon.

—

The rainy day turned into beautiful, pink-and-blue-skied night.

I was wearing bluejeans and white shirttails, walking down the hospital's cobblestone road again. It was 8:30 that same evening and I'd been asked to come back to Bowditch.

A bear-bearded, rabbinical-looking attendant was assigned to record and supervise my visit with Ben Toy. A ring of keys and metal badges jangled from the rope belt around his Levi's. A plastic name pin said that he was MR. RONALD ASHER, SENIOR MENTAL HEALTH WORKER.

The two of us, both carrying pads and pencils, walked down a long, gray-carpeted hall with airy, white-curtained bedrooms on either side.

Something about being locked in the hall made me a little tense. I was combing my hair with my fingers as I walked along.

"Our quiet room's about the size of a den," Asher told me. "It's a seclusion room. Seclusion room's used for patients who act-out violently. Act-out against the staff, or other patients, or against themselves."

"Which did Ben Toy do?" I asked the attendant.

"Oh shit." Big white teeth showed in his beard. "He's been in there for all three at one time or another. He can be a total jerk-off, and then again he can be a pretty nice guy."

Asher stopped in front of the one closed door in the hallway. While he opened it with two different keys, I looked inside through a book-sized observation window.

The room *was* tiny.

It had gunboat metal screens and red bars on small, mud-spattered windows. A half-eaten bowl of cereal and milk was on the windowsill. Outside was the stockade wall and an exercise yard.

Ben Toy was seated on the room's only furniture, a narrow blue pinstriped mattress. He was wearing a black cowboy Stetson, but when he saw my face in the window he took it off.

"Come on the hell in," I heard a friendly, muffled voice. "The door's only triple-locked."

Just then Asher opened it.

Ben Toy was a tall, thin man, about thirty, with a fast, easy, hustler's smile. His blond hair was oily, unwashed. He was Jon Voight on the skids.

Toy was wearing white pajama bottoms with no top. His ribs were sticking out to be counted. His chest was covered with curly, auburn hair, however, and he was basically rugged-looking.

According to Asher, Toy had tried to starve himself when he'd first come in the hospital. Asher said he'd been burly back then.

When Toy spoke his voice was soft. He seemed to be trying to sound hip. N.Y.-L.A. dope world sounds.

"You look like a Christian monk, man," he drawled pleasantly.

"No shit," I laughed, and he laughed too. He seemed pretty normal. Either that, or the black-bearded aide was a snake charmer.

After a little bit of measuring each other up, Toy and I went right into Jimmie Horn.

Actually, I started on the subject, but Toy did most of the talking.

He knew what Horn looked like; where Horn had lived; precisely where his campaign head-quarters had been. He knew the names of Jimmie Horn's two children; his parents' names; all sorts of impossible trivia nobody outside of Tennessee would have any interest in.

At that point, I found myself talking rapidly and listening very closely. The Sony was burning up tape.

"You think you know who shot Horn up?" Toy said to me.

"I think I do, yes. A man named Bert Poole shot him. A chronic bumbler who lived in Nashville all his life. A fuck-up."

"This *bumbler*," Toy asked. "How did you figure out he did it?"

His question was very serious; forensic, in a country pool hall way. He was slowly turning the black Stetson around on his fist.

"For one thing," I said, "I saw it on television. For another thing, I've talked to a shitload of people who were there."

Toy frowned at me. "Guess you talked to the

wrong shitload of people," he said. He was acting very sure of himself.

It was just after that when Toy spoke of the contact, or bag-man, involved with Jimmie Horn.

It was then also that I heard the name Thomas Berryman for the first time.

OUT NOW

NYPD Red 3

James Patterson
& Marshall Karp

A chilling conspiracy leads NYPD Red into extreme danger.

Hunter Alden, Jr has it all: a beautiful wife, a brilliant son and billions in the bank. But when his son goes missing and he discovers the severed head of his chauffeur, it's clear he's in danger of losing it all.

The kidnapper knows a horrific secret that could change the world as we know it. A secret worth killing for. A secret worth dying for.

New York's best detectives, Zach Jordan and Kylie MacDonald, are on the case. But by getting closer to the truth, Zach and Kylie are edging ever closer to the firing line . . .

CENTURY

THE *SUNDAY TIMES* BESTSELLER

Hope to Die

James Patterson

I am alone, I thought. Alone.

Pain knifed through my head. I sank to my knees, bowed my head, and raised my hands towards heaven.

'Why?' I screamed. 'Why?'

Detective Alex Cross has lost everything and everyone he's ever cared about.

His enemy, Thierry Mulch, is holding his family hostage. Driven by feelings of hatred and revenge, Mulch is threatening to kill them all, and break Cross for ever.

But Alex Cross is fighting back.

In a race against time, he must defeat Mulch, and find his wife and children – no matter what it takes.

THE END-GAME HAS BEGUN.

CENTURY

Burn

James Patterson
& Michael Ledwidge

**Detective Michael Bennett is coming home to New York.
And a world of unimaginable evil awaits.**

Having brought an end to the vengeful mission of the ruthless crime lord who forced the Bennett family into hiding, Michael is finally back in New York City.

However, Bennett is thrust straight back into a horrifying case: a witness claims to have seen a group of well-dressed men holding a sickeningly depraved and murderous gathering in a condemned building.

The report reads like the product of an overactive imagination. But when a charred body is found in that very same building, the unbelievable claim becomes all too real...

CENTURY

Invisible

James Patterson
& David Ellis

My nightmare: it's the same every time. I'm trapped in my bedroom with an inferno blazing around me.

It started eight months ago, when my sister was killed in a house fire. Her death was written off as an accident, but I know she was murdered.

There have been dozens of 'accidental' fires across the US over the past year that are all too similar to be coincidental.

I've never been more sure of anything.

One of the worst serial killers of all time is being ignored.

And it's up to me to stop him.

arrow books

NYPD RED SERIES
NYPD Red (*with Marshall Karp*) •
NYPD Red 2 (*with Marshall Karp*) •
NYPD Red 3 (*with Marshall Karp*)

STAND-ALONE THRILLERS
Sail (*with Howard Roughan*) • Swimsuit (*with Maxine Paetro*) • Don't Blink (*with Howard Roughan*) • Postcard Killers (*with Liza Marklund*) • Toys (*with Neil McMahon*) • Now You See Her (*with Michael Ledwidge*) • Kill Me If You Can (*with Marshall Karp*) • Guilty Wives (*with David Ellis*) • Zoo (*with Michael Ledwidge*) • Second Honeymoon (*with Howard Roughan*) • Mistress (*with David Ellis*) • Invisible (*with David Ellis*) • Truth or Die (*with Howard Roughan*) • Murder House (*with David Ellis, to be published September 2015*)

NON-FICTION
Torn Apart (*with Hal and Cory Friedman*) •
The Murder of King Tut (*with Martin Dugard*)

ROMANCE
Sundays at Tiffany's (*with Gabrielle Charbonnet*) •
The Christmas Wedding (*with Richard DiLallo*) •
First Love (*with Emily Raymond*)

OTHER TITLES
Miracle at Augusta (*with Peter de Jonge*)

FAMILY OF PAGE-TURNERS

MIDDLE SCHOOL BOOKS

The Worst Years of My Life (*with Chris Tebbetts*) • Get Me Out of Here! (*with Chris Tebbetts*) • My Brother Is a Big, Fat Liar (*with Lisa Papademetriou*) • How I Survived Bullies, Broccoli, and Snake Hill (*with Chris Tebbetts*) • Ultimate Showdown (*with Julia Bergen*) • Save Rafe! (*with Chris Tebbetts*) • Just My Rotten Luck (*with Chris Tebbetts*)

I FUNNY SERIES

I Funny (*with Chris Grabenstein*) •
I Even Funnier (*with Chris Grabenstein*) •
I Totally Funniest (*with Chris Grabenstein*)

TREASURE HUNTERS SERIES

Treasure Hunters (*with Chris Grabenstein*) •
Danger Down the Nile (*with Chris Grabenstein*)

HOUSE OF ROBOTS

House of Robots (*with Chris Grabenstein*)

HOMEROOM DIARIES

Homeroom Diaries (*with Lisa Papademetriou*)

MAXIMUM RIDE SERIES

The Angel Experiment • School's Out Forever •
Saving the World and Other Extreme Sports •
The Final Warning • Max • Fang • Angel •
Nevermore • Forever

For more information about James Patterson's novels, visit www.jamespatterson.co.uk

Or become a fan on Facebook

MEET THE WOMEN'S MURDER CLUB

Four women sit at their usual table in Susie's bar, and the conversation, as always, is murder…

LINDSAY BOXER

A homicide detective in the San Francisco Police Department, juggling the worst murder cases with the challenges of being a first-time mother. Her loving husband Joe, baby daughter Julie and loyal border-collie Martha give her a reason to protect the city. She's not had the easiest start in life, with an absent father and an ill mother, and she doesn't shy away from a difficult career. Keeping control of her head and her heart can be tough, but with the help of her friends, Lindsay makes it her mission to solve the toughest cases.

CLAIRE WASHBURN

Chief Medical Examiner for San Francisco and one of Lindsay's oldest friends. Wise, confident and viciously funny, she can be relied on to help, whatever the problem. She virtually runs the Office of the Coroner for her overbearing, credit-stealing boss, but rarely complains. You may hear her called 'Butterfly' thanks to a tattoo just below her waist. Happily married with children, her personal life is relatively calm in comparison to her time in the Women's Murder Club.

CINDY THOMAS

An up-and-coming journalist who's always looking for the next big story. She'll go the extra mile, risking life and limb to get her scoop. Sometimes she prefers to grill her friends over cocktails for a juicy secret, but, luckily for them, she's totally trustworthy – most of the time ... She's just published a book, somehow finding the time to write between solving cases, writing articles for the *San Francisco Chronicle* and keeping her on–off relationship with Lindsay's partner, Rich Conklin, together. Other than reading, she loves yoga and jazz music.

YUKI CASTELLANO

One of the best lawyers in the city, and desperate to make her mark. Ambitious, intelligent and passionate, she'll fight for what's right, defending the underdog even if it means standing in the way of those she loves. Often this includes her husband – who is also Lindsay's boss – Lt. Jackson Brady. Her friends can barely get a word in edgeways when she's around, unless she's got a Germain-Robin sidecar in her hand!

WHEN YOUR JOB IS MURDER, YOU NEED FRIENDS YOU CAN COUNT ON.